Testing for Disaster

EMBERWOOD
BOOK II

NICOLE CAMPBELL

Testing Recipes for Disaster

NICOLE CAMPBELL

Copyright © 2024 by Nicole Campbell

All rights reserved. No part of this publication may be reproduced, stored or transmitted in any form or by any means, electronic, mechanical, photocopying, recording, scanning, or otherwise without written permission from the publisher. It is illegal to copy this book, post it to a website, or distribute it by any other means without permission.

This novel is entirely a work of fiction. The names, characters and incidents portrayed in it are the work of the author's imagination. Any resemblance to actual persons, living or dead, events or localities is entirely coincidental.

First edition

Editing by K.F. Starfell
Cover art by Margaux @caravelle_creates

To all my fellow neurodivergent b*tches—
I hope your pillow is always on the cool
side and someone pays for your coffee
today.

—Nicole

Content Warning:

- This book contains depictions of romantic and sexual interactions meant for readers ages 18+.
- Discussions of doctor visits and ADHD diagnosis.
- Brief depictions of modern-day witchcraft.
- Brief conversations about past drug use.
- Depictions of family estrangement.

Prologue—Jeremy

Spring

My eyes were sweating. The spring air was warmer than it should have been when Lauren and I walked out of *Books and Broomsticks*, and this had to be the reason for the watery eyes.

"Do you need, like, a hanky or something, Jer?" Lauren asked, keeping up with me easily on the way to my car, though I had no idea how with the heels she was wearing.

"I have *allergies*, Garrett. It's a well-documented medical condition that—"

"That makes you cry when you see your best friend down on one knee, proposing to the woman of his dreams? You're allergic to commitment? Or love? Or—"

"All of the above, maybe. But fine, it was *nice*. They were both really happy and…"

Jesus, I thought, my voice already tightening again, thinking about Jesse's stupid proposal.

"It was nice, Laur. I'm sorry I don't have a heart of stone like some people," I said pointedly as we reached my GTI.

Her lips quirked up, but it didn't light up her face like her smile usually did. Guilt formed in my chest. I wasn't sure what I was guilty of—giving each other shit was what our entire friendship was based on. That, and the fact that her brother was my best friend.

"Thanks for the ride," she said as she slid into the passenger seat. "I wasn't excited to get a ride home from the happy couple. Or my mother and her tears, though you're now making me think I didn't escape much of anything."

Her smile was a little bigger with that insult, and I huffed dramatically and put the car in reverse. I opened my music app the moment silence settled around us and started a playlist that I thought she'd like.

Quiet with Lauren and me was dangerous for too many reasons. I'd crossed the line from friendly to flirting more times than I cared to admit, and even if Jesse seemed to have calmed down somewhat about it, his disapproval was fine with me. I wasn't operating under the delusion that I was let-him-date-your-sister material.

"You can change the song if you want," I said, desperate for something benign to fill up the ride to her townhouse.

"It was nice."

"Hmm?"

"The proposal. It was kind of perfect. I did sound… negative, before. I'm not. My best friend is going to be my actual, legal sister. And they're so happy…"

"I know, Laur. I was just giving you a hard time. Sorry if it bothered you."

Things were getting far too serious, and we still had at least four minutes until I dropped her off. My hand gripped the gearshift to keep from reaching for hers, but I let my eyes drift to her pretty green ones. Her red hair was pulled away from her face and curled down her back. She looked gorgeous, and it killed me not to tell her that.

"No, I know. I…whatever. I wanted to say it out loud, I guess."

She bit her lip like she wanted to say more, but instead, she rolled down her window and let her fingers glide over the night air. I sighed, wishing I had the right words or was the right guy to get her out of her head, but I didn't, and I wasn't.

I pulled into her complex and got out. I realized too late that I would never do that for a guy friend I was dropping off at home, and this looked like a date, but there was no turning back now.

"You're upholding the ideals of chivalry, Jer? It's like I don't even know you."

"I don't want you to fall over in those heels and be held

responsible for your concussion. It's a liability issue."

She rolled her eyes, linked her arm through mine, and leaned against me. Even in those shoes, she barely reached above my shoulder. Her hair tickled the back of my arm enough that goosebumps rose in response.

"Your castle, milady," I said with a bow and a horrible British accent.

"Thank goodness you don't have an accent. That would be unfair in the grand scheme of things."

"Because I'm otherwise nearly god-like in my perfection?"

"I was going to say you were cute, but you took it off the deep end, there."

"I'll take 'cute' coming from you anytime. You look gorgeous tonight, Laur."

Fuck. This is not the plan.

I'd done so well keeping my mouth shut all night.

She fished her keys from her tiny bag and stepped closer to her door before stopping. Her eyes searched mine for an uncomfortably long moment.

"Do you wanna come in?"

She might as well have asked me to diffuse a bomb with how quickly my heart rate jumped. Every part of my body was screaming at me to already be inside with her back pressed against the door, finding out what she felt like under my fingers. But there would be no coming back from that, and we both knew it. It would put a definitive end to this game we played.

"Please don't ask me that," I got out, though it was barely above a whisper.

Hurt flashed across her face, and I hated it, but the hurt would be so much worse if I crossed the threshold—both literal and figurative.

"Fine, Jer. Have a great fucking night."

And with that, she was inside; the door slammed and locked in an instant.

I stood there stupidly for several moments, paralyzed with indecision about anything I could possibly do to make the last ten minutes disappear.

Instead, I shoved my hands in my pockets and made it my mission to kick any stray pebbles on the walkway back into the nearby landscaping. It was safe to say that I would *not* be having a great fucking night.

Chapter 1 - Lauren

Three months later: Summer

A nagging sensation had been wrapping its way around my spine while I got ready to tone my client's hair.

What am I forgetting? I pleaded with my brain as Sarah chattered up at me from the shampoo bowl.

She was talking about her high school reunion coming up next weekend over the Fourth of July, and I felt myself smiling and nodding about the dress she bought with the slit up to her hip as I started coating her newly lightened hair. Then, it finally dawned on me that this was *not* the toner I should have been using.

Shit shit shit. I tried not to let my racing heartbeat and the cold, slimy feeling dripping down my back show on my face. *You can fix this, no big deal.*

"Hey, Sarah? I think I have a better idea for a toner for you that will get us closer to the photo you brought. I forgot it even existed—because we *just* started carrying this line—but if you're okay with it, I think I'm going to rinse you and go mix up the other. I honestly think you'll be so happy with it."

I was already wetting her hair as I spoke.

"Oh! Okay, yeah, that sounds fine. I trust you!"

Maybe you shouldn't, I thought.

My brain was not here. It wasn't even *there*, it was *everywhere*. My thoughts felt like the carnival that would be rolling into town next week—the lights, the sounds, the fireworks, the smells of fried food—all of it happening at once, and I couldn't temper them. I rinsed Sarah as she changed topics, now chatting about her son and his handprint art he'd brought home from preschool.

Breathe in and out and fucking focus, Garrett.

I left her at the bowl and went to mix up the *correct* toner, which was absolutely not a new brand, paying extra close attention this time. Christian eyed me suspiciously from his station when I came back with the new bottle, and I tried to convey to him what an idiot I was without speaking. He quirked a perfectly lined brow to let me know I'd have to explain later, but he eased back into his conversation with his client.

My heart rate came down within a more normal range after I corrected my error. Sarah's hair ended up looking perfect, and she left me a hefty tip I didn't deserve. It was a good thing I had an hour break between appointments to get my shit together.

My iced coffee was sufficiently watery, but caffeine had the opposite effect on me as most, and I needed it.

Christian floated gracefully into the chair next to me in the back room and picked up his own coffee, taking a long drink before facing me. His eyeliner was still winged to perfection, even after the three clients he'd seen today.

"Spill," he demanded.

"How does your eyeliner stay on your face after blow-drying? It's not fair."

"I'll teach you, Grasshopper, after you tell me what you did."

His rich brown eyes widened in impatience, his dark lashes and arched brows playing along.

"I mixed up a toner that would have been disastrous on her. Like, I didn't even think about it, just threw it in the bottle and went on my merry way like an asshole. Thank god I realized it almost as soon as it touched her head, and I made something up about having a better idea from a new line. I need to get my brain together before I screw up something I can't fix."

"It happens to the best of us, Darling. Don't beat yourself up."

"Oh yeah? When's the last time you almost had a client walking out of here a brassy blond?"

"Never, obviously. I wasn't referring to myself because my work is impeccable. But you know, everyone *else*." Another sip of iced coffee.

"You're a little bit of a bitch, you know?"

"Takes one to know one. Anyhow, I'm going to get a salad; you want anything?"

"Grilled cheeeeeese."

"You have the tastes of a toddler."

I grinned and shook off what remained of my mistake so that I didn't make another one when my next client arrived.

* * *

This pattern of swinging from feeling like I could fall asleep standing up to being so awake I had no choice but to paint my guest bathroom at one in the morning had to stop. I *knew* there was a limit my brain would hit where I wouldn't be able to function, and my mistake at work only proved it.

I was *good* at my job. I didn't make careless errors like that, but lately, it seemed like I could not settle on a single train of thought. My brain was Grand Central, and all the trains were there at once.

I dipped the paint roller back into the fuchsia color that resulted from me mixing all the red and pink paint I had left from my *I wanna paint hearts all over my wall* project. I compromised with myself that I'd only paint one wall, and then I'd force myself to lie in my bed and close my eyes and not open them until morning. I was going to kick insomnia's ass.

Interestingly, the thing about sleeping after weeks of *not*, was that I slept for fourteen hours straight. There were texts from my mom, Sam, Jesse, and Christian, and even two missed calls. Everyone knew not to call me unless they were dying.

Uuughhhh.

So much for accomplishing anything on my day off. I slid out of bed and talked myself into at least throwing in a load of laundry to the wash.

See? You can do things.

I put a mini-pizza into my toaster oven and slumped over on

one of my barstools.

SAM: Are you off today? I'm only working this morning and kinda wanna go look at dresses. There's a lady who hand makes these gorgeous gowns in Centerville.

LAUR: Fuck, I just woke up. If you're still in a shopping mood I can be ready in 30 minutes

SAM: Eh, she closes at 5 and I got wrapped up designing invitations anyway. Happy hour at The Bar?

Guilt settled in my stomach. I was her maid of honor and should be taking more initiative in helping her with wedding planning.
Add it to the list of shit you should be doing.
The pizza dinged, and I bit into it far too early, the sauce rendering my taste buds useless for at least three to five business days.

LAUR: See you in an hour.

The thought of washing my hair was wholly overwhelming, but I made myself get in the shower to scrub off the rest of the fatigue still clinging to my body. I shot off a text to Christian, who'd only sent me a *Clueless* meme, letting him know he should meet us. He and Sam had met a few times, but I needed to make them *friends.*

LAUR: Will my brother be gracing us with his presence?

SAM: I know you're REALLY asking if Jeremy will be joining us to see if you need to have an excuse to bail at the ready, but no, Jesse is doing training for new coaches tonight.

I only validated her message with a middle finger emoji. She didn't appreciate how much creativity it took to avoid him in a town this small, especially when he was Jesse's best friend. I'd made up early appointments I didn't have and home projects that didn't exist, all in the name of making sure I'd only seen Jer in passing since the night he drew his line in the sand. He'd attempted to make two appointments through the salon website, and I'd canceled them and sent him a form message. Because I was petty.

After that disaster, I'd decided that if he had the balls to flirt with me for almost a year, then he should have had the balls to follow through. I ignored the simmer of mixed emotions in my stomach when I thought about what would have happened if he *had* agreed to come in that night.

Maybe you wouldn't have flipped out and tried to pretend it never happened. It's possible you would have fallen in love and gotten married and lived happily ever after.

My inner voice didn't even believe its own delusional words. But I wasn't prepared to admit that he might have made the right call. There were plenty of very cute tourists in town for the Fourth that would happily come in if I asked them.

Never mind that you have turned down the last several guys that've hit on you.

I frowned involuntarily.

I put my plate in the dishwasher and decided I should leave now and arrive early. That *never* happened, but the guilt about making Sam miss out on a day of dress shopping was weighing on me. I could get a table and buy the first round of drinks.

I checked my appearance briefly, satisfied with how my homemade halter top had turned out, and headed to my garage and my little yellow Beetle.

After arriving, I plopped down at a high top in the back and stirred my vodka soda, wondering if it was always boring being early. I liked arriving once things were in full swing.

"Hey, can I get you another?" a voice asked to my left. My gaze landed on a probably late-twenty-something guy wearing khakis and flip-flops.

Definitely a tourist.

Emberwood was such a random place to be a travel destination, but the town had done a good job over the last fifty years building up events and quaint lodging near Lake Eerie. For a relationship-failure such as myself, it was helpful to have a rotation of cute guys pass through. But tonight, I was going to hype up Sam about her wedding without distraction.

"Ah, thanks, but I'm actually waiting on someone."

I shot him what I thought was an apologetic smile. He wasn't bad looking; I just wasn't going to make tonight about me.

"I don't see anyone yet…so what would one drink hurt?"

His grin widened, and he leaned too far into my bubble, accomplishing the opposite of his goal because now I was getting pissed off.

"Do you make it a point not to take 'no' for an answer, Chad? Because it's not a great look."

"Hey, baby, sorry I'm late," a familiar voice murmured in my ear, though certainly loud enough for Chad or Brad or whomever this guy was to hear.

Jer's arm wrapped around me from behind my barstool and made goosebumps erupt down my arms.

"Are you here to take our drink order, or should you be fucking off right about now?" Jer asked the guy, his voice as aggressive as I'd ever heard him.

The guy held up his hands like he was surrendering and scurried away back to a group of what I assumed was his flock of douchebags. Jeremy's hands left my body, and I sucked in a breath at the loss. I cleared my throat to hopefully cover it.

"You okay?" he asked, concern in his warm hazel eyes.

"Yeah. I'm good."

He stood for a moment, clearly warring with whether or not he was going to walk away.

"Listen, I know you're avoiding me, and you're doing a stellar job, by the way, but do you want me to hang out until whoever you're waiting for gets here?"

"I'm not *avoiding* you. I've been busy."

"Right. You're a horrible liar. You can own it; it's fine. I can sit here while I wait for my takeout, though. I won't even try to engage you in conversation, so maybe you can still count this as another day we didn't interact."

His tone was light, but the words held hurt anyway.

Join the club.

"Well, I would hate not to check off today on my anti-Jeremy calendar, but I guess you did me a solid, so I'll figure out how to deal."

He shot me a smirk that made me dig my nails into my palm. I still hadn't recovered from his arms wrapped around me, and he shouldn't be allowed to look at me like that.

"How are you?"

Chapter 2 - Jeremy

I thought about keeping the conversation light and getting out of there, happy she was speaking to me again. But I couldn't handle the thought of her continuing to avoid me, and I wanted to at least gesture at the elephant in the room.

"I'm okay. Look—"

"Hey, guys! I didn't expect to see you here, Jer," Sam said, hopping up onto a barstool across from Lauren and me, followed by a guy I knew worked with Lauren, though I couldn't think of his name.

Not great timing, guys.

"Hey, Sam," I greeted. "I'm Jeremy," I said as the guy got settled and looked me over. "And I would shake your hand, but I can't promise I'm not still at least partially covered in grease."

"Don't threaten me with a good time," he said, grinning. "I'm Christian."

I huffed out a laugh at that.

"Are you staying?" Sam asked, and it sounded like a genuine invitation.

I'd hung out with her and Jesse quite a bit lately but never with Lauren for longer than ten minutes.

"Ah, can't. I am picking up food and then going home to shower long enough to forget my profession. Just wanted to say 'hey.' My food should be ready by now, though. It was good to see you both. Could I talk to you for a sec, Laur?"

I had nothing to lose, but I braced myself for her to tell me to fuck off. Instead, she nodded and slipped down off her barstool.

She was so short. I forgot sometimes since her personality was terrifying. She was wearing a black halter top that looked like it used to be a Fleetwood Mac concert t-shirt and jeans with the biggest flares I'd ever seen, her yellow sandals barely peeking out.

"Thanks. For the rescue. I didn't say it before," she said once we were out of earshot.

"Anytime, Garrett. Just…"

Her green eyes looked up at me expectantly. Why was this so hard? I supposed she couldn't avoid me *more*, so I might as well bite the bullet.

"I miss you. I'm sorry for…" I didn't know how to finish the sentence without making things worse, being that we'd never technically acknowledged anything between us. "For not handling things well," I offered. "But I want to be able to hang out again. I also *really* need a haircut, and for some reason, my appointments keep getting canceled. It must be a glitch with the website."

I was *begging* her to let us go back to some semblance of normal.

"Hmmm, that's so odd. None of my other clients have said anything."

"Probably an error on my part. I'm known to screw things up."

She gave a laugh and half-rolled her eyes. I felt like I was being appraised for auction before she spoke again.

"Fine. I'll make sure your next appointment doesn't accidentally get canceled. But… damn it, Jer."

"I know," I murmured.

"Whatever. If we're *friends*, then act like it. I'll see ya."

Instinctively, I reached for her wrist to keep her there, though I had no rebuttal. I didn't *want* another friend. But that's what I needed to be for her, or she'd learn how truthful I was being when I said I was known to screw things up. She looked up at me, and I dropped her hand.

"Thanks, Laur. I'll see you soon."

She nodded and made her way to the bar. I didn't miss her downing a shot after I finally got my to-go order. I glanced around to make sure the country club rejects had vacated the area, not trusting a single one of them around Laur or Sam with their drinks out in the open. I finally made it to my car, even more exhausted than when I'd walked in.

Today had been fucking *brutal*. Two guys had called out "sick" from the shop, meaning they were watching *The Price is Right* and nursing hangovers. Being the owner's nephew, *that* meant I got to work all day. I normally bounced back and forth between being under cars and being in the office, but today had been all oil changes and new brakes and starting on rebuilding a transmission. All I wanted was to eat my burger and take the world's longest shower. I hadn't planned on getting caught up trying to build a bridge back to something that looked like friendship with Lauren, but I was glad the night turned out that way.

A legitimate groan slipped out of my mouth when I finally made it to my apartment and peeled off my shoes.

Because I was classy, I ate my burger standing up, leaning over the sink in my kitchen. That shit was messy.

The knowledge that I was only a shower away from being able to pass out gave me the motivation to drag my ass into the bathroom. My apartment was average—one-bedroom, tan carpet, oak cabinets, linoleum that'd seen better days, but the water pressure was top-tier, and I'd never been more grateful. I got out to a text notification from my uncle.

UNCLE NICK: Hey kid. I wish I could give you tomorrow off, but the best I got is that you don't have to come in until eleven. Get some sleep.

I felt my shoulders drop. I'd hoped he wouldn't need me at all tomorrow. The thing about being a mechanic was that it was a decent job. It was honest work, it paid okay, and my uncle being the owner was usually a perk. But the thing about being a mechanic when you *hated* working on cars was that it was dirty, unforgiving, physical labor, and I was spent.

JER: Got it. I'll see you then.

The only thing I did before closing my eyes was put in an appointment request at *The Dollhouse* for the next week, hoping she meant it when she said it wouldn't mysteriously get canceled. I punched my pillow and shut off the bedside lamp before the appointment confirmation email arrived. That softened the blow of everything else, and I was dead to the world.

Chapter 3- Lauren

"Sorry, that took longer than expected."

After my chat with Jer, I'd ordered an ill-advised shot and gone to the bathroom to process the feelings I shouldn't be having. I was determined to get myself back to normal before devoting the night to wedding talk and cheese fries.

"No worries, I convinced Sam to do a quick reading while we waited," Christian assured me, popping a fry into his mouth.

"Oh? And?"

"I am going to open a stunning salon and be insanely successful. Those aren't my words; those are my *spirit guides*. We'll see."

"Any salon you opened would draw people from every corner of the tri-state area, Chris."

I eyed him sincerely. He was toned down tonight in jeans and a tight green t-shirt that set off his deep brown eyes.

"I agree," a bright voice chimed in.

Genevieve took the empty seat next to me and grinned. Sam had met her at *Books and Broomsticks* a while back and ended up designing a book cover for one of her romance novels—the one we were all celebrating the night Jesse proposed. She'd since become a recurring guest star in our friend group.

"Eeee! You made it," Sam squealed happily. "I'll get your first drink," she offered, holding up her own beer as a visual aid.

"Hold up. Since when do you drink beer? I demand a margarita or a fruity something," I interrupted.

"I know, I know. I've been trying different types so that I have something to order at baseball games. Jesse's only just now feeling okay being a spectator at minor or major league games, so I want to do the whole experience. Hot dogs, beer, peanuts, whatever. It's only okay. I promise I'll order a marg next time."

"Well, I suppose that's an admirable endeavor. But you can't spring these kinds of changes on a girl and expect immediate acceptance."

"Well, I'll order a marg," Gen offered, flipping her honey blond hair over her shoulder.

She had such thick waves I'd originally thought she had extensions, but *nobody's* extensions looked that good. She was simply blessed.

"*Thank* you."

"I will be certain to run my drink choices by you next time," Sam assured me, grinning before going to order Genevieve's drink.

I'd originally hesitated to embrace a new friend, having only gotten Sam back a year ago, but she made it easy to like her. She was generally up for anything and had a similar love of late 90's rom-coms, so she was A-OK in my book. I tuned back in to Christian explaining the vision for his hypothetical salon.

"I feel like a glitter waterfall would be appropriately shocking."

"I couldn't imagine anything *more* appropriately shocking. I could make it for you! We could use rhinestones and LED lights and glitter paper and glitter fabric," I said, refocusing.

"Speaking of shocking, maybe we could chat real quick about you and Jer looking cozy over here after three months of radio silence," Sam interjected, her blue eyes lit up.

Christian and Gen leaned in, invested. They'd all been trying to get out of me exactly what happened with Jer, but I was uninterested in explaining how I got rejected on my doorstep. Only Sam got the basic rundown because she'd earned it after decades of friendship.

"There was a whole situation with a douchebag tourist guy who wouldn't take my flat out 'no.' I was handling it, but Jer overheard and came over to pretend to be my boyfriend and tell the guy to fuck off."

Gen sucked in a breath. "Did he say something like '*touch her and die*'?"

"No, not everything is a romance novel."

Gen pouted a little, and Christian raised a brow.

"Fine. He did get a little aggressive with the guy, and it was objectively hot. I can admit he's attractive without being *attracted* to him."

"Sure, Darling. You keep living in your little fantasy land," Christian said, sipping his drink.

Sam only clapped in apparent glee.

I shook my head before responding. "I am fully grounded in reality. He's not interested, and I don't find that to be an attractive quality in a man. I'm delightful. And hot."

I tried to tamp down the swell of embarrassment that still existed from him turning me down. I wasn't used to being rejected, and I sure as hell wasn't going to give him the chance to do it twice.

Friends it will be.

"Oh, he's in a fantasy land, too. You're both delusional, and it's a little infuriating," Sam lamented.

I only rolled my eyes and took another shot. I knew I'd regret it in the morning, but I wanted to forget the goosebumps that broke out when his fingers grazed my stomach because I couldn't remember the last time a guy had an effect on me like that.

Why does it have to be him?

Why couldn't the guy sending literal shivers up my spine be interested in me? Sam wasn't wrong. It *was* infuriating.

"Whatever. You know I've made a recent vow to only hook up with tourists anyway. I suck at breaking things off, and they come with a nice built-in expiration date. Even if I *were* attracted to Jer, the whole thing has the potential to be a recipe for disaster."

Sam sighed, resigned to my stubbornness, at least for tonight.

"Now, let's talk about these dresses you want to go see. I want pics."

Wedding talk was a surefire way to get Sam going, and I relaxed into my role. I was going to be the best maid-of-honor anyone had ever seen from here on out.

Christian left us at the bar shortly after we dove into talk of veils because we were only a pre-game for his date later.

Because everyone has someone but you! Yay!

The shots were a bad idea.

Bad, bad, bad.

The room was a little wavy. Or maybe I was swaying. Either way, it was time to go home.

"Maybe in the future, you could admit you have big, messy, unresolved feelings for your brother's best friend instead of taking shots of tequila."

"Don't you judge me! You're marrying your brother's... best friend's... my brother!"

"No judgment here, Laur. I maintain that I like you guys for each other. The two of you are just masters of weaving unnecessary webs of complications."

"Blah blah blah, 'I'm a psychic.' You ask my spirit guides why they cock-blocked me the night of your engagement party!"

I groaned and pressed my face to the cool glass of Sam's car window. She only snorted.

"There is more than one thing wrong with that command. And it's not your spirit guides; it's all you and Jeremy, standing in your own ways. You both like to pretend the problem is Jesse, and it's not. He really is over his hesitation about whatever happens between the two of you. He knows better than to contradict my intuition."

"*Hesitation?* You mean *forbiddance*. I don't know if I believe you. Is *forbid-dance* a word?"

This conversation was making me nauseous.

Maybe that's the shots.

"But maybe Jer rejecting me was just as well. I'm a dis-saster, and I'd end up getting turned off if he liked me back and gh-ghosting him." I was now hiccupping through my words, another reminder of how much my body hated tequila. "How do you ghost your brother's best friend? He's *around* all the d-damn time. Where

I have to look at his st-stupid eyes and his stupid biceps. Have you seen his arms? I mean, *really* looked at them. I want to bite them."

Sam was now shaking with laughter, and I grinned in spite of myself.

"Whatever. Fuck him. Do you know how hard I've had to work not to s-see him for three months? I'm ex-hausted."

"We will be discussing your little *disaster* comment more in-depth when you're sober. For now, you're home."

I glanced up and saw that we were, indeed, at my townhouse.

"Let's go, drunky."

I heaved my butt out of Sam's car, annoyed that I'd have to go get mine tomorrow. She linked our arms and let me lean on her.

"Thanks for driving me. And not judging me."

"Anytime. Do you want me to get you water and ibuprofen and tuck you in?"

"I promise I will hydrate and make it to bed. I'll text you."

"Love you, Laur. I'll pick you up at nine to get your car before work."

"Love you too! If you see Jeremy, tell him…I hate him."

"I'll be sure to relay the message."

I let her hug me tightly before I lumbered to the kitchen for the water and painkillers and then up the stairs to my room.

Going to sleep fully clothed and in my makeup sounded like the absolute right decision. I pulled my phone out of my pocket to text Sam that I was safe in my bed and decided that another right decision would be to text Jeremy and let him know where he stood.

LAUR: I hate you a LOT. And your eyes and your arms. Goodnight.

Chapter 4 - Jeremy

My muscles were unhappy about the amount of time I spent either under a vehicle or hunched over a hood yesterday. I stretched before grabbing my phone. My alarm hadn't gone off yet, so that might've meant I had time to make a decent breakfast.

A grin spread across my face when I read Lauren's text. Her sending me drunk, sassy messages beat the silent treatment any day of the week.

It was only eight, meaning I had time to make breakfast *and* drop a muffin off at the salon as an apology for my eyes and arms.

I'd bought lavender from the specialty grocery in Centerville, picked up fresh lemons and some local honey, and it was possible these muffins would be so good that Lauren would forgive my offending body parts on the spot. I'd perfected my base muffin recipe a while ago—round, golden brown on the top and fluffy inside, but I'd been trying out more flavor combinations. Next, I'd try the same flavors in cookies and a cake.

My tiny kitchen smelled like sugar and lemons by the time I got them in the oven. Paula, the instructor for most of the baking classes I'd completed in the final semester of my program, would have been happy with these.

Are you ever planning to do *anything with the skills from said program?* I thought, knowing the answer was *probably not.*

I shaved and got dressed. I was thankful today would be more office work than being in the garage. It was boring, but I could listen to music or baking podcasts in my headphones while I worked. No headphones were allowed on the garage floor.

I made a smoothie while I waited for the muffins to bake and took the time to clean up my mess. While I washed mixing bowls and beaters, I tried to shake off the negativity that came with thinking about work. I knew that I was lucky in the grand scheme of things.

After high school, I'd decided to take the fuck-around-and-find-out route for a while.

If 'a while' is three years.

What I found out was that spiraling into a routine of doing illicit drugs on random Tuesdays after (hell, during) work, getting into screaming matches with my ex, and generally having little regard for myself or others did not leave a lot of room for upward mobility. Instead, those years left me fired from my serving job, in possession of a couple of misdemeanor charges, kicked out of my parents' house, and overall, out of options.

At the insistence of my grandmother, who was maybe the only family member not to write me off after all of that, my Uncle Nick reluctantly put me up on his couch and put me to work. I knew a fair amount about cars from my dad—he was always a car guy—and Nick filled in the rest. I had no right to bounce back as quickly as I did. While I wouldn't ever say it was *easy*, I knew it was a lot harder for my former friends who didn't have a grandma or an uncle like mine.

I blew out a breath. Thinking about my life from not-so-many-years ago was always a sobering experience. I tried to tell myself I wasn't that guy anymore and shake it off.

But you could be. A few missteps, and you'd be right back there fucking up everything you touched.

"Nope," I said aloud, refusing to let myself get dragged into that place. It helped that the timer dinged and gave me something else to focus on.

"Yesssssss."

I breathed in the subtle floral scent of the lavender and knew they were going to be good. I took a photo and sent it to my grandma. After only a little hesitation, I sent it to my mom, too. She and my dad moved to Toledo a few years ago, shortly after shit hit the fan. While things were still pretty much no-contact with my dad, my mom and I texted. Sometimes. Or even talked on the phone if it was, like, my birthday or Christmas. It was slow progress, was the bottom line.

While they cooled, I finished getting ready for work and shot off a text to Lauren. The knot in my chest when I thought about her had loosened after last night, and I wanted things to go back to how they were.

No, you really don't. You want her. End of story.

My jaw clenched at my too-honest inner monologue, and I promptly ignored it.

JEREMY: I'm going to go out on a limb and say your choice in beverage last night has you hating life right about now. I have a present to drop off for you as an apology from my eyes and arms. See you in a bit.

LAUR: Bringing me a present is an odd response to me saying I hate you. But I'm not gonna complain.

JEREMY: Good girl ;)

LAUR: It would be a shame if my very sharp scissors slipped while cutting your hair next week, ending in a tragic severing of an important artery.

I should have deleted that reply instead of sending it, but it was so hard to resist when I knew I could get her worked up. *And* when I knew she was thinking about parts of my body while drunk last night. My grin faltered when I remembered what she said about acting like a friend if I wanted a friend. I'd kind of been hoping she wasn't serious, but I also didn't want her to go back to pretending like I didn't exist.

Not off to a great start.

I resolved to do better.

JEREMY: Sorry, I couldn't help myself. You don't have to resort to murder. I'll be appropriate. Scout's Honor.

She only sent back an eye-rolling gif, but again, any response was better than the silence. Armed with baked goods and a plan to pick up coffee, I headed out to my car and appreciated the warmth of the sun as I slid into the driver's seat.

The salon had just opened and wasn't too busy yet. The receptionist said Laur was in the back and would be out soon. I'd been there so many times over the past year she knew who I was and commented on my absence. My hair had never been so well maintained in my life up until recently.

I walked back to Lauren's station and set the bag with the muffins on the vanity slowly, hoping if I took long enough, she'd come out and I could make her try one to see what she thought. I sank into her chair and spun around while I waited. Checking my phone, I sighed, knowing I had to leave to get to the shop.

"Is that my present?"

I looked up and found her leaning against the wall, dressed in a ruffly sort of yellow top and her hair done in two twisty-looking braids.

"It is. And if you hurry up, I can watch you open it before I go."

She eyed me suspiciously as she walked over to peer in the bag.

"You bought me muffins?" she asked, surprise in her voice. "They smell amazing. Just not what I expected."

"Ah, no. I *made* you muffins. Lavender, lemon, and honey. Now I need you to try one before I'm late for work."

"*You*...made lavender, lemon, and honey muffins. From scratch. This morning."

Her tone was disbelieving.

"Tasting first, questions later, Garrett."

She shook her head but took one out and peeled the brown paper wrapping.

"It's weird that you're watching me eat, but whatever."

She sank her teeth into the muffin and let out a little moan while she chewed.

"Jer. When the fuck did you learn to bake?"

She picked another piece of the muffin top off with her nails and popped it into her mouth.

"I told you I was taking classes at ECC."

That may have been true, but I'd sort of kept my whole certificate program very vague to most people. It felt like an opportunity for me to fail with an audience. Again. Thankfully, I didn't fail, but now it was a little odd telling people what I'd been doing for almost two years.

"Okay, totally honest, when you said you were taking some sort of cooking classes, I envisioned like a basic 'how-to-grill-chicken-breast,' college-level home economics type of course. Not for you to be making little pieces of lavender clouds that melt in your mouth. Jesus, this is good."

I felt the satisfied grin spread across my face, and it only made me happier that she had powdered sugar on her nose. I stood and stepped into her space, brushing my thumb to remove it.

"I'm glad you like it."

She looked at me for a beat before drawing in a breath and stepping back slightly.

"Ah, thanks. I, um… yeah, it's great. I guess I'll forgive your arms and eyes or whatever. Sorry, I was a little drunk last night."

"I'm trying very hard to be appropriate, so I'm not going to make a joke about how you insulting what are arguably two of my best features was a very interesting approach for a booty call. But I want you to appreciate my restraint."

As it happened, I was very bad at being 'friendly.'

"You're the literal worst. Thank you for the muffins."

"I brought one for Christian, too, if he's here. His compliments were much more straightforward than yours last night."

"He's off today, but even if he weren't, I wouldn't share. Now go to work."

"I'm going, I'm going."

I turned to head out of the salon.

"And Jer?"

"Yeah?" I replied, turning around.

"If you decide to come to happy hour tomorrow, I don't think I'll have to leave early. My schedule has recently cleared up."

That was probably the closest I'd get to her admitting she'd been avoiding me and, dare I say, an almost-apology.

"I'll be there."

And with that, I felt more like myself than I had in months.

Chapter 5- Lauren

Pulling back the foils and watching an entire goddamned rainbow appear was magical. My client had decided to go for it today after a year of being afraid of vivids. It kicked my ass but looked *so* good. I was floating. On days like these, it was easy to forget that I was only cosplaying as a person with their life together. Today, I felt like my hot-mess self was my Hyde instead of Jekyll, and I totally had that bitch under control.

To congratulate myself, I put tight spiral curls in my hair, giving off very Julia-Roberts-in-*Pretty-Woman* vibes, and I pulled out a lilac sundress with a sweetheart neckline that I'd thrifted over a year ago and never worn. Was it overkill for the only establishment in Emberwood to offer happy hour? Yes. Did I care? Absolutely not. Life was too short not to be the best dressed person in the room. It had nothing to do with the fact that Jeremy and I would be in the same room for a whole evening for the first time in months.

And if it did *have something to do with him, it would only be to make him regret his life choices that he didn't kiss me when he could have.*

Revenge clothing was my favorite kind. But then I was thinking about how close he was to me yesterday morning when he brought me muffins. Fucking gourmet, delicious muffins that I would now compare all other breakfast baked goods to as long as I lived.

Screw him for ruining breakfast for me.

Picturing him in an apron, measuring out crushed lavender, had me in a chokehold. He was shirtless under the apron in this daydream, the veins running over his biceps on full display.

Get.It.Together.

The clock let me know that I was running an expected number of minutes late, so I slid into a pair of heels and headed to my car.

Thankfully, Sam was as consistently early as I was late, so I never had to worry about us getting a table. She and Jesse were looking perhaps too cozy for a public setting, so it was my job to interfere with that.

"Try not to make everyone else bear witness to your little bubble of love all the time, yeah?" I demanded, sliding in across from them.

"Try not to make everyone else feel inferior by showing up to The Bar looking like you're headed to a Parisian café. Jesus, Laur," Sam replied, checking me out in the friendliest way possible.

"I had a good day. Ergo, I do pretty hair and wear a pretty dress." I shrugged.

"Mhm. Nothing to do with the company on this particular night."

I glared at her.

"You shut up, Sam Marsh. And also, don't talk to my spirit guides or whatever. I declare a boundary or a magical contract forbidding you from doing so."

I'd meant it to be funny, but she looked a little hurt like I was accusing her of something.

"You know I don't—" she started.

"I know, I know. I'm sorry. It was a joke, honestly." I cleared my throat, hoping to move on.

"Back to this 'company,' who is coming tonight that I don't know about? Do you have a date?" Jesse interjected.

"No. I just decided to clear my *very* busy calendar to prioritize you guys, and, you know, whoever else comes to happy hour. Friendships are important, Brother."

"Right. You're here to prioritize your friendships. Not because Jer is coming. Because it's not a date."

He schooled his expression into something neutral, and it was clear that Sam had something to do with his non-judgmental tone, even if it was strained.

"It's not, Jesse. He's made it perfectly clear that he doesn't want it to be." I could have stopped there, but I felt like testing my brother's newfound commitment to being *fine* if I wanted to date his best friend. "And if it *was*, you'd have to zip it because if you hadn't noticed, you're about to marry my best friend, and I never made a peep about it. The hypocrisy, honestly."

Jesse had the decency to look sheepish.

"Well…" Sam started.

"Gah! Fine! *One* peep. Sue me."

"Who is suing you and why?" a voice interrupted from behind me. I ignored the anticipation that wound around my spine.

Sam jumped in, saving me an awkward explanation.

"I am. For her showing up looking like *that* while the rest of us are stuck being mere mortals."

Jer's eyes roamed over me, lighting up nerve endings I didn't know existed. My brother muttered something that sounded a lot like *not making a peep* before he claimed he was getting us all a round of drinks. Sam not-at-all-subtly jumped up to follow him.

That shook us out of whatever trance we were in, and Jer slid in next to me. He leaned over even further, the scent of fresh laundry and cinnamon overwhelming me. I wondered if he'd been baking before he left.

"Are you trying to kill me?" he murmured in my ear, sending goosebumps down my arms.

"I already told you I was. I threatened to slit your throat and make it seem like an accident not two days ago."

He sighed. "This tactic is more painful."

I met his eyes, and he did look almost pained, but he was grinning regardless. I simultaneously needed to lean into him to feel his hands on me again and also drag my chair to the other side of the table because I had already made up my mind about him.

Friends. Friends. Friends.

I settled for scooting my chair a few inches to the left, making him look at me like I'd popped his balloon.

Why can't this be easy?

Jesse and Sam finally returned with not only drinks but also cheese fries *and* mozzarella sticks *and* pretzel bites with queso.

Suspicion rose in my chest. This much bread and cheese was usually reserved for heartbreak.

"What, were they out of pizza and grilled cheese?" Jer asked, his brows furrowing. Maybe he was also aware of the implications of this combo.

"We can get that, too! If you want, I mean," Sam said.

"Nope! You're not this cheerful. Spit it out," I demanded while shoving a pretzel bite into my mouth.

She glared at me.

"I can be *cheerful*."

"Babe…you may have overdone it," Jesse agreed quietly, making Sam roll her eyes.

"Fine. We have to tell you guys something, and we aren't sure if you're going to be thrilled about it or not," she admitted.

"If you are *pregnant*, and I have to find out the same time as Jer over *cheese fries*, I will seriously consider revoking your title and status because—"

"I'm *not pregnant*," Sam ground out, telling me to shut up with her eyes.

I stopped talking and grabbed another pretzel.

"So," Jesse started. "We're getting married—"

"*What?!* Congratulations! How'd you keep it a secret?" I interrupted. My snarkiness was apparently out in full force tonight.

Now both my brother and Sam were shooting me annoyed looks. I jumped as I felt an arm wrap around me and a hand clamp over my mouth.

"I got it, guys. Go on," Jeremy assured them.

I thought about licking his hand, but I couldn't decide if that would deter him or not. I sighed in defeat and listened.

"We've decided to get married on Equinox," Sam got out, not giving me any more chances to delay.

Jeremy uncovered my mouth.

"Remind me what Equinox is," he said.

"Oh, there's a fall and spring equinox. It's when the day and the night are the same length, like a marker between the light and dark half of the year," Sam explained.

"And you mean *spring*, right?" I asked, starting to understand why they said I might not be thrilled about this.

"We do not," Jesse said. "We're getting married on September twentieth."

"It's already *July*!"

I wondered if it was possible neither of them had looked at a calendar recently before making this decision.

"That's cool. I am so confused. Why this is an issue?" Jeremy looked at me for clarification.

"Lauren's brain is going to explode because most people take a year to plan a wedding. And while we've done a little bit, we're essentially going to do it in ten weeks," Sam explained.

I nodded emphatically like this was the most obvious thing in the world.

"And in order to do that… we're going to require a fair amount of help from our maid of honor and best man," she finished, offering an apologetic smile.

I took in a slow, deep breath and consciously fixed my face.

This is fine.

I could help my best friend and my brother plan a wedding in ten weeks with no prior experience in doing so. It would simply have to become my new all-consuming hobby.

"Okay, then. Perfect. Let's make some lists, shall we?"

The relieved smile that immediately spread across Sam's face was all I needed to know; I'd do whatever I had to in order to make sure this wedding was everything she wanted.

And sure, Jesse, too. Whatever.

I'd have to figure out how to do it on my own, though, because being in close quarters with Jer on a regular basis for the next three months was a surefire way to lose my mind.

Chapter 6- Jeremy

I couldn't remember even attending a wedding before. Maybe my aunt's when I was a kid? I had a vague memory of my mom putting a little bowtie on me and telling me how handsome I looked. I shoved that memory into a box and pushed it to the back of my brain while I tuned back in to Sam and Lauren rapid-firing ideas at one another. Jesse shot me a sheepish look and a shrug while he tipped what was left of his beer into his mouth.

"Okay, so… you want a joint wedding shower, joint bachelor/bachelorette party, the rehearsal dinner is at the shop, and the ceremony is in Zin's garden. She is dealing with catering and booze for the actual wedding?" Lauren repeated back in summary, Sam nodding her head.

"Um, I'm sorry, could someone, like, write down my role? Or give me a checklist?"

"Don't worry about it, Jer. I'll handle it," Lauren said, waving off my question.

Sam looked pointedly at me as Lauren went back to her notebook.

"Not an option. Sorry, Laur."

She sat up slowly and turned to me.

"*What's* not an option?" There was a challenge in her voice.

"You doing everything, and me doing nothing. This is probably the only time I'll be a best man, so let's do it right, you know? Why not?"

"You want to help me plan a wedding shower and a joint bachelor-slash-ette party?"

"More than anything in the whole world, yes."

I almost hoped steam came out of her ears because her face was screaming at me.

"Okay. Awesome. Tell me, Jeremy, what do you think we

should do for the shower? Venue, theme, games?" she asked, plopping her chin in her hand like she was ready to watch me squirm.

Sam held up a finger. "Ah—no games. Just to interject that. I hate shower games of all kinds."

Lauren glared momentarily at Sam but turned her ire back to me quickly.

"Well, I'm not sure what all goes into a wedding shower, though I'm sure the internet can help. But I could make desserts. It would be great for my portfolio if I could do a whole variety… maybe some tea cakes, macarons, whatever you want, honestly. If you'd trust me, I'd love to do the wedding cake itself."

"Can you use edible glitter?" Sam asked, her eyes growing big.

"In any color you can imagine."

Jesse mouthed *thank you* from behind his fiancé, and the fight in Lauren's eyes dwindled, realizing I was committed to being a part of this thing, and consequently, her life, for the next ten weeks.

What could possibly go wrong? I thought ruefully, knowing I hadn't even made it a whole twenty-four hours of trying to be appropriate with her since she started talking to me again.

* * *

Sam and Jesse left shortly after, citing early games for Jesse's Little League teams the next morning, but it was more likely that Sam wanted to force Lauren and me to talk. Sam was a puppet master.

A psychic, witchy puppet master, I thought, which was even more terrifying.

Lauren was still scribbling ideas into her notebook, and I wasn't sure she even noticed we were alone.

"You know we don't have to plan everything *tonight*, right?" She stopped and looked up, then around, and I thought my assumption might be correct.

"Jer."

"Laur."

"This is insane. You get that, right? Like, I love Sam and my brother more than any people on earth, and I understand she has this vision of some sort of universal balance of the equinox, but this is craaaaaazy."

She flopped her notebook closed and downed the rest of her now-watered-down drink.

"I'll admit, I am not well-versed on wedding planning procedures. But I think it's going to be okay. They're not planning on having, like, five hundred people or something. Let me help."

I carefully pulled the notebook over to my side of the table, worried I might spook her if I moved too quickly.

"There are so many details. And my brain already can't hold onto the details of my everyday life, and now I'm going to trust it to ensure my best friend's wedding day, one of the most important days of her life, is magical and perfect? This thing cannot be trusted, Jer," she insisted, tapping her temple.

Her words rushed out, and it was like seeing behind the curtain. Her confidence was usually front and center, and I'd never seen her defeated. Even the night at her front door, she went straight past vulnerable to angry.

"How about this. You can be the idea man, er, woman. You can throw out all the creative ideas or scribble them in this notebook, and I will organize them into something that looks like a reference sheet. A multi-tabbed spreadsheet even."

"You do spreadsheets?" she asked, clearly suspicious.

"I do a lot of office work at the garage for my uncle. It's usually turning documents into PDFs, but yeah, I also do spreadsheets."

"Did you just make document conversion and Microsoft Excel seem hot?"

"Absolutely. If you want, I'll roll up my sleeves *while* I work on the spreadsheets so you can see my arms, which apparently get you all hot and bothered."

"I would punch you if I wasn't so relieved. Also, you're driving me home. Let's go."

I wondered why Lauren ever bothered to drive anywhere, but I counted myself lucky that she was no longer glaring at me or looking like she might launch into a panic attack.

I understood where she was coming from a little because I was already picturing the desserts I wanted to run by Sam for the shower. My program had ended a month ago, and it was the perfect time to force myself to get serious about my portfolio and look for even part-time work with a caterer or a bakery. The idea of coming home covered in flour and sugar every day instead of grease was enticing.

"What are you doing for the Fourth?" she asked as soon as she plopped into my passenger seat.

"Avoiding tourists, like every year. You?"

"Ordering a ton of food and watching the fireworks over the lake from my back patio."

"You have a decent view?"

"Yeah, I'm, like, in the perfect spot on the hill to see over the trees. You should come."

"Are you drunker than I thought, or are you legitimately inviting me over?"

"Maybe both." She giggled and rested her head against the window. "But we can iron out at least the big things for the shower. Time, place, aesthetic, and food. Yeah?"

There was no trace of sarcasm in her voice, and I wasn't sure how to take this version of Lauren.

"Yeah, that sounds good. What can I bring?"

"I wouldn't complain about more of those lavender muffins."

"Ah, I do have some leftovers, but you may be excited to hear that I've now perfected a fluffy, cakey lavender, lemon, and honey cookie. I made, like, two dozen, so I'll bring some of those."

"This is how you get girls to drop their panties, isn't it? It's not the arms or the eyes or your stupid voice, it's the baked goods."

I choked on air, but the coughing fit turned into a laugh, though her face was completely serious.

"As cool of a scheme as that would be, you are the only girl I've ever brought baked goods to. Except my grandma. She taught me how to bake, though, so that seems fair."

Lauren let out a sigh that I couldn't quite decipher as I pulled into her complex.

"Do you need a ride in the morning?"

"Yeah, but Sam will come and get me."

"I don't mind, Laur. And I'd bring you a muffin."

She swore under her breath. "Be here by nine."

With that, she slammed the door, and I watched her disappear into her townhouse. I'd thought about walking her up, but it seemed a whole lot safer not to press my luck.

Chapter 7 - Lauren

I was so screwed. I had to figure out a way to make him *less* attractive for the next ten weeks. Part of me wondered if he was insisting on being involved to annoy me, but he seemed genuinely excited about working on the menu and trying out new stuff for his portfolio, and damn it if his excitement wasn't adorable. Yes, it was odd to think of a six-foot-three hulk of a man as adorable, but he was.

LAUR: Can I put Jer in the freezer? Or his name, you know? How we did with your old douche-bag boss? Or like, is there a spell to make him less *him* for the next 10 weeks?

SAM: I mean, if you've decided to work together, I think putting him in the freezer would only make things more difficult and cause communication issues?

LAUR: Okay, no freezer. A spell? An anti-attraction potion? Something?

SAM: You do know that I'm not like a Hocus Pocus, Bewitched, Sabrina type of witch, right?

LAUR: What I know is that you're a very unhelpful witch.

SAM: Lol, fine. I can pull some crystals and make you a sigil that will help you keep a level head when he's around. Assuming that's what you want.

LAUR: Finally. Yes, I want. Sigil it up!

SAM: You're ridiculous.

LAUR: And you lovvvvvve me. Night!

SAM: Night

But did I sleep? Absolutely not. There were Pinterest boards to be made for the shower and the rehearsal dinner. I was less worried about the joint bachelor party thing because that honestly seemed like what we already did every Friday at happy hour, only with a few more people.

There were so many pretty themes—a fairy garden, boho, whimsical, goth, a Mad Hatter tea party?! I wasn't certain I wanted to get married, maybe ever, but I definitely wanted to throw myself fancy parties. Whatever I didn't use for Sam, I was using for my own birthdays for the next ten years.

The last time I looked at the clock it was around three a.m., and I woke up on my couch with my laptop still on my lap sometime after sunrise.

This might not have been the best idea.

I dragged my ass to the kitchen to make coffee and decided I had time to jump in the shower before Jer picked me up. I at least had to get yesterday's makeup off my face. Getting in the shower was my least favorite thing. But, also, getting out of the shower was my least favorite thing. It was a real conundrum.

I stayed under the scalding hot water for too long, but there weren't enough reasons to turn it off and be cold when I got out.

A towel warmer would be excellent. I should see how much those are. I could probably make one if I wanted to… it's gotta be like a heating element and some pipe?

A look at the time when I finally exited the shower pulled me out of my next project, and I realized I had too much on my plate as it was. I quickly twisted my wet hair into two Dutch braids and put on the bare minimum of makeup. I grabbed a somewhat clean pair of jeans from the floor and a purple *Emberwood Cheer Camp* t-shirt I'd had since freshman year of high school. It was so soft, though; I couldn't get rid of it.

I was looking for my sneakers when Jer knocked on the door.

"Hey, I'm almost ready, come in."

I left the door open and him standing outside, assuming he'd follow. One shoe was eluding me.

"You know I've never been in your place before?" he asked, walking in slowly and taking it all in.

My house was a lot. I had giant Pop-Tarts that I made from papier-mâché hanging on my wall instead of normal things like photos. My kitchen cabinets were bright blue, and I'd covered my appliances with pink vinyl. I'd spent years curating a massive collection of frames so that I could cover a whole wall with them in a rainbow gradient. Each frame had a key in it. Those were also thrifted; I liked the look of all the mixed metal inside the bright colors.

Every wall in my little townhouse had its own flair, and together, it sort of looked like Lisa Frank and Rainbow Brite consulted on the design. I watched him look around for a moment before I finally found the shoe hidden in my basket of blankets.

Because that's where that goes.

"I get it. It's not for everyone," I said, anticipating the comments that pretty much every man ever made if they came back to my house. About how they could never live somewhere so "*girly*" and "wasn't I worried about *resale value*?" No. Nothing concerned me less than resale value. I wouldn't want to sell this place to someone with no taste anyway.

"Seriously? I mean, I get that some people are boring, but this is like living in a pop culture museum. It's fantastic. Did you *make* this?" he asked, referencing the strawberry Pop-Tart on the wall.

"Yeah. I saw a painting somewhere like that... maybe in a magazine or on a blog? Anyway, I had to have some. The wild berry one is my favorite."

I stuck my foot in my shoe and grabbed my purse, wondering if I was going to be able to pull him back outside. He was now looking at each of the keys in the frames.

"Do these keys go to something? Or are they—"

"I will explain my décor to you another day. We can work on wedding things over here if you want, and you can poke around at all of it. But we both do have to work."

"Don't remind me. Yeah, let's go. I like your hair by the way. I was appropriately distracted by your house, but the braids are fun."

"You're not going to make any suggestive comments about pigtails being—"

"I was *not* going to say that. I'm charming and flirty, Laur, not pervy. I hope, anyway."

I laughed and hopped into the passenger seat of his car. His car was always so clean it was almost unnerving. Not a single fast-food wrapper anywhere.

"You're right, you're not. Sorry to have suggested otherwise," I said.

"You might have to earn my forgiveness. Three months of the silent treatment ought to do it!" He side-eyed me hard.

"The past is in the past, Jer! Let it go. And you promised me muffins."

"I did, I did."

He reached into the back, pulled up a white paper bag, and placed it on my lap.

"Also, you weren't a cheerleader," he proclaimed, gesturing to my t-shirt. "I would have remembered you in the uniform."

"Don't act like you know everything about me. I'm mysterious. I also *was* a cheerleader for two whole weeks before freshman year. But they practiced *really* early, so I quit before the school year even started." I shrugged. "Am I not allowed to eat in your car? It feels like that would be a rule?" I asked him warily, wanting to eat one of those muffins. He huffed a laugh.

"I work at a body-shop. I'll vacuum it out while I'm there if I need to. It's a nice ego boost when you like my food. But did you ever wear the *uniform*, Laur? This is important information."

"No, now stop it. You said you weren't pervy. And thank god, I'm starving."

I promptly pulled out the largest of the three, bit off a chunk of the top, and groaned.

Just as good as I remembered.

Chapter 8- Jeremy

If she did not stop moaning about my damn muffins, she was going to see how quickly I could cross into pervy territory. I white-knuckled the steering wheel and thought about doing tire rotations.

"I'm not discounting your talent at your job or anything, but can I ask how you bought your house at, like, what, twenty-one?" I asked, always wondering how she pulled that off.

"You don't think I'm raking it in as a small-town hair stylist? Rude."

I started to backtrack. I'd only been trying to steer the conversation away from the sounds she'd been making.

"Nah, it's fine. And uninteresting. My grandma left Jesse and me money and said in the will that it had to be used for a home, school, or travel. I bartended through school, and I hated not being able to paint or decorate my apartment. The market had bottomed out like a year before, and I ended up getting an insane price on the townhouse. So, now I get to decorate how I want, and my mortgage is lower than my rent ever was."

"I... well, I guess that makes perfect sense. You don't give off the vibe of a real estate mogul, but I could see it."

"Totally."

"What'd Jesse do with his money?"

"Nothing, as far as I know. He had a scholarship for school. He's probably saving it for something smart like his future kids' college funds."

"Boring."

She let out a light laugh.

"So, did you think about cakes last night? I'm impressed that you're that good. I bet you could get your own show on The Food Channel. They love hot guys who bake things," she said, eyeing me covertly.

"Well, you don't know that I'm that good yet, but the fact that you're complimenting me already this morning is a positive sign. I usually have to go through seven levels of sarcasm and a couple vodka sodas before we get here."

"*Right*. Like you're unaware of what you look like. You're so ridiculous."

She rolled her eyes and prepared to pop the last piece of muffin into her mouth, but her words made me feel bolder than usual. I grabbed her hand and pulled it to my mouth, eating the piece off her fingers.

"You can't take the *last* bite! That's basic food sharing etiquette, Jeremy Ash!"

"Whoaaaa, I wasn't prepared for my full name. I'll make sure to only take the second to last bite next time, I swear. But there *are* two more in the bag."

"Yes, but I was anticipating *that* as my last bite, and I was going to savor it. Now I have to eat a whole other one!"

"What a hardship. I'm so sorry, Laur. Truly."

She swatted me on the arm, and regretfully, I pulled into the parking lot where she'd left her car. She unbuckled her belt, and I had a moment where I felt like maybe I could lean over and kiss her, and we could skip all the awkwardness of figuring ourselves out and jump ahead to being comfortably *together* like Sam and Jesse. It was a nice moment.

"Thanks for the ride. And breakfast."

"Did you mean it when you invited me over for fireworks?" I asked abruptly.

I had kind of planned on letting that go, but now the idea of sitting with her in the dark and watching the show over the lake was something I needed.

"Oh! I did say that, huh?"

Her silence was a beat too long, and I was ready to bow out.

"Well, yeah. Come over before sundown. I don't know if Sam and Jesse are coming. They *really* like carnival rides, so they might stay at the fair… and it might just be you and me. If that's okay, then I'll see you Monday."

"I'll see you Monday. Er, wait. Don't I have a hair appointment tomorrow?"

"Possibly. If it didn't get canceled. I can't be held responsible for the whims of technology, Jer."

"Well, I'm going to assume that technology has taken one look at my almost man-bun and decided to let this one stand."

"Yeah, yeah. Maybe. I'll see you *tomorrow* then. Are you sure you're not stalking me? This feels like we're seeing a lot of each other."

"Stalkers are usually stealthier than making appointments on a website using their real name. I think. I can't be sure."

"Perhaps." She gave me a silly side-eye and bounced off to her little yellow Bug, and not even the looming number of oil changes I had on the schedule today could bring me down.

* * *

"Are you *smiling* while being here before ten on a Saturday?" Rachel asked when I walked through the front of the shop to get to my closet-office.

I didn't have a job title so much as doing whatever my uncle needed me to do. Sometimes, that meant ordering, checking on special orders, filing invoices, and sometimes, that meant spending the day doing seven million oil changes. Today would be mostly the latter, though I had to follow up on one phone call from the day before.

"For sure not. I must be having some sort of facial tic or something."

"Did you have a date? Are you over Lauren? Oh my god, was the date *with* Lauren?" Rachel asked, her voice getting louder the further down the hall I went.

My relationship with Rachel went back to middle school, when we were always friends by association. She'd dated several of my friends over the years, actually. When she started working at the shop, she was coming out of a shitty relationship, and I was still barely getting my life together. We quickly fell into a someone-to-listen-to-my-tragic-life-story situation, and we hooked up all of one time. It should have worked because we got along well, and she was hot, but it just…didn't. We were better off for it anyway, and we never stepped a toe over that line again.

I heard her shoes tapping down the hallway toward me.

"No. No. And no. Does that clear things up?"

"Also, no. Because you can't even stop smiling when you're being a dick to me. *Something* happened. I'll take you to lunch soon. You can tell me alllll about it."

She grinned confidently and turned on her heel to return to her perch at the front desk, her wavy black hair flipping as she did.

Rachel had started dating one of the newer mechanics recently. I liked him for her—he settled her down. But now that she'd found someone, she was insistent that I did, too. She was now the biggest supporter of me getting over myself and trying to make a go of things with Laur. But as much as she joked, she didn't push. She knew my hesitation, and probably better than anyone, she knew my history. I sighed in resignation that I'd have to explain to her that I was all lit up because Laur liked my muffins and invited me over to plan a wedding shower. This did not sound like forward progress. This sounded like I was becoming her newest gal pal.

Not great. Not great at all.

I tried not to let that little revelation dampen my buzz, and I reminded myself that I got to research complicated cakes later, so today would be a work sandwich, bracketed on each side with either Lauren or baking.

Better.

Chapter 9 - Lauren

"I brought you the best breakfast you'll ever eat. You're welcome," I said in greeting to Christian when I walked past him to drop my bag in the back.

"Oh?" he asked when I returned. "From where? Because if you baked it, I might let you keep that all for yourself."

"I can *cook*. I survive living on my own, don't I?"

"You survive on bar food and the taco truck down the street."

"That's a lie. I have pasta and frozen meatballs at home for when I'm feeling fancy." I was gifted with a light clap. "But *no*, Jer made these. He went to baking school or something."

"I accept. He has good vibes."

Christian held out his hand, and I delicately placed the muffin into it and awaited his thanks.

"Damn. That tastes like a family of elves baked it," he muttered.

"Right? You're welcome."

I was a little jealous when Christian told me what services he had booked—his clients were adventurous. He was doing a set of extensions, a mermaid balayage, and then some normal cut and colors.

I want to do a mermaid balayage, I pouted in my head.

"Think I should put some red, white, and blue tinsel in my hair?"

"Really? Patriotism in *this* economy?" he asked incredulously.

"You're probably right. I'm bored with my appearance, I think. Wanna dye my hair?"

"No. I don't dye naturally red hair anyway; you know this. Channel your boredom into planning the wedding shower you're freaking out about."

"Damn it! How do I keep forgetting that's the only item on my agenda?!"

Christian sighed, shook his head, and went to greet his client. I got a diet soda from the fridge in the back and downed it, excited to see Gen this morning. She'd started coming to me shortly after we met, and she was a dream client. Her hair was awesome, and she claimed she was mostly here for the socializing.

I opened Pinterest while I waited and tried to narrow down the gazillion ideas I had for the shower theme. Maybe I'd let Jer choose based on what desserts he wanted to make. That would help tremendously with my decision paralysis. I took some screenshots and dropped them in a text with the labels A, B, C, or D.

LAUR: Choose your favorite theme based on the delightful things you want to bake.

He did not immediately answer, which was the most annoying. He was probably under a car or something. My mind wandered to him in a tight white t-shirt, sweaty, and spotted with grease.

God, why is that hot? You should ask Gen to write a mechanic romance.

"I'm here! And I brought you iced tea with lemon. You like this, yes?"

"I like all forms of caffeine, yes. It calms me down."

"Ah, so you're one of those people who can drink three coffees and take a nap?"

"Yes!"

"My sister is the same way. You'll have to let me know your favorite drink for next time."

She plopped down in my chair, and I secured her cape.

"Before I forget, I need you to write a mechanic romance. Asking for a friend, obviously. And also, tell me what we're doing today."

"For a friend, huh? Is there anyone I should use for my inspo board for said mechanic?"

"Nope, totally up to you. You know, art imitating life or

something."

"Riiiiight. I'll get that outlined for you."

She grinned widely before taking out her phone to show me pictures. Her hair was a lovely honey-colored blond, and the photos showed the same base color with chocolate and caramel lowlights.

"Girrrrlllll, this is sexy."

"You think? I like the darker vibes. I kind of feel like I'm entering my villain era. Or, at least, Penn thinks so. I might as well roll with it, right?"

I stepped back on my heel and cocked my head at her. Penn was Gen's husband. Yes, we teased her that their names rhymed. But we'd only met him twice; he hardly ever came out. I wasn't around him enough to form an educated opinion, but I was happy to make snap judgments at any time.

"Not that I'm opposed to a villain era, but *why* exactly is Penn under this impression?"

"It's a long story," she said with a sigh.

"It's a good thing this color's going to take a while then, huh? I'm going to go mix up. I'll be right back."

I mixed carefully, still reeling from the error I'd made last week. Plus, now that I knew Gen was feeling yucky, her hair needed to be that much better.

"Timer starts now, so get to talkin'."

I laser-focused my attention while I started putting on color and folding foils. She took a deep breath, and I knew this was going to be something heavy.

"I don't know. He's stressed about money, I guess. And my last book did okay, but the ones before that have kind of slowed down in sales...and preschool teachers don't make very much. So, he wants to move to Toledo, because his company is opening a branch, and for me to look for another job once we're there, but I don't want to. Is that selfish, you think? I mean, if we had anything serious going on, like we were racking up debt or not paying our bills, I get it. But we're okay. He wants a bigger house, a nicer car, fancy vacations. And I just don't care. That does sound kind of villain-esque when I say it like that."

She bit her lip and looked nervous. Little did she know that even if she *did* sound like the villain, I was bound by hair stylist code to support her evil efforts one thousand percent. As it happened, she wasn't, though.

"Hmmmmm. I'm not getting villain. Sorry."

"Yeah? I love my littles at school, and having breaks and summers off gives me time to write, and I can't imagine going to a job I hate every day to drive a different car? And I *like* my tiny rental house. It's cozy."

"I'm totally with you on the job thing. I had to explain this to Sam last year when she was thinking about going back to a design firm that it's not necessary to hate going to work. Some of us like our jobs most of the time."

"Ugh, it's so good to hear someone else say that. I feel like I'm banging my head against a wall with Penn. He only sees one version of success, and that's dollar signs."

She sighed, and I could tell that maybe we needed to steer into happier topics now that she'd gotten it off her chest. I was going to send her husband a glare or two the next time I saw him, though; that was for sure.

"Well, I happened to read your last three books, and I can tell you that you successfully made me lust after a football player, a cowboy, and an architect. So, I say mission accomplished on that front."

She laughed, and her eyes lit up at the compliment.

Back on track.

I finished up her color and left her to sit while I went to grab a snack.

"I was eavesdropping," Christian said, settling in next to me in the back room.

"I would expect nothing less."

"I am *incensed* at the audacity of her husband."

"I, too, am incensed. That's an excellent word."

"Good. We can be incensed together. And you've already planned to glare at him should he show his face at a happy hour, correct?"

"How do you know me this well?"

"We're Geminis, darling."

"It makes so much sense."

I wandered back out to check on Gen's color after mixing up her toner, *correctly*, and as predicted, it was looking *amazing*.

"You are going to be *so* happy with this!" I squealed.

She looked genuinely excited, and I was going to add some pretty layers around her face for fun if she wanted. I rinsed and toned her and took her back to my station.

"So, do you want me to turn you around so you can be surprised at the end, or does that give you anxiety?"

"Oh! No, let's do the surprise."

I clapped because makeover reveals were what I lived for. I got to work, and I had to say that I still had the ability to amaze myself. The new color perfectly complemented her skin tone.

"I am so very good at my job. You ready?"

She only nodded quickly, and I spun her around, elated to hear her gasp.

"Oh my *god*, Laur, I look like a different human!"

"Yes, but still pretty you."

"I'm obsessed. Seriously, thank you so much. Maybe this will take Penn's mind off everything else."

She grinned, and I hoped that was true. She was the nicest girl; she deserved an equally nice husband.

"He would be a fool not to fall all over himself, yes."

"Agreed!" Christian called out from his station, confirming my analysis.

"You guys are so good for the ego. I'll see you at happy hour next week, maybe?"

"I hope so! Enjoy looking at yourself in windows," I called after her as she left.

I sank into my chair and twirled around, sipping what was left of my tea.

"Shouldn't you be utilizing your time to get back to planning?"

"Damn it!"

Chapter 10 - Jeremy

I pulled into the salon parking lot about ten minutes before my appointment, and it was surprisingly empty for a weekend. Lauren was cashing out a client when I walked in.

"It's not just me, right? Like, isn't this place usually hopping on a Sunday?" I asked, leaning on the reception counter.

"You're not wrong, but, holiday weekend. There's one other girl working today, coming in around eleven, but it's always slow on long weekends like this. I usually get a tourist or two wanting something done before a barbeque or a boat adventure, so I figured, why not?"

So, the two of us. Alone. Where she will be forced to stand extremely close to me. Perfect.

"That makes sense. Well, shall we get to it? My hair is becoming oppressive."

She rolled her eyes but led me back to her chair.

"A trim? Or are we doing a mohawk today? Full buzzcut, maybe?"

"You're hilarious. I don't know if you can even call it a trim since it's been months. I could be in an 80s hair band, Laur."

I demonstrated by headbanging to no music and letting my hair swing back and forth. I liked it long*ish*. Not ponytail long.

"It is a little overgrown, I'll give you that," she admitted, combing her fingers through it. I had to have a brief mental argument with my dick that this was not the time to barge into a conversation where he was uninvited. The hands in my hair were professional, not recreational.

"Let's get you shampooed, anyway. You big whiner."

"I'm sorry, I missed that. You said I have a big—"

"Ego. I said you have a big ego."

"Neither assumption is incorrect," I added almost under my breath, but she shook her head in admonishment, letting me know she heard me loud and clear. I shrugged and got as comfy as I could in the shampoo chair. There had to be an invention that made this less awkward. I didn't fit right.

Her nails on my scalp and the citrusy scent of whatever products she used were relaxing, though. Sadly, she finished up, and I followed her back to her station.

"So, friend. How's life? I feel like I haven't talked to you in months," she began, coming in hot.

"Well, friend, I guess it's all right now that I'm not being left as the third wheel in all group activities. Plus, I'll be back to my gorgeous self shortly."

"Assuming the scissors don't slip."

"Right. I feel okay about that assumption."

She shrugged.

"Are you seeing anyone new?" she asked, her tone light.

The question was innocuous for one friend to ask another. It felt like a ticking bomb coming out of her mouth. I let out something between a strangled laugh and a cough. Because *no*, I wasn't. I *wasn't* because it felt weird to think about other women when all I wanted to think about was *her*. Lauren's scissors stopped moving, and she looked apologetic before opening her mouth to deliver what would have likely been an awkward apology.

"Nope. You know me, anyway. I don't really do relationships, and the tourist thing feels like watching the same movie over and over again after a while, so, no. I needed a break."

She seemed to un-pause and go back to focusing on my hair once I got out my little declaration.

"Why is that, anyway?"

"Why is what?" I asked, afraid. She had me cornered, and I very much wanted this conversation to be over.

"The no relationships thing. I mean, I get it. I, too, am a relationship-school-dropout. I mean… you used to date a lot in high school. And there was Kat…"

I swallowed and told myself to keep to my lighthearted story about not wanting anything serious, wanting to have fun, but it felt so tired, especially with Lauren. I also knew *why* she was asking. Because I'd said no to her, and she wanted to know if the *no* was because of me or because of her.

"Well. Since you are the one with the sharp instrument near my throat, tell me which answer you want. The standard one or the real one."

This is not your best idea.

"The real one, obviously. I have to keep it confidential anyway; it's in my oath."

I chuckled at that, imagining her swearing an oath over a blow dryer.

"Oooookay. But when I'm a total buzzkill, you must take responsibility."

She nodded her assent, still trimming away.

"I did used to date in high school, and the stakes were low, and it was mostly fun. Well, dramatic, but in an exciting way, I guess. And Kat and I were the *most* dramatic, even then."

Lauren's raised brows let me know she at least remembered some stories. She was a year behind me, but our school was tiny. Everyone knew everyone.

"I made... poor decisions, we'll say, after graduation. I was serving at La Cantina in Centerville and making what I thought was a massive amount of money. Kat was, too, and we thought we were invincible or something. Doing a lot of coke does that to a person," I explained, not wanting to lie by omission.

I was not a good guy then. I didn't know if I was a good guy now, though, I tried a lot harder.

"Oh," Lauren said, her tone purposely neutral.

I wondered if they taught that at hair stylist school, too. How to respond when your clients say awful things.

"It didn't start out that intense, I should say. This is, like, over years of kind of spiraling. We ended up in this toxic place where what used to be innocent drama turned into screaming matches and her putting a hole in the wall of my room at my parents' house with my baseball bat. And that later turned into me getting kicked out because my parents found my stash after the whole incident and me losing my job because Kat had also been sleeping with our manager, so…"

The only sound for several heartbeats was the snipping of scissors. I'd even left out the part where I got arrested for kicking my manager's ass after said firing.

"I'm not gonna lie, Jer. I was unprepared for that story. I'm… I'm sorry that's how life went after graduation."

I waved my hand, realizing I'd clearly told the story wrong.

"There is nothing you should feel sorry for after that incredibly condensed version of my post-high-school life. I realize I made Kat sound like the villain there, but I brought all of it on myself. I was not good to her, either. I was sarcastic and mean and, well, high, most of the time, and I openly flirted with other girls because I am a dick. If pity is the emotion you're feeling, then I'm not explaining it right.

"But I don't do relationships because I don't want to do that to someone else. Bring out their worst with my worst, I guess. I don't know if that makes sense."

She stood still, a look of understanding crossing over her face, and I at least felt that I'd hit home the fact that our earlier encounter was a *me* issue and not a *her* issue.

"You don't think it would be different now because *you're* different now?"

She'd stopped snipping completely by this point.

"It's an assumption that I'm any different now. I mean, I don't do illicit drugs anymore, so that's an improvement, for sure. But I have no other proof that I'm a different person. The only evidence I have is that I was not a version of myself that I liked very much when I was in a quote-un-quote *serious* relationship. And it's been a few years, and that seems like a long time, but it also feels like I'm still getting my feet under me sometimes. I decided it's better that I don't go there."

Her expression confused me now. She almost looked defeated.

"So, you don't think people can change?"

"I don't claim to know anything about what other people can do. Just me."

She nodded, her chin jutting out slightly like she didn't like my answer.

"I told you I'd be a buzzkill."

She huffed a laugh and seemed to realize she was no longer cutting my hair but instead standing and talking to me in the mirror.

"Sorry. You're distracting."

"How about you? Anyone new?"

Part of me wanted her to say yes so that I'd be forced to be appropriate and get over this urge to feel like I could have *things* with her. Happy, stable, long-term things. At least she'd started cutting again, and I wasn't sure if I was relieved or annoyed that she was almost done.

"No. Maybe I'm on a break too."

"Well, your phone has buzzed sixty-seven times since I've been sitting here, so *someone* wants to get ahold of you."

She grimaced.

"Tourist I hooked up with last year is in town again. I am being very mature and ignoring him until he goes home."

"Ah, I never thought about one coming back to haunt me. You've unlocked a new fear."

"Right? That's supposed to be clear-cut! Whatever. Maybe I'll block him."

"Not good enough for a repeat performance?"

"That's sort of my issue, in a nutshell."

I looked at her quizzically, wondering if I was about to get to see a Lauren without her walls up.

"Pity I have to blow dry you now, and you won't get to hear my whole failed relationship history."

She smirked at me, looking more like herself now as she flipped her dryer *on*, effectively ending all communication. She was sneaky.

I narrowed my eyes at her in the mirror, but it was fine. I'd said what I'd needed to say; I hoped she understood better why I couldn't cross that line with her. All I felt with her was light, and I had no desire to turn into some sort of monster who diminished it because I couldn't stay in the friendzone where I belonged.

She finished, I paid, and it seemed like whatever little oversharing space I was in had dissipated. We were back to our normal banter again.

"I'll see you for fireworks tomorrow. Bring cookies, or I'm not letting you in."

"I promise. Thank you for making me look less like a Yeti. I think I lost five pounds in hair."

"Well, try not to wait so long between appointments next time. Self-care is important, Jeremy."

She grinned widely at me, and I left shaking my head, feeling like maybe we'd found some equilibrium.

Chapter 11 - Lauren

There were a lot of emotions making a sort of panic smoothie in my stomach after that appointment. Not only because of Jer's story. I knew some stuff went down with him and Kat, but Jesse had already left for college, and Jeremy and I weren't friends without my brother as the common denominator then, so I didn't *really* know.

I struggled to imagine him the way he described himself, and I guessed I could see the part where he flirted with other women... he was a pathological flirt; it's part of why he was fun to hang out with. But the rest... it was hard to reconcile his version of himself with the one I saw. I didn't think he was *that* great of an actor, so my hypothesis was he *had* put in the work to be better, even beyond being clean.

He was always working, either at the garage or in class, and he only ever drank, like, one beer anytime we went out if anything at all. He'd taken my ass home more than once and brought me baked goods. He was helping me plan a wedding shower, for fuck's sake. This was not a man who brought out the worst in people. At least not anymore.

It helped that I understood his history, though. His hesitation with me had always gone beyond some half-hearted objection from Jesse about it being weird seeing his best friend with his sister. This made more sense. The annoying, persistent little thought that had popped into existence during his speech, though? I hadn't anticipated that. I had tried to squash it out of existence during my next client's service, but there it remained hours later as I tried to sleep.

This is what happens when you ask people serious questions. You get serious answers, and now you must think serious thoughts.

I yanked my pillow over my head, knowing it would do no

good at all, and I started making a mental list of what I needed to do for the shower. Invitations would be the natural next step, but graphic design savant that she was, Sam insisted on creating them herself. I needed to arrange for rentals.

I can send out emails at one a.m. That's acceptable, right? It's not like I'm calling anyone and waking them up.

I decided that logic was sound, and I got out of bed and began filling out contact forms for every local rental place I could find for tables, linens, and heaters. At least my insomnia was productive.

* * *

I finally passed out somewhere around three-thirty and slept like the dead until noon. My phone had notifications, but coffee came first. After I began to wake up in earnest, I scrolled.

SAM: Get me your schedule for this week. Dress shopping for real!

LAUR: I'm off Wednesday! Consider it planned.

She sent me back no less than fifteen clapping emojis.

LAUR: Are you and Jesse coming over for fireworks or are you going to stay at the fair?

SAM: Fair. We totally missed the fun last Harvest Festival because of my mother, so I've insisted we bribe the Ferris wheel operator to put us at the top for fireworks. You're sure you won't come?

LAUR: I'm sure. I'm not in a carnival mood. Jer's coming over so we can work on wedding shower things anyway, so I'll have someone to ooh and ahh with over the finale anyway.

SAM: Am I allowed to make a comment about how there are many other things you could ooh and ahh over with Jer alone in your house?

LAUR: Permission denied.

SAM: You used to be fun!

LAUR: You used to be nice!

SAM: That's an outright lie. I've never been nice. Have fun tonight. Allllll the fun.

I sent her a single middle finger emoji and moved on.

* * *

I'd cleaned my house with the music at the loudest volume I could get away with while avoiding one of my neighbors knocking on my door to complain. My house was typically clean, and I knew where *everything* was. Except for important items I needed daily. Namely my keys, my shoes, my phone, and, for some reason, my hairbrush. Today was not an exception. I knew my phone was in my house because it was streaming music to my speakers. But *where* in my house was a mystery.

I occupied myself with fun eye makeup and turned down my speaker so I could hear him knock on the door if he arrived early. I originally thought about red, white, and blue shadow, but for a night in, that seemed like maybe a lot. So, I went with straight-up glitter instead because: fireworks. I was nothing if not a theme lover.

I found my phone tucked into the shorts I was wearing earlier and pulled it out, victorious. Christian had sent me pictures of his own eye makeup, and, of course, it was insane and made mine look like a child's art project. He also went for fireworks but with expertly drawn silver glitter lines exploding from his eyeliner. He zoomed out and got his shirt in the frame that said **FUCK THE PATRIARCHY**, so I guessed he was going for balance. I sent back twelve fire emojis. The next messages were from Jer, and that little whisper of a thought I'd been squashing all day waved hello in my brain.

Shut up.

JEREMY: You said sundown, but that's not a time.

JEREMY: Maybe it is. I looked it up and it says 9:05, but I'm pretty sure fireworks start at 9. So, I'm going to assume you meant to come over at some point as the sun is setting. I have unilaterally decided that means 8:30. See you then. I have cookies but let me know if you want me to pick up anything.

He sent a photo of said cookies as proof. I looked at the time, and my heart gave a slight sputter. It was 8:25. I grabbed the sigil Sam had made for me to help me keep a level head. Whatever that meant.

LAUR: I realize this response is late, but yes, 8:30 is fine.

JEREMY: Glad to hear it. I just pulled in.

I went to unlock the door and figured I'd wait. He parked and stepped out of his car wearing a tight blue t-shirt and jeans, a hoodie thrown over his shoulder, and his tattoos peeking out beneath his sleeves. His hair looked good, falling along his jawline. That wasn't a compliment for him; it was a compliment for me. I was very talented.

"You like what you see, Garrett? I feel like you're undressing me with your eyes."

"You'd like that. I was admiring my incredible skill with your hair."

"Sure, you were. It does look good, though."

He handed me a container of cookies, and I could already smell them. I directed him inside and offered him a drink.

"Can I have, like, a gigantic glass of water? I can feel my body begging for hydration. I got caught up in our project today and sort of forgot to eat or drink things for, you know, survival. But you should have the beginning of a super sexy spreadsheet in your inbox. And I ordered ingredients for the desserts for the shower. So, I'm winning at that."

"I feel this struggle on a very deep level. Yes, water, and I have Chinese being delivered in, like, five. I figured Chinese restaurants might be less busy today."

"Hot *and* smart. You are killing it at wooing me. I like it."

He winked at me like he was a movie star leading man, and I wanted to make fun of him, but my body was a big fan of the compliment and the wink.

"I'm not wooing you. I don't *woo*."

The food arrived at that moment, and I had to abandon my defense. As soon as he'd said it, I realized I hadn't eaten all day either, and my mouth started watering.

He took one look at the collection of paper boxes and scoffed.

"If this isn't wooing, I don't know what is, Garrett."

He helped me open everything up and attempted to give me forty bucks to pay for it, which I refused because Sam and I never worried about who paid for food, and Jer and I were supposed to be friends, too.

"You can get next time, then. Stop pouting," I said after he kept complaining.

His smile returned, and I proceeded to inhale crab rangoons straight from the bag as I loaded up a plate.

"We have to go out on the porch to see the show, so hurry

up."

He heeded my warning, scooped noodles onto his plate, and followed me out to my patio. It was tiny but cute. It matched the rest of the house in that everything was bright and mixed patterns, and I loved it.

We plopped onto the cushioned bench and consumed our calories in silence. The temperature had dropped with the sun, and I zipped up my hoodie and grabbed a blanket from my couch. Because he was very, very manly, Jer declined a blanket, but after approximately two more minutes, he tugged on the corner of mine and declared that sharing was caring.

"I have other blankets, is all I'm saying."

"But I like that you're under this one, too," he said, flirting shamelessly, bumping his shoulder into mine.

I rolled my eyes and ignored the warmth of him against me. At least his boundary of flirting and nothing more made more sense now. It was less infuriating. Thinking about his story from yesterday made me sit up a little straighter as I consciously tried to push that annoying notion away again.

"Sorry," he muttered, scooting back out under the blanket. "You told me to act like your friend, and I have been doing a shit job of it. I'll go get a blanket."

"Oh, shut up," I started, wishing the fireworks would start and interrupt the word vomit I knew was about to come out of my mouth. "You can sit under the blanket. Jesus."

"Okay... you seemed, whatever. I'll stop talking."

He scooted right back in where he'd been.

"I just... the way you were talking about yourself in relationships yesterday? I kind of feel the same. I think. I've been trying *not* to think about it, which makes the stupid thought pop up even more."

"What do you mean you feel the same?" he inquired, his tone curious.

"Not in terms of, like, a baseball bat incident. Thankfully, I don't have one of those. I tend to… go from hot to freezing at the drop of a hat. And then I'm done, and I feel bad because it's never a good reason. Like, I'm putting these guys through unnecessary drama or confusion. I'm not sure how to put it. But most of the time, they're decent guys.

"So, when you said something about not liking yourself in a relationship, it kind of struck a chord. It's a lot easier to think that there's something wrong with everyone else, and it's a harder pill to swallow to admit that the common denominator is me. Or like I cause harm to other people, even if it's not intentional. Sometimes it is intentional, though."

I bit my lip, disliking the direction I'd taken the evening so far.

"It's not even like I don't *know* that I'm the issue. It's why I mostly hook up with tourists, but it's another thing to hear it out loud. Bottom line, I think I should also stay away from relationships. So, thanks for that."

I tried to end it lightly and took a large drink of water.

"Laur… there's nothing *wrong* with you," he started.

"It's fine. I wasn't fishing for a compliment. And to prove my point, I ghosted the last guy I went out with, who was somewhat local, because he said his favorite movie was *Fight Club*. I mean, it's the most cliché 'I'm trying to sound like an alpha' answer, so I don't apologize for rolling my eyes, but otherwise, he was okay for the whole three or four dates we went on. But no, never to be spoken of again."

Jeremy laughed and chewed thoughtfully on his orange chicken.

"It might have been a little harsh, but that answer *could* have been indicative of a whole host of other red flags. Maybe you dodged a bullet, you know?"

"Yeah, maybe. Except I do that shit a lot. So, am I constantly dodging bullets? Should I be concerned that someone has a hit out on me?"

He laughed again but was quiet for a few uncomfortable beats after. When he finally met my eyes, I was worried he'd say something judgy and make me regret my existence for the past ten minutes. Instead, a serious expression settled over his features.

"We're kind of a mess, Laur."

A small giggle escaped my mouth, and then another, and then the gates opened. It was completely ridiculous. He joined me in laughing too hard at how screwed up the two of us were. The giggles subsided, and I wiped tears from my eyes.

"At least we're *hot* messes, you know? I look good while I'm fucking everything up," he insisted.

I opened my mouth to respond as the first firework went up.

Thanks for nothing, I thought, noting they were starting ten minutes late.

Just long enough for me to overshare. But I guessed it all ended up as well as it could have. Both of our attentions refocused on the show over the lake. The reflections were as lovely as the fireworks themselves, and it didn't matter how old I got, they always felt magical.

I felt Jer move impossibly closer and put his arm around my shoulder. I should have shrugged it off. I wasn't sure if this was out of pity that I sucked at relationships, but it felt more like commiseration about our abject failures with the opposite sex. Plus, it felt good having his fingers rub circles on my upper arm. The shiver that echoed through me had nothing to do with being cold.

If we're enjoying it, then we might as well really *enjoy it.*

It was in that spirit that I took out the little piece of paper with the magical sigil and tore it in two as discreetly as I could. There was no room for rationality with the way I was feeling.

I set my plate down on the little table and drew my knees up, curling into his side and letting his arm drape over me and pull me tighter. As the sparkles in the sky popped, he played with the hem of my jacket and brushed his fingers over my hip, creating ripples in the shivering effect. I gripped his shirt in my hand, needing something to keep me from floating. He didn't seem to mind.

The finale began, and a smile spread across my face because I couldn't be unhappy during a Fourth of July fireworks finale. Jer's free hand loosened my grip on his shirt and intertwined his fingers with mine as the colors blazed in the distance.

The show ended, and we could hear the cheers from down by the lake drift up. We let the cocoon around us linger for a moment before awkwardly disentangling ourselves from each other.

"I suppose we need to tend to very important serious wedding shower business?" he asked, clearing his throat and picking up our plates to bring inside.

I nodded affirmatively, following him back in the house. I did spare one last look at the bench, wishing maybe that show had gone on a while longer.

Chapter 12- Jeremy

"That was a good show," Lauren said, her voice coming out a little strangled.

"Right. Top tier fireworks."

My own voice was lower than I intended, and I swallowed to make it go back to normal. This was both *exactly* what I'd wanted and exactly what I had been trying for so long to avoid. Because now we were alone, I'd willfully crossed a line, and I had no logical escape plan.

There's got to be some sort of fireworks on a summer night clause that equates to "What happens in Vegas," I thought. *If there isn't, there should be because this is unbearable.*

Laur zipped and unzipped her hoodie awkwardly before clearing her throat.

"Do you want, like, water? Beer?"

Alcohol would do nothing to make my judgment any better, but I also might not survive the evening without something to take the edge off. The edge was *sharp*.

"Ah, beer, sure."

I dropped down onto her couch. It was some sort of soft material. Way better than the couch I'd gotten from Craigslist for free.

"Here," she said, thrusting a bottle at me from as far away as she could stand. "And the cookies you brought. I'm sure fancy cookies and cheap beer are classy in some cultures."

"Oh, it's a deeply engrained custom in the Ash heritage. Cheap beer is practically our holy water," I assured her, taking a gulp in hopes it would dull that edge soon.

She shot a grin at me, a smidge of her rigidity fading.

"Let me get my laptop and notebook, and we can get started."

I nodded, pulling up the stuff I'd saved on my phone. Upon

her return, she looked at the spot next to me and then at the rest of the seating options in her small living room, a desperate look on her face, like a magical solution would appear.

"You can sit on my lap if that cushion is offensive," I blurted out, however inadvisable.

Giving in was so much easier than resisting, and I was still operating under a fireworks clause.

"You're ridiculous."

"You're the one looking around like you don't know where to sit in your own house."

I shrugged and gulped more of my drink. She narrowed her eyes and sat next to me, though there was a good ruler-sized distance between us.

"Excellent," I said.

"So, you chose none of the options I sent you, but it's fine because none of them were right."

"Technically, Sam sent me photos of cakes and stuff, and I wasn't sure which of your categories they fit into."

"She sent *you* cake photos?! Let me see them."

"I am making the cake, Princess. Calm down."

"Do not call me *Princess*. It's condescending. And I'm merely *surprised*. But she did send me bouquets and dress ideas, so I guess I feel fine about it."

"Sorry, you were acting a little entitled. You know, like a princess. But okay, Cupcake. Let's get to it."

She almost growled at me, and I tried to press my lips together to keep from grinning when I passed her my phone so she could see the cakes. It did not work.

"Well, I suppose you're right that none of my categories fit this look specifically. *This* is Persephone walking on the edge of the underworld and the world of the living. Sam's a bit of a genius. It's the perfect representation of equinox."

She was talking more to herself than me now, or, at least, I hoped so because I was lost.

"I'm going to nod like that makes sense. I've got a general idea of a mash-up between a starry night and dusk-colored florals—like dark greens and pinks and purples."

"Right. Like I said. Persephone."

"Right."

I downed the rest of my beer and got up to grab another, offering to get something for her as well. She only held up her nearly full glass of wine and continued to scrutinize the cake photos. I opened her pink refrigerator and popped the top off my drink when the oven caught my eye.

"Uh, Laur?"

"Yeah. Do you need help with the bottle opener or something?" she asked, irritated.

"Shut up. You have a Bosch convection oven?"

"Yes? I don't know what's special about it, but I got it for a steal, according to what they normally list for. Some rich lady on Kelleys Island was remodeling a kitchen in her million-dollar house after it had been redone, like, three years before, I think she said. My years of stalking thrifting chats and Craigslist paid off that day. Pain in the ass to get it here, though," she mused.

"When you say a *steal*..."

"500 bucks."

My jaw could have been scraped off the ground.

"Laur. Have I ever told you that you're the most amazing woman I've ever known?"

"No. But that's not shocking. Are you going to enter a courtship with my oven, or are we going to make a list of venue choices for this Persephone-inspired wedding shower?"

"I will do literally anything you want if you let me bake in your kitchen."

"Oh. Um, sure, whatever. Are you messy, though? Because I am a tad neurotic about my space."

"I will clean your entire townhouse. And your car. Jesus."

I traced the edge of the oven and promised I would see it later before I returned my attention to the mildly annoyed redhead.

"Got it. Venues."

We narrowed our choices to a couple of restaurants with available outdoor seating and plenty of space heaters, but the most enticing option was the Garrett family deck. It sat nestled in the woods with a creek alongside it and no neighbors behind.

When she was this focused, Lauren's energy was electric. I was fairly certain that I'd experience a shock if I touched her. God, I wanted to touch her. Her hoodie had been forgotten, and she had on a flimsy excuse for a tank top, the lace of her bra easily distinguishable under the fabric.

Stop staring at her tits.

"Well, that seems like the most obvious answer. Besides renting some tables and heaters, it would be mostly free, and it's close, and we could take our time setting everything up," I offered.

"And it comes with the added bonus of my mother giving me unsolicited advice the whole time," she said, taking a deep breath. "But yes, that seems to make the most sense. Plus, if we're buying something permanent like solar lights or dishware, my mom will probably pay so she can keep them. I'll deal with the comments for that."

"Your mom's like the nicest lady ever," I countered, never having heard a mean word come out of the woman's mouth.

"She is. Therein lies the problem. She… she so desperately wants me to be happy. And that's supportive and wonderful, but it's a lot of pressure to try to appear happy all the time."

"I guess I get that. I'll run interference for you, then."

She shot me a grateful smile before we moved on.

"Email the list or the links or 'pins' or whatever, and I'll get everything sorted. You want an afternoon tea?" I asked.

"Mhm. Ending at sunset. It'll be gorgeous. We won't do *only* tea, but there will be pretty teacups. And champagne and wine and sparkling water with berries and finger sandwiches and what do you think… macarons? The lavender cookies? Do you think we need a cake, too?"

"I was thinking petit fours in blues and purples with pink and cream flowers on top. And edible glitter at Sam's request. She said no big cake for the shower."

I heard Lauren mutter a curse under her breath.

"What, do you not like that idea? I'm open to suggestions; I've never even been to a wedding shower before."

"Ugh, you're so obtuse," she grumbled. "Don't make me compliment you. Your head won't fit through the door on your way out."

"I'm willing to risk it. Compliments from you are becoming addictive."

"It's a great idea, okay? You're rapidly becoming an asset to this whole process instead of a hindrance, and I don't' know if I'm happy about it."

She let her eyes drift over to me and then rolled them at the huge smile now residing on my face.

"Tell me more about how perfect I am."

I reached forward to grab the last cookie from the plate and awaited her words.

"I said the *idea* was—what?! No. We've discussed you taking the last bite of things, Jer. That was *my* cookie, and I don't have anymore! You can make more."

"I have no recollection of this discussion. And I'm pretty sure the accepted legal precedent is that possession is nine-tenths of the law, and well, this cookie is in my possession."

I took a gluttonous bite and let out a moan.

"I'll show you possession, you selfish ass," she claimed, and she lunged for the cookie.

Unfortunately for her, my arms were much longer than hers, and I easily held it out of her reach, though now we found ourselves in the predicament of her leaning across my lap and the smell of her shampoo invading my senses. She did not seem as affected by said predicament because she doubled down, planting her knee painfully into my thigh and reaching again for the cookie. With one hand on her waist, I held her at bay and stretched my arm up.

"You are positively *feral* this evening, Laur. Accept defeat with some dignity."

She huffed out an angry sigh and sat back, now fully straddling my lap, her knees bracketing my thighs. My dick twitched at the immediate images flashing in my head.

Fuck.

Flirting—and even snuggling—was one thing, but this kind of proximity was entirely another, and my brain was empty of all rational thought. She crossed her arms but seemed to realize the situation and moved to slide back to her cushion. I wrapped my left hand firmly around her thigh and kept her exactly where she was, the cookie now forgotten on the side table.

"What are you doing?" she whispered.

"Being a selfish ass," I answered, my voice heavy with the knowledge that she hadn't consented to the fireworks clause.

She inhaled sharply, waiting for me to continue.

"Do you think... that the Fourth of July, with the fireworks and whatnot, creates some sort of portal where two people can do stupid, absolutely unwise things, and there be no real-life consequences the next day?"

My fingers traveled as I talked, my thumbs tracing the bottom of her ribs over the joke of a shirt, and the goosebumps that broke out across her skin made my heart run away with the horses stampeding through my chest cavity.

"I believe Sam has mentioned some kind of astrological occurrence on the Fourth that does exactly that, yes."

Her voice was still hushed, her green eyes locked with mine, each of us begging the other not to pop this bubble. I wanted her so badly there was every chance I wouldn't last forty seconds if she touched me, but it would be worth the embarrassment.

"That makes perfect sense."

"Obviously."

We had come to the end of the road for our banter, and my body acted before my brain caught up. I grabbed her ass firmly and pulled her into me, my face now level with her tits, but I was a gentleman and looked up, her red hair falling over her shoulder and forming a curtain, like we were hidden from the reality of this decision.

Her fingers tugged gently on my hair, her nails trailing deliciously along my scalp, and I pressed my lips to hers, half expecting her to leap off my lap and disappear. But she didn't. She opened for me and traced her tongue along mine, a hint of lavender and honey still between us. It took everything I had to let her explore and set the pace. I matched her pressure and intensity as it became more demanding, her breathing shallow and quiet, contented sounds dropping from her mouth.

The lacy bra she was wearing was practically begging to be pulled down, forcing her breasts up on display. I groaned before tugging a perfect pink nipple into my mouth and sucking, relishing her gasp and the harder tugging on my hair that followed. Almost involuntarily, and by that I meant completely on purpose, I rocked up against her center, wanting her to know how fucking hard I was under her.

"Keep doing *all* of that," she murmured.

"Whatever you say, Princess."

I turned my attention to her other nipple and held her hips tightly, grinding her against me. Her shorts were so very thin, and it made no sense why I still had jeans on.

"Damn it, why is it hot when you say it *now?*"

That made a laugh rumble out of my chest, but she swallowed it with a kiss, her pace now hurried. I tugged at her shorts, and she stood, shimmying out of them. Lauren looked well and truly undone, her bra askew, her hair wild, her lips pink.

"You're fucking perfect," I got out before I pulled on her hand to bring her back to my lap.

She stopped short and dropped to her knees instead, working on my pants.

"Hey, hey, Laur…"

She stopped and looked up, and I almost died inside from seeing her at that angle. This would be fueling my shower sessions for months.

"This can just be about you. I can stay exactly like this and make you feel good. I don't want you to think I expect—"

"On the rare Fourth of July portal night? You must be joking. I've been dying to see if your confidence is earned or not for months. Now, take off your pants."

I almost called her 'princess' again, but I wasn't sure it would accomplish me being inside of her faster, so I settled for complying with her request.

"Get back over here," I insisted this time, knowing that if she so much as breathed on my dick, it was over. I needed a minute to think about chairs or recite a recipe in my head.

You are not a fucking fourteen-year-old boy. Get yourself under control.

She straddled me again, and I let my hands roam freely while I kissed her, appreciating parts of her body I only usually ogled from a safe distance. I tugged at the ends of her long hair gently, pressing her chest further into me and baring her throat. I sucked and bit my way up her neck, simultaneously wanting her to keep wiggling and stop for a second. I went back to a spot that had made her shiver and bit lightly again. Her hand, having made its own trail over my body, reached down and gripped me firmly through my boxers. She groaned, and I laughed.

"Is my confidence earned or not? And please lie if the answer is not."

"I wish I was lying," she bit out breathlessly. "It's not fair. Please tell me you don't know how to use it, and this is about to be a wholly disappointing experience."

"You *want* me to fail to get you off."

"It would be so helpful."

She couldn't hold back her grin then, and she gripped me again without warning, making something unintelligible leave my mouth.

"I did say I would do anything to use your oven, but I can't, in good conscience, do that."

Instead, I brushed over her underwear with my fingertips.

"And I'm doing *something* right because you're so wet, Laur."

She opened her mouth like she was going to offer some sort of alternate story, but I pulled her panties to the side and sunk a finger inside her, effectively ending her sentence.

"Well played," she got out, now back to gripping my hair and widening her knees to give me some room.

I kissed her more roughly and added a second finger, finding her g-spot and staying there, my thumb taking over circling her clit. My mind was racing from her letting out breathy moans and gasps in my ear, wondering if she was loud when she came, and hoping she was.

"Don't stop," she directed, and I ensured that I changed *no* variables in that moment and let her ride my hand.

"*Fuck*, Jer," she let out as she shuddered around me, her nails almost painfully digging into my shoulders.

I pulled back when she slumped against me, wondering if she'd leave our no-consequences bubble in her post-orgasm state, but she still wasn't leaping up or tensing like this was a mistake.

"You're so hot, baby," I said into her neck, not sure where the *baby* came from. It sort of popped out, and I expected her to call me on it.

"Jesus. Are you making your voice lower on purpose?"

"I don't think so? This is just my voice."

"Damn it. Why does everything you say sound so fucking good?"

I took it that the question was rhetorical because she pulled off my shirt quickly and unhooked her bra. I ran my fingers over her nipples and pinched slightly, listening for any indication it was *too* hard, but her tiny gasp and instant hardening between my fingertips indicated that it was just right, actually. I did away with my boxers and guided her underwear to the floor.

The Fourth of July, with its magical astrology, had become by far my favorite holiday.

Chapter 13 - Lauren

No one. Repeat: *no one* had ever made me orgasm that hard with only their fingers.

Holy shit.

I hadn't been kidding earlier. It would have made things so much easier if he was bad in bed. Because, after tonight, I would *know*, and knowing might have been worse than wondering. I moved next to him on the couch and bent over his lap, wasting no time in running my tongue up the underside of his cock. The way his body tensed told me he hadn't expected it, which made it that much better. He recovered quickly and rested one hand gently on the back of my neck, running his fingers up and down, not pushing.

Thank god, I thought.

I'd ghosted guys who thought they were porn stars in the bedroom. But Jer… he was *sweet*. It should have been awkward, but having him compliment me was kind of hot.

"Your mouth is perfect," he murmured, encouraging me to take him even deeper. "Too perfect. Come here, baby."

I popped off him with an audible sound, and he groaned again, crashing his mouth into mine, more frantic than he'd been before, the kiss a flurry of tongue and teeth and exploring and sucking and biting. He attacked my neck again, finding the place that made a little lightning effect domino through my limbs, and he repositioned us so that I was lying flat, him hovering above me. I hooked my heels around his back and pulled him toward me, wanting friction that he was *not* giving me. He chuckled and didn't even budge despite the considerable effort I was putting in.

Fucking Viking lumberjack, that's what he is.

"Is there a problem?" I asked, getting impatient.

"Mmmm, I'm not done with you yet. I have to take full advantage of the portal."

My heart sped up and fluttered against my ribcage. He kissed his way down my body, and apparently, he was finished teasing me by the time he got there because his tongue pressed firmly around my clit over and over and over, joined by his fingers slipping back inside me until I was pretty sure the fireworks from outside had made their way in. I was lightheaded as my second orgasm crashed into me.

My legs were shaking, and I couldn't feel my fingers as I came down, having not been prepared for that one to hit as hard as it did. Jer looked at me with a mild expression of concern as he ran his hands over my thighs.

"No, I'm good. It's a—good. Why can't I think of other words than good? You've stolen all my words."

This made him laugh in that stupid, low voice again. He was lying earlier. He *definitely* had a sex voice that was deeper than his normal voice, and it did things to me.

"I'm glad you're good. Do you want to take a break? Or stop?"

"What? No. Why? Do you want to stop?" I asked, a slight panic creeping into my voice.

I hadn't known that would be the last orgasm, or I would have savored it more, much like the last bite of muffin or the last cookie.

"Does it *feel* like I want to stop?" he asked, coming back to hover right above me, placing my hand over his length, now *aggressively* hard.

"No," I said, breathing.

"Okay. Tell me, then. Break?"

"Ten deep breaths. Go get a condom from my nightstand drawer and don't pay attention to anything else you see in there, got it? First door on the right at the top of the stairs."

He huffed out a laugh at my instructions and made his way stark naked to the staircase. I did not hate the view. That man. I refocused on my breathing and getting my limbs to calm down. My eyes were closed, but I heard him come back into the room and kneel next to the couch. Next was the sound of the condom wrapper, then the sensation of his hands, gentle and warm as he touched me. He smoothed my hair back from my face and peppered kisses from my temple down my jawline, bringing back my goosebumps. I opened my eyes and sat up slightly to meet him in the middle, immediately pulling him back to me to finish what we'd started.

"You're sure?" he whispered.

I knew he was afraid to break the spell we were under. I was fucking terrified. But if this was the only chance we had, where we were both willing to check our baggage, then I was taking it.

"Very," I said against his mouth.

He devoured me with his next kiss, his hand reaching between us to guide himself into me. He pressed in slowly, an inch at a time, and it was delicious. His large hand wrapped around the back of my thigh, and he hitched my knee up to my chest, deepening his angle and making me cry out something that may not have been English. He was more vocal than any man I'd ever been with, but not in the way that made me cringe. He told me how amazing I felt, and how he had wanted to touch me for so long, and that I was even better than he imagined. The praise rolled over me, making all of my nerve endings buzz to life.

The last orgasm built slowly, so at least I was prepared this time. He rocked into me, his free hand making circles on my palm as he held it above my head, the other tracing my jaw between kisses.

"I want to see you come apart one more time," he said roughly in my ear, and I knew he was close, too.

His hand put pressure exactly where I needed it, and the orgasm ripped through me, stealing the breath I still had and rendering me boneless when it left. He followed with a mixture of cursing and praise, and he finally half-collapsed on top of me. I twisted so we could face each other and so that he didn't crush me underneath him. He rested his forehead on mine, and we existed for a minute in our portal.

He slipped out a minute later and murmured something about

getting rid of the condom and getting water. I padded to the bathroom to clean up and maybe tame whatever had happened to my hair during our little adventure. I made my way back out to the living room with a messy bun and a satin robe wrapped around me, preparing for him to already be gone. I wouldn't have blamed him. We'd agreed that either of us in a relationship was a bad idea, but it was hard to remember the reasons why right now. I hoped that with some space, I would remember them. In the moment, it seemed completely appropriate that he would stay here forever, and we could do *that* as many times as we wanted.

He wasn't gone, but he was pulling his shirt over his head, already dressed from the waist down.

"Here," he said, handing me a glass of water from the coffee table.

I took it and drank, happy for anything to do with my mouth other than make words come out of it.

"I feel like I should offer you food, but this is your house, so I'm not sure what to do with that." He gave me a sheepish grin and sat on my couch, now pulling on his socks.

"That's all right. I'm not hungry."

I didn't know how to say *stay* without breaking the rules we'd set.

But we made up the rules! We can change them! my subconscious screamed at me.

But the speed with which Jer had dressed made me think that would not be reciprocated. And he'd already rejected me in my own house once; I wasn't looking to do it again.

"Laur," he started.

"It's fine, Jeremy. We agreed to the Fourth of July portal, whatever. It's okay. You can go. I'm fine."

My voice almost broke on the last fine, but I was proud of myself otherwise. He breathed out a deep sigh.

"And if I'm not? Fine, that is," he asked, his gaze cutting to me sharply.

"I... I don't. I'm sorry if you feel like this was a mistake," I said, shaking my head. "I'm not sure what to say to that."

My heart went from zero to sixty in the time it took for him to make that comment. I was fully prepared for the consequences on my end. I knew I'd be wrecked and want more even though I knew I was not a *more* girl. I hadn't considered that maybe he'd feel regret or pull back from us even being friends.

His face fell.

"That's not... I mean, this might have been a colossal mistake, Laur," he laughed. "But I think we both knew that. I don't regret it, that's not what I was trying to say. Maybe we leave this here for now. I feel like talking about it in the state I'm in is a bad idea. Is that okay? We can talk more. Whenever you want. If you want. I think I need to breathe a minute, yeah?"

I found myself nodding without knowing what I was agreeing to. Everything he said made some sort of sense, even if I didn't know exactly why.

"Yeah, of course. It's late anyway. You're good to drive?"

"Yeah, I'm fine. I..." he trailed off and let the sentence hang there. "I'll update the spreadsheet tomorrow with the organized list of stuff. Okay? And we'll figure out when we can meet next."

I nodded again. I was becoming an excellent mime. He stepped in close to me, the scent of him overwhelming my space.

"And I have to arrange a time to come over and use your oven. You might never get rid of me, honestly."

I cracked a genuine smile at that. At least I knew he wasn't going to disappear completely, not when I had this holy grail appliance.

"Yeah. I'll talk to you then."

He didn't move for a beat, but then he tilted my chin up with the pads of his fingers and leaned down to press one soft kiss on my lips before walking to the door without a backward glance. My fingers traced that kiss for too long after I heard his car start and leave, wondering maybe, if I stood very still, he might come back, and we could drop this whole portal pretense. He didn't, and I eventually went to bed, hoping sleep would come easily after the physical and emotional toll of the night.

Chapter 14- Jeremy

Fuck.

Chapter 15- Lauren

Fuck.

Chapter 16 - Jeremy

Silence was the enemy. Keeping a constant stream of noise directed at my ear holes was key. It didn't matter what it was. Metal, grunge, country, sports radio, podcasts, fucking show tunes. Because anytime there was silence, my mind wandered. Sometimes it took the scenic route through images of how fucking amazing that night was. It didn't feel real because she was a goddess. Mostly, though, it preferred an off-trail path of all the ways I'd screwed up—how awkward this was going to make things when she inevitably realized I was a mistake, how I would likely lose my best friend in the whole ordeal as well when Jesse rightly took her side, and on and on and on.

I had emailed her the stupid updated spreadsheet and added enough emojis to hopefully seem normal. She sent back a simple thanks, and that was that. I had typed out too many messages yesterday without sending any of them because I couldn't decide how to play it.

I hadn't been lying. I wasn't fine. Leaving her standing in her living room had been the hardest thing I'd done in a long time. I wanted to stay and hold her and, honestly, go another round. But if I'd stayed, the idea of leaving would have become impossible. And the whole god damned crux of the issue in the first place was that I wasn't that guy. She deserved that guy. This delightful spiral was what I had to look forward to any time the noise stopped.

The holiday weekend was over, and I was happy I had to be at work. The more distractions, the better. I went in *early*. I didn't take out my earbuds, knowing that if I stopped to talk to Rachel, she'd immediately call me on my ridiculous attitude. Thankfully, she was helping a customer, and I didn't have to deal with it. I didn't want to talk to her about Lauren. That made it feel like I was bragging or like I'd done something worth acknowledging when all I'd done was fuck myself over so royally I might never recover.

Bravo.

I did need to go out, though. Jesse and Sam were both out of the question. I needed a full three business days before I could have a good enough poker face to talk to either of them, maybe more for Sam and her fucking psychic abilities. I shot off a text to Danny, a mutual friend of Jesse's and mine, to see if he wanted to grab a drink after work. We hadn't ever hung out, just the two of us, so it felt a little like I was asking him out or trying to arrange a playdate, but I was desperate.

JEREMY: Hey man- are you around after work to grab a beer or something?

DANNY: Yeah, I'm around.

JEREMY: Anywhere but The Bar. I'll buy the first round.

DANNY: Reds game is on at 6, and there's a new sports bar in Cloverdale.

JEREMY: Sweet. Send me the info, and I'll meet you there.

Okay. That would help. Sitting at home alone after work was no longer on the agenda.

I managed to avoid Rachel and her increasingly invasive questions until I could clock out, a headache forming behind my eyes, likely from having my earbuds in all day long. I knew I looked like shit, but I also didn't think Danny was going to be expecting me pretty and ready to put out, so I drove straight to Cloverdale to whatever new wing spot had opened.

He wasn't there yet, so I took it upon myself to order a shot. Then another. Then another. Then a beer.

"Hey, man. Qué pasa?"

"Hey. Not a lot. Just needed to get out. I'll get you a drink."

I came back with a Dos Equis in hand.

He eyed the beer suspiciously.

"It's because I'm Mexican, isn't it? Like I can only drink beer that's in Spanish?"

I almost choked on my own breath.

"Wha? No, no. Last time we were all out, you ordered a Dos Equis, so I figured—"

"Yeah, I'm fucking with you. Thanks for reacting perfectly."

A shit-eating grin spread across his face, and I could have punched him.

"You're a dick."

"Eh, your reputation precedes you. Takes one to know one. Cheers."

He clinked his beer with mine, and I slid onto the barstool, deciding Danny and I could be actual friends if he'd already called me a dick within five minutes of the first time we'd really hung out.

"Ah, for the record, what does Dos Equis mean? I mean, I know *two*..."

"I can't tell you that. It's a cultural secret. Reds are down already in the second?"

I shook my head, sinking into my chair and focusing on the game. I played everything in high school. One, because I was a big guy with a modicum of athletic ability, so they'd put me on whatever team, but two, because it kept me out of my house and, therefore, away from my dad. I never had the raw talent for any sport, though, that Jesse did for baseball. Scholarship offers did not come in for me, especially as a barely-C-student. I didn't have a particular emotional attachment to any one sport, and I was able to enjoy just being a fan. I absolutely got my Jesse's struggle with watching pro-baseball after his injury, but it was kind of nice to drink a beer and watch a game.

The three shots and two beers had hit my bloodstream hard, being that I rarely had more than a single drink when I went out anymore, and it was becoming clear they were a bad idea. Rather than drowning out my thoughts about Lauren, it only amplified how fucking badly I wanted her. I tried to focus on Danny talking shit about the ump and something about him working to get his contractor's license.

"You should do it. Get the license, you know? I bake now. I mean, I got, like, a pastry certification. To make cakes. They're good."

Danny was shaking with laughter.

"You are *lit up*, man."

"Fuck. I am. Don't let me text her."

I had enough of my brainpower left that I knew I should *not* drunk text Lauren. Or anyone.

"Well, everything makes more sense now. Who am I not letting you text?"

"Lauren," I grumbled.

"Garrett? Like, my boss's daughter? Jesse's sister?"

"That's the one."

"Give me your phone."

"Why?"

"I'm not going to be responsible for you doing some dumb white-boy shit, like drunk dialing her for a booty call or throwing rocks at her window or something. I have benefits at that job, bro."

I slid my phone across the table at him, and he pocketed it, still chuckling about my baked goods.

We watched the rest of the game, and I got myself a lot of water, sobering up a bit. Danny swore when he checked his phone a bit later and asked to settle his tab.

"I gotta go. I'll drive your ass home, but you're going to have to bribe someone else to bring you back in the morning because I'm off tomorrow, and we're not ride or dies yet, you know? But hold out hope because you don't annoy me. Much."

"I'll stare at the phone waiting for your call, Danny."

"That's the spirit."

"Everything okay? With whatever that text was?"

"Ah, my sister. My niece's father—and I use that term loosely—bounced without a word again a couple weeks ago. Mari doesn't wanna tell our parents, meaning I'm call number one when shit goes wrong. Daniela spiked a fever and needs meds."

"Oh, shit. I can get another ride if you need to—"

"All good. There's that 24-hour pharmacy by your place, anyway."

He shrugged like this was not the first time he'd needed that information. We listened to what I was pretty sure was mariachi music on the drive, and I was eighty-five percent certain he was fucking with me. He did get me home at a reasonable hour and gave me back my phone, so all in all, he was a gentleman.

"Good luck with your best friend's sister. I'm sure that won't be messy at all. Vaya con Dios!"

He sped off, and I stumbled into my apartment. Since there was no danger of me arriving at Lauren's townhouse and throwing rocks at her window, I figured a single text couldn't hurt. Or it might hurt a lot, but I felt like I deserved it.

JEREMY: Can I come bake at your house on Thursday?

JEREMY: Also. I'm still not fine.

LAUR: Sure, I'm done at 2 on Thursday.

LAUR: I don't think I'm fine either. Night, Jer.

JEREMY: Night, Laur.

Chapter 17 - Lauren

Why did it make me feel better that he said he wasn't fine? I had been booked solid yesterday, so I didn't have a lot of time to obsess over our little road trip across the line until he'd sent that message. Thinking about it this morning, the line was hazy. More like a chalk line around what had been our boundaries because they were dead and gone.

At least on your end. Who knows what he's thinking?

But... now, at least, I knew he wasn't feeling footloose and fancy-free, whatever that meant. What I needed was a project. Something I could throw myself into so completely I forgot to eat or sleep. That would make sure Jer stayed locked in the recesses of my mind until I was ready to deal with him. Or until Thursday when he came over to use my oven. What was that even going to entail? Was I supposed to, like, sit at the counter and watch him measure ingredients and use a mixer?

That set me back a good ten minutes: imagining him in my house, shirtless, making my kitchen smell delicious, and feeding me baked goods.

Project.

I looked around my house, determined to find inspiration. My gaze zeroed in on my stairwell. It was one of the only areas that still had the original dust-colored paint. This was because I didn't have a ladder tall enough to reach the top. I could borrow one from my dad, absolutely. The problem was that every time I got the inspiration to paint that wall, I wanted it done *right then*, and coordinating a ladder pick-up didn't fit into my impulsive decision-making process.

Well, that would be my focus today after Sam and I got done dress shopping.

Shit.

I looked at the time and realized my little daydream had made me late. I threw on a simple yellow t-shirt dress and a pair of black sandals and determined I'd do basic makeup in the car. I texted Sam that I was on my way, and I hurried to my garage, hoping she'd end up driving once I got to her house—my car desperately needed some time and attention, but I was stretched thin as it was.

Sorry, little car.

I got my wish, and Sam granted another I didn't even know I had when she handed me an iced caramel latte as soon as I got to her door.

"Bless you, child."

"I'm older than you, but you're welcome."

"Yeah, yeah. I'm so excited to look for your dress I could pee my pants."

"Please don't because Jesse cleaned out my car, but secretly? Same." She grinned, her eyes literally sparkling with fine silver glitter.

"Let's goooooooo."

Sam was not a white-dress bride. She wanted to look like a celestial goddess, and I was there for it. She had done the work and called boutiques and tailors and dress shops for the past two weeks to figure out where we could realistically drive in a day, and which shops carried dresses in stock in her size (fuck the fashion industry for their lack of clothing above a size eight. But that was a rant for another day).

I made her stop at the gas station on the way out of Emberwood and bought snacks like we might never return, but it was going to be a great day. The complicated *situation* with Jer was barely a blip on my radar.

* * *

"I swear to god I like every single dress you put on better than the last one," I said, taking a picture.

It was a shimmery purple with an asymmetrical sleeve and had gorgeous lace sewn on top of tulle that all floated gently to the ground.

"There have been so many pretty ones. Maybe I'm being picky? I feel like a lot of them could work."

"I mean, it's nice to have a list of things that could be good, but maybe you need to see photos side by side, you know? And you can think about it."

"Yeah, maybe you're right. Do you have it in you to do one more stop on the way back to Emberwood? It's a shop that does cosplay costumes and is, apparently, a great spot for secondhand stuff, too. It's kind of a stretch for a wedding dress, but who knows?"

"Like you have to ask if I have the stamina for more shopping. Especially recycled fashion. You're speaking my love language, sister."

Her face lit up, and we upped our caffeine intake with some large drive-thru iced teas before getting back on the highway. She'd asked how planning with Jeremy was going, and I gave a five-star performance of "It's fine. Really." I did *not* shift focus to myself and my questionable decision-making.

We pulled up to the shop, adorned with only a simple sign that read *Carrie's Cosplay Creations*. Sam pulled open the door, and it was like entering a Dungeons and Dragons fantasy world, but with the addition of glitter and tulle. There was a *lot* of secondhand inventory, somewhat sorted into categories based on type of character. I felt renewed energy buzz through my system. I'd been training for this since I discovered my first designer dress at a thrift store when I was fifteen.

I looked at Sam and could tell she was a little shell-shocked. I didn't blame her; the store looked deceptively small from the outside.

"Girl. Go look at jewelry. I'll pull five things to get you started and keep rotating out. Go," I insisted when she looked like she might protest.

About that time, a middle-aged woman, whom I assumed to be Carrie, came out and greeted her. I could hear them chatting about jewelry, but I was on a mission. I turned out anything that looked remotely adjacent to the vibe Sam was going for that was in her size range, but I didn't take anything off a rounder until my second pass through.

There was one dress that I knew was for sure coming into the dressing room, so I went back to it first, then grabbed four more based on look and quality and made my way back to the front.

"I have your choices! Please try this one first," I said, holding up the one that had called to me the most.

Her eyes widened when she saw it, and she nodded excitedly, excusing herself from Carrie.

"You aren't looking for a job, are you?" the woman asked me, her expression impressed. "Most people don't have the eye or the patience to do what you did."

"Sadly, I do hair full time, but this place is amazing. I'll be back for myself."

"Oh! Do you do intricate hairstyles? My customers who do all the big cons in the region are always looking for a stylist who can do various fantasy character looks."

"I have taken extra classes in stylistic braiding, mostly because I like to do my own, but I can't say I get asked to do it very often. Around prom, usually."

"Well, leave me a stack of cards, and I can guarantee you you'll get more."

I pulled out the small stack of business cards I always had in my bag and handed them to her.

Well, that was a happy coincidence, I thought, even more glad we'd decided to come.

"Can you come lace me the rest of the way up?" Sam's voice called above the dressing room curtain.

I hurried in and grinned, knowing my instincts on this one had been right. I tried not to gush too much until she got out on the pedestal and the big mirror. I laced the corset to cinch in her waist and push her boobs to an almost obscene amount of cleavage.

"I'm fairly certain you were a lady in waiting on a royal court in your past life."

"Likely a servant. You can do a past life reading another time, Sam. Focus."

She nodded. I grabbed the back of the giant skirt and carried it out behind her. She stood up on the pedestal and fell silent.

"Is this real?" she whispered.

"Certainly not," Carrie said, having joined us. "It's otherworldly."

The off-the-shoulder gown had a dusty blue satin bodice that met the largest tulle skirt anyone had ever seen. It started in the same blue at the top and deepened into a midnight blue so dark it was almost black at the bottom. Exploding from the layers were plumes of purple tulle ranging from lilac to plum, and the whole skirt was sprinkled with silver beading that shimmered under the lights. Sam pulled her dark curly hair off her neck and turned, getting as many angles as possible.

Carrie stepped up and asked permission to put add some things to the ensemble. She clasped a multi-strand necklace with tiny rhinestones and amethysts, but then she brought out the pièce de résistance, which was a thin crown that looked like vines woven together made from silver, meeting in the center at a small sparkling crescent moon. The woman positioned it in Sam's hair and fanned her curls around her. When Sam turned, the tears were instantaneous. From both of us.

She sent the photos to her mom, who immediately called and paid for all of it over the phone. I was glad Nora had the self-awareness not to insist that she accompany Sam to dress hunt. They were getting better, but Nora was still on my list.

Carrie packaged everything up and sent us on our way, both of us giddy and singing and laughing all the way back home. I agreed to keep the dress at my townhouse until she took it somewhere to be hemmed, lest Jesse see it before the wedding. But not before she got to show her aunt. We stopped at *Books and Broomsticks* before I finally made it back to my car and then home. We'd been gone for eight hours, and I was *tired*.

Maybe I won't even have to start my painting project tonight. It's possible I'll fall asleep while eating dinner.

* * *

Unfortunately, as soon as I ate, hydrated, and completed my ready-to-watch-tv-in-bed routine, my brain decided *now* it was time to think about all the ways things with Jer could go sideways. If Jesse found out we had a one-night stand, his newfound casual indifference might crumble. I wasn't worried about me; he was stuck with me. But I didn't want him to be pissed at Jer and make things weird between them.

Another reason to keep quiet to Sam.

I didn't *think* she would say anything to Jesse if I asked her not to. I had no reason not to trust her with everything; I just…her marrying my brother had a million positives, but there were a few drawbacks. This was one.

I also couldn't shut down the scenarios in my mind about how tomorrow was going to go when he showed up here. Some of them were so hot I considered a cold shower or a trip to my newly relocated toys, but that stairwell was still calling my name. I ventured to the haphazard collection of supplies on my garage shelves and prayed that any and all spiders would have the decency to leave me alone while I looked at all my leftover paint from other projects.

Aha! I found a nearly full gallon of a pretty hyacinth purple. It was purchased on a whim for my closet until I decided I owned too much purple clothing, and it would blend together. However, it would be perfect for the stairs. I would get started, get paint on the wall, and hope that my penchant for a cohesive aesthetic carried me through whatever was necessary to finish it. Painter's tape in my teeth, roller and paint tray in hand, I went to work.

Painting was one of my least favorite tasks to do, but my most favorite to have completed. In one day, I could change the vibe of a space with almost no budget. I hadn't ever painted a stairwell before, though.

Taping the carpet down was a pain. Making sure I got paint below the carpet line was a pain. Cleaning the drops I inevitably got on said carpet was an even bigger pain because it could have been avoided if I'd planned and gotten a drop cloth, but again, I had no control over when inspiration struck. I got the first coat finished for everything I could reach. This left about the top third of the wall still dirt-colored, and I frowned. Partly because it annoyed me to see it encroaching on the majestic purple that now took up residence on the bottom two-thirds of the wall, but also because I could feel that same inspiration retreating at lightning speed.

No, no, noooooo. I need *that motivation.*

I hadn't texted my dad yet about the ladder, and now it was too late. I also needed to get another gallon of paint for sure to finish at least two coats on the whole space, meaning the energy *had* to stick around until tomorrow. I lied to myself and said I'd take a quick break, do a second coat on the bottom, type out a text to my dad so I'd only have to hit 'send' in the morning, and make a run to get paint during lunch at work tomorrow.

Easy peasy.

I even wrote it down in a bullet point list on a sticky note. Everyone knew you had to do it once it was on a sticky note. I peeled off my now-sweaty t-shirt and flopped on my couch in my sports bra and leggings, remote in hand. Re-runs of *Bewitched* were on some cable channel I'd never heard of, and I settled in. There was almost nothing better than Endora being an absolute queen.

It was eight seventeen when I opened my eyes and checked my phone, still on the couch, and I had to be at work at nine-thirty.

Stellar.

I stared angrily at the semi-painted wall on my way to my room, knowing it was going to be stuck like that until the urge came back around. It might be tonight; it might be three months from now. No one knew. Dry shampoo would be my friend again today, it seemed. I briefly wondered if I could convince Christian to give me a blowout if he had a break in his clients, but I could already imagine the disdain radiating off him. It might be worth asking to see how well it matched the real-life version.

* * *

I'd been right about Christian refusing to give me a blowout. He did take pity on me, though, when I gave him a dramatically vague version of being tangled in a complicated web with Jer and him coming to bake at my house that afternoon. I ended up with killer eye makeup and still-dirty hair. It was better than nothing.

In a shocking turn of events, I neither texted my dad nor went to get paint. I spent my lunch searching Pinterest for inspiration for my bridesmaid dress. Sam had given me carte blanche to dress myself and Jer since we were the entire wedding party. Now that she had her dress, other things could fall into place. I should probably have been focused on the shower that was scheduled in a few weeks, but dresses were less stressful. I was counting on Jeremy and his spreadsheets to kick my ass into gear when it got down to the wire.

I changed into loungewear when I got home. Then changed, again, into very short jean shorts and a sweatshirt I'd altered to hang off one shoulder. I was still comfy, but I wanted him to be a little pained when he looked at me. Still with no idea how to act or what to do when he got there, he knocked and forced me to wing it.

Chapter 18- Jeremy

I almost texted her to cancel four times that day. It didn't help that I had the day off, and no one else I knew was around. I spent the morning with myself and my own thoughts; it was a blast.

I did call my mom to check in. This didn't make the day more fun, but I felt like I'd put in effort in at least one area of my life. It had been over two years since I'd had anything stronger than a drink, but our relationship hadn't recovered.

Yet.

I wasn't ready to write off getting things back to some semblance of normal with my mother. When I was young, she had been my biggest fan, and I shattered that into a hundred pieces. It was hard to put *those* back together while also trying to put my *life* back together. But I thought it could be done. My dad? He wouldn't even get on the phone with me, and he'd conveniently have to work the few times my mom and I met up for lunch or dinner.

I'd thought about scheduling a meetup for a midnight snack to see if he'd be more creative in his excuses, but I didn't have the energy. Today, my mom had chatted with me about her garden and what they'd done for the Fourth. It almost felt like a normal conversation. Except for the fear on the edge of her voice when she asked me what I'd been up to. As though I might casually tell her I'd decided to throw away the last two years of rebuilding my life to do to a line.

Whatever. It's progress.

All of that meant I was feeling like a fuck-up before I even got to Lauren's door, and I had no idea how to act around her. My general plan was to pretend the hookup never happened. We were friends who casually flirted, and that was it. Except now, I knew what it was like to be with her in real life, and I *wanted* to kiss her as soon as she answered the door. I may not have been doing illegal drugs, but I was for damn sure developing an addiction.

Fuck.

I pulled up to her townhouse and grabbed the bags from my trunk. I figured if she was going to be cool about me baking over there, I might as well stock up and keep supplies in her pantry until she kicked me out. Because there was no way she had decent bakeware. Or maybe not any bakeware. Today, I was going to start working on cake flavors for Sam and Jesse to try for their main wedding cake, and I'd freeze squares of all the flavors to do the petit fours for the shower.

That's perfect. Focus on the cake. Talk about cake. It'll be great.

I set one of my bags down and knocked, my stomach doing some sort of calisthenics I had not authorized.

"Hey," she offered when she opened the door.

Her eyes dropped to my very full bags.

"Are you planning to stay the week?" she asked, her voice slightly higher.

"Ah, sorry, I figured I'd bring everything rather than realize I needed something and not have it." I shrugged.

She was in a sweatshirt and shorts, but it made me want to pull her into my lap and snuggle with her on the couch, and that was more dangerous than the want of kissing her. She shrugged back and turned, walking toward her kitchen. I assumed I was to follow. She watched me curiously as I started to unpack and set things on her counter.

"You know I have, like, cake pans, right?"

"Well, no, I did not know that. And I also need to make sure I use the same pans each time so I can recreate—"

She opened a drawer and pulled out almost an entire collection of aluminum bakeware—some from Sur La Table and others from Williams Sonoma.

"I have these," she said, her brow raised.

"Why do you have these if you don't bake?"

She was an enigma.

"I got them at several estate sales. I like nice things, Jer, and I don't bake *today*, but you never know what my next project is going to be. I want to be prepared. You're welcome to any of it. I'll be over there, ignoring my stairwell."

She gestured behind her to a now partially painted purple wall.

"I don't think I'm going to ask. But if today isn't good, I can come back—"

"Do your thing. It's fine. I do get to try all the stuff, though, yes? Like, that's part of the agreement?"

"Of course."

She nodded and sidled away, plopping down on her couch and turning on the TV. That interaction was far too polite for my liking, but we did at least survive without anything supremely awkward happening. We also had addressed zero things about the elephant in the room, but I supposed he'd be there later. AC/DC was blasting in my earbuds, and I started measuring wet ingredients and got to work on a vanilla cake.

Once everything was mixed, in the pans, and in that beautiful oven, I looked over to see that Lauren was no longer on the couch. My gut tightened, and I wondered if that was because she knew I'd be able to talk while I waited for them to bake.

"Shit," I said quietly.

We should have gotten this over with before. The night it happened even. This was torture. I started washing bowls and beaters when she re-entered the kitchen.

"It smells good."

"Thanks."

Her eyes narrowed at me, and I wondered if she was going to call out this ridiculous atmosphere where we couldn't even have a conversation. Instead, she continued to her pantry and pulled out a package of strawberry Pop-Tarts.

"Do you want one?"

I shook my head.

"You're going to eat that when I am going to offer you cake in about twenty minutes?"

"I fail to see how those two things are related. I will eat these now. Cake later."

I laughed lightly.

"Okay, but those aren't even *good*. You're going to ruin your taste buds, and you won't be able to fully experience the cake."

"You shut your mouth in front of the Pop-Tarts!"

She gestured to the adjacent wall where her giant pastry art hung.

"Do they have ears?" I asked in a hushed voice.

"They have *feelings*, Jer."

My shoulders tentatively relaxed; this felt like familiar territory.

"I'm sorry, I take it back."

She shot me a side eye that said *good call*. While we were on this precarious ledge, I decided to jump off it.

"Laur…"

"Oh god, don't."

"Don't what?!"

"Whatever you're going to say. Stand there and look pretty and don't talk, please."

"I don't know whether I'm offended or turned on, honestly."

She glared at me. Hard.

"I know you want to talk. And I just don't. Because nothing has changed about either of us since the Fourth. It's awkward, but we're going to have to get over it. Unless you have some epiphany to share with the class?"

"I… no. No epiphany to speak of."

I didn't know why the first emotion to work its way through my chest was disappointment. I knew I couldn't offer her a relationship, and I should have been glad that she was willing to let the hookup be what it was, but I also hated it.

Do you want her to beg you to be someone you're not? So, what, you can turn her down? That didn't sit well, either. *What are you doing?*

She nodded, a hardened look taking over her face, and took

her Pop-Tarts back to the couch.

"Bring me cake when it's done."

I refocused my attention on cleaning everything up and leaving her kitchen as I'd found it.

Chapter 19 - Lauren

That little speech hurt more than I thought it would. I didn't expect it to go any differently. I didn't even think it would have been good if it had. If he had said that he wanted to be with me, I would have agreed because he was funny and stupidly hot and unfairly good in bed. And then, eventually, one or both of us would ruin it.

So, in reality, this is good. He can bake, and I can watch TV, and someday, we'll go back to how we were before.

We had to wait out the awkwardness. No problem.

He was cleaning the kitchen, and I was very involved in my trashy reality show—so much so that I had no idea what it was called or what was going on. It was clear he had run out of things to clean because he was pacing slowly in my kitchen like he was afraid to approach me.

"You can come sit while you wait if you promise not to interrupt my show. The plot is very important."

He looked relieved and sat down a respectable distance from me on the couch. We sat in silence for a minute or two or three hundred because the tension was so thick, I felt like I was in an alternate universe where time had no meaning.

"This show is awful. I kind of love it. Why is that girl separated from the rest of the people?"

"She broke a house rule or something."

"So, she's in time out?"

"Yeah, I guess. But now you're interrupting."

"Sorry, sorry."

To his credit, he watched the awful show until his timer went off, and then he was back to work. My entire house smelled like vanilla, and it was amazing. He sauntered back with plates and what looked like a cup of frosting.

"I'll have you know this is sacrilege," he said as he sat back down, his leg now brushing up against mine and making me wish

I'd worn pants. I shifted to put inches between us.

"Cake? No. Cake is a religious experience if done right."

"Well, we agree on that. But I mean me cutting off these pieces before it cooled. However, it's only going to be cut into squares for Sam and Jesse's tasting or the petit fours. So do not think that I'll always bring you cake straight out of the oven. Today is an exception. And I brought buttercream that I made yesterday at home. You must have the whole experience."

A grin spread across my face. I took the fork he offered, scooped out a ridiculous amount of frosting, and plunged it into the small square of cake. I unceremoniously shoved the whole thing in my mouth.

"Mmmmmmsofkgd."

"I take that to mean good, but you're *supposed* to savor it. Heathen."

"This is how I savor," I said after I'd swallowed and gulped down my water.

He ate his own like a civilized person, I guessed.

"And you call *me* a princess."

He choked on the bite he was eating and coughed, reaching for his water.

Maybe bringing up the name he called you in bed wasn't the best move when you're trying to ignore that it happened. Honest mistake.

"Sorry. I didn't mean to almost kill you."

"Lies," he rasped.

I suppressed a laugh but gave him a shrug instead.

"You'll never *really* know, I guess. Anyway, what's your timeline for baking? I figured we could make a schedule to make sure everything gets done. And when I say *we*, I mean *you*."

"I'd kind of picked up on that, actually, since every time we talk about the spreadsheet, you change topics."

I almost argued, but I did do that. It was just so much information.

"But before I can do that, I need to know if you're amenable to me baking here when you're not home, or, um, if that's weird? I just don't know if I'm making a schedule based on me or based on both of us. In which case, I need your work schedule."

"Oh. I guess that's fine, yeah. It would probably be easier for you. My schedule sometimes changes if I have walk-ins or cancellations anyway. If you could, ah, let me know when you'll be here, so I don't think there's a murderer in my house when I get home, that would be good."

"Are there murderers who also bake for you?"

"There could be. I don't *know* all the murderers."

"Fair enough. I will send you my baking schedule so I can get everything done before the shower. And I took the liberty of making a one-page checklist of the other tasks that need done based on your tornado of sticky notes, text messages, and emails. You can check off the ones you want to do, and I'll do the rest. I got the feeling the spreadsheet was a bit much."

"Can't you be an asshole or something?" I muttered.

It was hard to move past all of this when he was acting like the center of a cinnamon roll.

"What's that?" he asked.

I only shook my head because he heard me loud and clear.

"This is a lot to get done. Okay."

I started to rattle off the things I would do, which included making sure we had table linens, dishware, flatware, adequate lighting, teacups, heaters, and a rain contingency plan for inside the house. Jeremy was dealing with pretty much everything food and beverage related.

"You got it. Are you sure you want to pick up the heaters? I guess you can borrow a truck from your dad or Jesse as easily as I can from the shop, but they're kind of bulky."

"*Yes*, I can handle it."

He held up his hands in surrender, and I took that opportunity to steal the cup of frosting from his plate and promptly eat it with my fork.

"I *would* have given it to you if you'd asked."

"More fun if I feel like I got away with something."

"Sometimes," he agreed with a laugh.

He found a place in my pantry to keep some of his things so that he didn't have to lug them back and forth, and then he was gone. We had done it. We had successfully navigated being alone together. No one kissed anyone, and everything was relatively fine.

Great.

Chapter 20 - Jeremy

I wanted to believe that Lauren was genuinely busy when I went over there to bake. It had been more than three weeks, and I'd seen her all of twice at her house. The progress I was making was great, but I felt more like a tenant than a friend using her space. She'd still been showing up to happy hour, but she always seemed to need to leave after about thirty minutes. Just long enough that I couldn't quite call her on avoiding me. Every single interaction was more of *almost* ordinary, and then taking two steps back into awkward and stilted. I'd hoped after some time, things would feel normal again, but I knew, at least on my end, I still thought about what she tasted like when I kissed her. I was wrecked.

I'd finally gotten together all the samples for Sam to try and was headed to *Books and Broomsticks* to do the tasting there since I didn't exactly have a shop front. I still had everything plated on long white ceramic dishes, so it looked somewhat professional. This whole experience was showing me how much work I needed to do if I wanted to do this for a living, even part-time. Every time I turned around, there was something else I needed.

I had to admit that my ears perked up when Sam said Jesse was leaving the cake up to her so we could do the tasting around her schedule. I wasn't *planning* to ask about Lauren to see if she'd said anything about me, but that plan got a little murkier when it was only Sam. Not only because she was a psychic and asked *really* specific questions, but she was easy to overshare with.

If Lauren didn't tell her, you sure as fuck can't tell her.

I'd have to feel her out once I was there.

I parked, carefully got the cooler out of the back seat, and made my way into the shop. I had only been there a couple of times, the last being Sam and Jesse's engagement, but it was kind of a cool place to be.

"Be right there!" Sam's voice called from behind a shelf.

She bounded around the corner, her eyes lit up to see me. Well, more likely my cooler, but it was *my* cooler.

"Hey, Sam. You ready to try some cake?"

"There has never been a time in my life where the answer to that question was no."

She smiled and gestured to a table she had cleared. I pulled out the sampling dish and discarded the plastic wrap; thankful everything seemed to be as it should. I'd taken photos before I'd left, to be safe, but I wanted a couple more with the shop as a backdrop. Sam indulged me before we got into it.

"Okay, so, as requested, I've got vanilla, chocolate, and lemon, two of each—one with buttercream and the others with either a raspberry, chocolate, or lemon filling. And you didn't ask for these, but I have a spice cake with a cream cheese filling, because it will be the beginning of fall, and, I don't know, that sounded fall-ish, and a caramel cake, which is a recipe of my grandma's."

Sam's eyes got wider the longer I talked, and I thought maybe I should write this stuff out for clients so they didn't feel like they should be taking notes. Another thing to remember on a seemingly endless list. All of it was kind of exciting, though. I felt like I was doing what I wanted, and people were interested.

"Can I eat now?" she asked.

"Yes. Tell me what you think after each one so I can write it down."

She nodded eagerly and sunk her fork into the vanilla cake with buttercream.

"Stoooooop," she said after chewing. "Ten out of ten. I think we're done here."

"You're going to make me blush. Continue," I insisted, making her laugh.

She judged every sample on a scale of ten, but the list of those with top marks was getting a bit long.

"How am I supposed to choose? Can you choose?" she asked.

"I mean, I *can*, but it's kind of your wedding."

"Right, right. Okay. We're good with the blue buttercream and the edible glitter and the flowers, yes?"

"Absolutely."

"Can I pick more than one?" She shot me a hopeful smile.

"Sure thing."

"I want the vanilla and the caramel. Just buttercream in the layers; no fruit."

"Perfect. I'll call my grandma and tell her that her cake convinced my first client."

"Hmmmm. She'll downplay it, but yes, she'll be secretly smug about it."

"That sounds like her, yeah."

"Shit, I'm sorry. Sometimes, things still pop through without me meaning to listen. I wasn't trying to read you."

"It's okay. I mean, I don't get it, but it's all good. If you've got any other predictions or warnings, feel free to lay them on me while I clean up."

I shot her a grin, figuring she'd go back to working. She did not.

"Well, that last one was from your grandpa. He's passed, right?"

"Er, um, yeah. Seven or eight years ago."

"He might be even more proud about the cake than your grandma will be. He's funny. I feel like he would have always had a story."

Goosebumps broke out over my entire body, and I sat my ass back in the chair.

"Yeah. He was known to spin a tale or two."

"He says you need to quit pussyfooting around and get yourself the girl. Something about, like, fear being part of life? Growing up?"

"Dreaming."

"Yes. He's very happy that you remember. Is that something he said a lot?"

"Yeah. Fear is part of dreaming, and if you're not scared, you're not dreaming big enough." Tears sprang to my eyes, and I let out a slow breath. "And the girl…"

Sam almost snorted.

"Right. We can pretend she's some random girl if you want. But your grandpa and I want you to know that you're completely transparent. I'll close this out now unless you have something else you want to communicate?"

"Oh, um, I miss him. And I hope, ah, I hope he's not too disappointed."

My voice broke on the last word. I hated the way it felt in my mouth and how the feeling settled in my chest.

Sam's voice was softer when she spoke again.

"There's nothing to be disappointed about. Be better tomorrow than today."

The tears fell in earnest now. That had been another one of his favorite sayings, and, god, I missed my grandpa. I knew he would have kicked my ass when I started fucking everything up, but I didn't ever think I'd get to hear his brand of wisdom again.

"Shit, Sam. Is this what you do all day? How is there not a line around the block?"

"Not all day, no. I also make displays for smutty romance books and pretty crystals."

"A woman of many talents."

"You want a hug?"

"If you're offering, yeah."

She leaned down and squeezed her arms around my neck.

"Thanks for letting me read for you. I don't always get relatives when I connect with someone's energy. I've never really considered myself a medium. But, it's special when I do. That was a good reading. I hope it helped."

"More than you can imagine. I'll see you at happy hour Friday?"

"Of course. Have a good night, Jer."

I nodded, repacked my cooler, and made my way back out to my car. My head was floating above my body as I walked, my limbs tingly. I wanted to call my grandma and tell her everything, but I thought maybe I should wait until my brain was connected to the rest of me again. I sat in my parked car for a good twenty minutes before I felt normal enough to drive, but I was looking forward to that conversation when I got home.

* * *

The encounter with Sam and my grandpa stuck with me. My grandma burst into tears when I relayed the whole thing, and when she calmed down, she told me not to screw up her recipe and have people thinking she couldn't bake. I assured her I wouldn't. She asked if I was going to share with my mother, and I decided I would, just not in a casual phone call. Conversations with my mom tended to stay surface-level, and that story was not.

The next week flew by in a mashup of petit fours, macarons, lavender cookies, oil changes, and trying to make Lauren laugh. We had moved painfully slowly along the road back to normal, and I found that I hated it a little bit. The longer we went, the easier it was to think the whole thing was a fever dream, and I didn't want it to be. The directive to *get the girl* echoed in my head the moment I woke up each morning, and I was struggling between wanting to latch onto that as a little mantra and tell Lauren maybe I *did* have an epiphany, and worrying that, in reality, nothing had changed.

Amid imagining being with Laur and what that would feel like, my brain liked to insert scenes of me losing my temper with her or making her look at me the way Kat used to, like I'd snuffed out her joy. I tried to cut those scenes short whenever I could.

I finally caught her at home for the first time that week on the day before the shower. We'd canceled happy hour because all of us were trying to get things ready.

She was near manic when I walked in the door, running

through the list of things she needed to do without taking a breath.

"Laur, whoa, whoa, everything is okay. Tell me what you need."

"I need someone who is an actual adult to come and do these things because I clearly am not, and I am going to ruin everything by not having any forks or something ridiculous."

She wouldn't look at me; she was roaming from room to room, fluffing a pillow, sending a text, rinsing a cup, without finishing any tasks. I put my hands on her arms, forcing her to stop.

"Okay. Give me the list, and let's see where we are."

We went through every item, and it wasn't bad. She hadn't gotten the heaters, but we surmised that could be done tomorrow morning. I had confirmed with the caterers that they were dropping food off at two; linens and teacups were already at the house and unpacked.

"I think we're okay. Like, everything is 90% done."

"Maybe that's the problem. I can't check anything off this godforsaken list because none of it is all the way finished."

I guided her to sit on a bar stool and poured her a glass of wine.

"It's two in the afternoon," she declared as she took a sip.

"We'll pretend it's five. You know you can call me if you get this stressed, Laur. I can help."

"Yeah, well. It's hard for me to call you. Maybe it shouldn't be, but it is. Thank you for showing up and helping anyway."

She took another long drink of her wine and cast her gaze anywhere but at me.

"Listen. I need to put the flowers on the petit fours, but then I'm essentially done until tomorrow. Do you want to watch a movie? We can order pizza and do that, and we'll get up early tomorrow and make sure everything gets done, and it'll all be fine."

She eyed me suspiciously.

"Any movie?"

"Any movie."

"And everything is going to be *fine* tomorrow?"

"To be honest, I think we could probably serve frozen waffles and juice boxes, and Sam and Jesse wouldn't care. If you haven't noticed, they're sort of in their own little bubble right now."

"Well. That would have been a suggestion to make *earlier*, Jer. My life would have been a lot easier."

"Next time we throw a wedding shower together, I swear, it's all Pop-Tarts and drinks from a box."

"Okay, good. You do what you need to do. I'll order pizza and hop in the shower. Then we're watching *How to Lose a Guy in 10 Days*."

"Never seen it. Can't wait."

Her shocked face and crossed eyes made me laugh, but she seemed better, calmer. I filled my piping bags and got to work, feeling further down the road to normal than I had when I walked in, so it was progress.

Chapter 21 - Lauren

If he hadn't shown up yesterday, I wasn't sure I would have slept at all. I knew I was in a tailspin, but it was like watching myself as a spectator and *knowing* I should calm down and not being able to fucking do it. And then he was there, and I was in the shower and eating for the first time that day and relaxing on the couch. He didn't make any comments about wanting to be under my blanket this time, but he did put a pillow down next to him and pat it when I started to yawn. I laid down, and his fingers eventually drifted to my arm and rested there like it was where they belonged. It felt like they did.

He left after the movie and insisted I didn't get up, but I thought that might have been more so that we didn't have an awkward goodbye at the door than him being polite.

I was in less of a panic the next morning, but I knew I had to get things done. I called the heater place and asked if I could fit them in my car or if I needed a truck. The guy said they should fit no problem, so happily, that cut a good half hour off my time since I didn't need to go pick up another vehicle. The weather was beautiful—a little cloudy but plenty of sunrays peeking through, and I was finally feeling excited instead of anxious.

Until I got to the heater rental place.

Because the guy I talked to on the phone assumed I was renting the small three-foot heaters, not the tall ones. My dad had already gotten the propane, so at least I didn't have to worry about that, but in looking at these things, I was pretty sure there was *no way* they were fitting in my Beetle. And I absolutely should have known that. Jer had even specifically said I needed a truck. I stood and chewed on my lip, my brain in decision paralysis. If I went all the way back to Emberwood to get my dad's truck, I would be hours behind.

Fuck it.

I directed the guy to bring them out to the front, and I would make them fit. He looked at me like I was more than a little crazy, but that only fueled my determination. I laid down all the seats and scooted the driver's seat up as far as I could while still being able to slide in. They might have been hanging off the back of my car, and I obviously couldn't close the trunk, but they were in. The useless sales guy loosely tied the hatch down with what might as well have been yarn.

Whatever. They're in.

The top of one of the heaters kept hitting me in the back of the head every time I hit the slightest bump. I was forced to drive backroads to Emberwood due to the open-trunk situation. I had horrible visions of these expensive metal heaters in pieces all over the highway. I was *easily* forty-five minutes behind schedule because I should have picked them up yesterday, and I didn't. Why? No reason. I couldn't make myself go get them because I knew it was going to be a giant pain.

Well, you were right.

But now, I was faced with getting these to my parents' house, setting everything up, and getting myself ready in about three hours' time. The only comforting thing was that I knew my mother would have already gotten most of the prep work done. It should have left me enough time to drop these off, get ready, and get back to set up and welcome guests. I tried to take deep breaths and tell myself I wasn't going to ruin this shower.

Until my car lurched twice and then sputtered. I managed to direct myself to the side of the road at the second lurch. Thankfully, I was on a straight section and not one of the curves, but what.the.fuck? I turned the key in the ignition, and nothing.

This cannot be happening. This cannot be happening.

My gas gauge hadn't worked in maybe four or five months, so I made sure to get gas once a week no matter what, and it was fine. I closed my eyes and tried to remember if I'd gotten gas on Monday, and I couldn't. All of the days in the past couple of weeks blended together, and I had no idea.

"Fuck!" I yelled, hitting my steering wheel.

What the hell was I supposed to do four miles from the edge of town with all these rented heaters in my car? If I walked, there was no way I'd get shit done for the party. Tears pricked at the corners of my eyes because this was not the time for this to happen, not when it didn't only fuck me over but Sam and Jesse, too.

God, I'm so tired.

I wanted to put my head on the wheel, ignore everything, and let someone else deal with the fallout. But I couldn't. I picked up my phone to call my dad, but the promise of his deep sigh gave me pause. So instead, I called another person I didn't want to, but at least I knew he wouldn't lecture me. Much. Jer picked up on the second ring.

"Hey, is everything okay? You never call."

"Ummm, no. Not really. Can you…can you come get me?"

"What's the matter?"

His voice was instantly concerned.

"I think I ran out of gas or something? I have the heaters in my car, and I don't even know what to do with them or if it's really the gas thing or that my car hates me. My gauge hasn't worked in months, so it's possible I'm wrong, and… I don't know. I'm so sorry, Jer. I know you're trying to get all of the food together, but I didn't know who else would come get me, and—"

"Laur, text me your location. I'll bring gas, but I'll grab the tow truck from the shop just in case. We'll get everything here in time. I swear."

"Okay. Thanks."

I texted him where to find me and then sat in silence. Why, of all weeks, did I choose this week to do this? I knew, rationally, that I hadn't slept properly in at least ten days, and I was surviving on diet soda, frozen pizza, and turkey sandwiches. It was not a recipe for thriving. I wanted to text Sam about how I'd "pulled a Lauren" and she'd never believe the predicament I was in now. But it was her wedding shower, and it made my skin crawl thinking about admitting to her I was this out of control. I was going to have to figure it out.

I started making plans in my head for how it was going to get done. I'd be making use of dry shampoo and extra deodorant and skipping a shower. I could ask my mom to arrange the flowers, get my dad to figure out the heaters once Jer and I got them to the deck.

It had been all of twenty minutes when the tow truck passed by and turned around so it could pull up behind me. I schooled my face into a determined expression and got out to meet him.

"Hey. You okay?" he asked, eyeing my overloaded Beetle suspiciously.

"I know. I shouldn't have tried to bring the heaters in my car. This is a problem I've brought upon myself."

"I'm not asking about your car or the party, Laur. Are you okay?"

I simply stood and stared at him, not even sure how to answer that question.

"Sure. I mean, right now is not great. But sure. Can we figure this out?"

He nodded. He popped my fuel door and the hood, added gas from a gas can, and tried the engine. It did try to spring to life, but the car was making a not-great noise. I saw Jeremy's brows furrow. He turned the car back off and went to do something under the hood. I sat on a tree stump while I waited, nervous he was going to tell me it was something awful.

"Hey, Laur?"

"What…"

"When was the last time you changed your oil?"

"Umm, I don't know? My dad used to do that until his heart attack, and then I started taking it to the place on Main, you know, but things have been crazy, so, a while ago?"

He went to my windshield to look at the sticker there and then got the mileage off my dash.

"You haven't changed your oil in about 7,000 miles. It's not catastrophic, just, you know, bring your car to me sometimes, okay? I think, right now, the issue is your fuel pump."

"Okay?"

My voice got tighter and smaller. I didn't know it could *be* catastrophic to wait too long to change my oil, and that was dumb because I was sure that was a normal fact that people knew. He got back into the driver's seat and peeled off the piece of electrical tape I had over one of the dash lights.

"You put tape over your check engine light?"

"It bothered me, and there didn't seem to be anything wrong with the engine, so I assumed it was an error. I always intended to get it checked out, though. I didn't want to look at the light."

"Okay," he said, and I could tell he was trying to keep his judgment at bay. "Laur… you can't ignore the check engine light or a faulty gas gauge. Okay? You could put yourself in a dangerous situation."

His voice was soft, and I knew he was trying to give me information, but *ugh*. I nodded because I knew my voice would shake if I spoke. I felt dumb. And that was not something I handled well. It brought back memories of many, many parent-teacher conferences when I was told I wasn't performing up to my potential.

I brought my feet up to the top of the stump with me and pressed my face into my knees.

"I'm going to secure the heaters to the truck bed and then hook your car up to tow. I might need your help to get them out so I don't scratch up your paint."

I nodded again. I got up, went to stand where he directed me, and helped lift the heaters where he wanted them. He maneuvered the tow truck in place to get my car hitched to it. There was a lot of unnecessary beeping, being that it was only the two of us out here. Once everything seemed secure, he hopped down from the back of the truck.

"You know, if you missed me, you could have just said. You didn't have to trash your car to get my attention."

He shot me a grin, and I promptly burst into tears. I thought I had been doing a pretty good job of calming myself down, but my brain couldn't tell the difference between laughing and crying at that point, so it all came out. I held my hands over my face and willed the water to stop.

"Oh my god, Laur, I'm sorry, I was only kidding. Your car isn't trashed. I mean, not irreparably, anyway. I'll fix it, and it will be fine. Please, please, don't cry over this."

He had reached for my hands twice and stopped. Things were weird between us, and I hated it. I hated all the things, actually.

"Well, then p-plug your ears and turn ar-round so you can ignore that anything's hap-penning. We're both real-ly good at that."

I sat back down on the stump, telling myself I needed a minute to cry it out before I had to turn my smile back on to host a party. I felt tears dampen my shirt sleeves, and I knew my puffy eyes were going to be a bitch to cover.

Jer knelt in front of me and gently tugged my hands away from my face and held them.

"Hey. Will you look at me, please?"

I shook my head and gazed at the sky instead, making him laugh.

"Laur, please."

I sighed and looked at him, his hazel eyes full of concern and his thumbs rubbing circles over my palms.

"I can tell you that ignoring what's right in front of me is one of the hardest things I've ever done."

I rolled my eyes, but he pressed on, touching my face and wiping my tears.

"I would love to dive into this with you right now, but I believe we have somewhere to be. So, here's how this is going to go: We'll take this whole truck to your parents' and drop off the heaters, leave your car at the shop, and then I'll take you home to get dressed and grab the cakes I made yesterday. I threw my clothes in the truck because I didn't know what exactly I was walking into. Your parents will help; everything will be fine."

I nodded furiously, like the more enthusiastically I agreed, the truer it would be.

"And whatever your car needs, I'll do the labor for free, so we'll get it fixed, okay?"

"Don't be ridiculous, you're not doing—"

"Yes. I am. Let me take care of it for you, okay? Please?"

I didn't say anything else, though I wasn't resigned to letting him do it. I stood up, and he breathed out and followed me to the truck, holding out his hand to help me get in. He directed us towards the body shop, and I let myself deflate into the seat.

"Thank you," I offered lamely.

"Laur. Are you okay?"

"I told you, I'm fine. Annoyed at myself."

"Lauren."

"Jeremy."

"Are.You.Okay?"

The heaviness of his words this time hit me somewhere different, and I couldn't quite get the answer out. I felt my breathing start to shorten again, and *damn it,* I did not want to cry anymore.

"I don't know," I got out.

He reached over and grabbed my hand, threading our fingers together and squeezing. I found the words spilling out of my mouth. The insomnia, the out-of-control feeling, the mistakes at work. How I could never finish anything even though I had a thousand ideas. Feeling like I was letting people down because I couldn't get my damn life together like everyone else seemed to. How I was lazy even though I hated being lazy. It felt like I'd been talking for an hour, but the dash clock suggested it had been five minutes.

He drove and rubbed his thumb over my hand while I talked, and he didn't interrupt me. He pulled into the main part of town as I ran out of words.

"Laur. You are the least lazy person I've ever met in my life. So, let's take that off the table right now. And I'm the last person to provide any sort of wisdom, but I think maybe you should talk to your doctor about everything you just said. My, um, well, Kat used to kind of describe her ADHD that way. At least pieces of it. And I'm not trying to, like, diagnose you or tell you something is wrong with you. I think, maybe, there's something else going on that isn't your fault."

"ADHD, like what eight-year-old boys get diagnosed with?"

He huffed out a laugh.

"I don't think it's age and gender-specific, but sure."

"You really think I should go to the doctor?"

"I think it couldn't hurt. I feel… very helpless right now because I can't make you see yourself how I see you. But I'm telling you that you're amazing at everything you do. Like, you blow me away. So, with everything you're feeling, it seems like something else could be happening."

"And Kat has this? Did she take medication or something? Did it help?"

"Yes to both. And I think so? Uh, she also sold her ADHD meds at times, so I'm not holding her up as, like, a beacon of mental health, but a lot of the feelings sound the same."

"Okay. I, um, well, I'll think about it. Thanks for listening to me have a little mental breakdown; I think I needed it."

I realized we were already sitting in my parents' driveway. He put the truck in park and turned toward me.

"Anytime, Garrett. Now, let's get to this wedding shower, shall we?"

We managed to get the heaters off the truck bed, and he mercifully let me stay in the cab as he hulked out and carried each one around to the deck. I did not want to have to explain my face or my car to my parents. We had under an hour and a half to get back and host the damn party. He still held my hand the whole way to the shop, and again in his car on the way to my townhouse.

When I'd called him, I thought I'd feel helpless or like a damsel asking him to come rescue me, but honestly, I felt grounded. I had been floating away in my thoughts; he brought me back to earth and was holding me there.

Chapter 22 - Jeremy

Everything seemed to spring into fast-forward once we got to Lauren's house. She shrieked when she saw herself in the mirror but declared I had to make her stop working on her makeup in twenty minutes no matter what, or we'd be late. She shoved me into her guest room-slash-office to get dressed. My outfit wouldn't be a surprise since Lauren had thrifted the vest and the blazer for me and told me exactly what to wear with it. Even when she was kind of avoiding me, she was committed to her aesthetic.

I pulled on a pair of charcoal pants, a cream-colored button-down, and a dark green vest. The woven blazer was different shades of gray, and I had to admit I looked good. I was glad I'd had the forethought to throw my deodorant and cologne into my bag, too, because carrying those damn heaters around the house had me sweating.

We were nearing the twenty-minute mark, so I went to her fridge and pulled out all the desserts. Everything looked great, but I was in my head about strangers eating my food. Before I had too long to think about it, though, I had to force Lauren to finish getting ready.

"Hey! We're at almost twenty-five minutes, just so you know," I called through her door after knocking.

"Can you come in here?" she called back.

I opened the door. The only time I'd been in her room was fumbling through a drawer for a condom, so seeing it in the light was a new experience. It was a lot like the rest of her house, full of color, but this room was a little softer. There was only one large abstract art piece on the wall above her bed and several lamps giving off low light.

"Can you get the rest of these buttons?" she asked, emerging from her bathroom.

I swallowed hard. She was in a dark green dress, similar to my vest, but it was sheer across her chest and down her arms and *fuck*, all the way down her back to her waist, I realized as she turned around. There were tiny buttons all the way up her back, and the top half was still undone. She swept her hair up to give me access, and I felt like a teenager because my fingers were shaking slightly, trying to put the loops around the buttons. I wanted to do the opposite of securing this dress on her. I cleared my throat.

"You look gorgeous."

"You don't look so bad yourself. You should think about adding vests into your wardrobe more often."

"For you? Anything," I agreed, finishing the last button. "You ready?"

"Against all odds, yes. Let's go."

* * *

As it happened, we made it there twenty minutes before everyone else. Lauren's mom had come through in the clutch, and we were able to step in and divide and conquer. I set up the dessert table, which had already been loaded with tablecloths, flowers, and delicate floral plates and platters.

"Don't forget to take pictures of everything set up before people destroy your creations," Lauren said as she breezed past me with even more vases full of peonies and other flowers I didn't recognize.

Shit.

I pulled out my phone and hastily took some photos.

"Guys… this is *beautiful*," Sam's voice said from behind me.

I turned in time for her to throw her arms around me.

"Did you doubt me?" I asked, knowing full well that *I* doubted me.

"Not for a second, no. But still amazing to see everything in real life. I'll have Zin get good photos before anyone touches it, promise. I'll even edit them for your portfolio."

She kissed my cheek and continued to see the rest of the space.

"I'm not going to kiss you. But thanks for doing all of this with Laur."

"You're missing out, but no pressure."

I grinned at Jesse and pulled him in for a hug. Seeing him and Sam as happy as they were after watching Jesse struggle through coming back from his injury was nothing short of heartwarming, and I wasn't at all embarrassed to admit that. It made me think maybe it was possible for a situation to change that drastically. Under the right circumstances, anyway. My eyes automatically scanned the area for Lauren, and I found her greeting guests as they made their way out to the back deck, directing them to find their tables and get champagne. No one would have known that she was in tears two hours ago.

Good.

She deserved to have a great night, too. I knew it was for Jesse and Sam, but we'd also worked our asses off making it happen, so it was fair that we had some fun too.

I recognized most people—it wasn't going to be a large affair, and it dawned on me that since Jesse and Sam had moved back to Emberwood, they'd built a whole community for themselves. Besides their families, there were coaches from the rec league, people from the hardware store, Christian and whomever his plus one was, Sam's friend Gen and her husband… it was small, but there was a lot of love all in one place.

Do not *cry.* I thought.

It was bad enough that I had cried at the proposal, but no one had even started making toasts or anything sentimental yet.

Jesus.

The feeling that settled into my chest wasn't jealousy, but it was a *want.* And that presented a problem because it directly opposed to everything I'd claimed to want for literal years. Regardless, that thought was going to have to wait until after tonight was over to sink its claws into me.

A small hand made its way into mine, and Lauren tugged me away from the table.

"Come, mingle, enjoy. You saved the day enough. You can relax."

My mouth quirked up into a smile. Saving the day was not something I was accused of often, but damn it if it didn't feel good.

Chapter 23- Lauren

I led Jer to his seat and left him with a plate of tiny sandwiches, cucumber water, and a glass of champagne. I didn't know how I was going to thank him for today, but feeding him and letting him relax felt like a decent first move.

"You are a magical fairy goddess princess," I told Sam, making her twirl around for the third time since I'd first seen her. The dusty lavender dress with her dark hair and blue eyes was straight out of a magazine.

"Back at ya."

Sam linked her arm through mine and rested her head on my shoulder.

"I'm so fucking happy, Laur."

"I know, girl. And you deserve it."

I put my cheek on her head and remembered why I'd done all of this in the first place. Not that I'd *forgotten*, but sometimes the details made the big picture hazy. In that moment, it was crystal clear. I felt some of the weight of the day fall off my shoulders. I was sure it would come back later, but I was going to enjoy this evening, too.

I was impressed that everyone had taken the theme to heart. Even Danny had come in a button-down and suspenders. The only person who didn't seem to want to be there was Gen's husband, but he was already on my shit list, so I didn't particularly care. I did resolve to glare at him until he was uncomfortable enough to fake it.

I was originally worried when Sam said no "regular" shower games because I didn't know what else to do, but we'd set out a cornhole set, and I'd made a ring toss out of pretty glass bottles, and it seemed like everyone was happy mingling and eating and playing. I changed the playlist from instrumental to a more sentimental mix so people could dance on the empty part of the deck if they wanted to.

"As I understand it, it's customary for the best man and maid of honor to dance," Jeremy's low voice murmured in my ear, nearly making me jump.

"At the *wedding*, sure. We don't have to dance now."

"That's not how I understand the custom."

He shrugged and gripped my hand to bring me into the small space, twirling me around and pulling me against his chest. I was vaguely aware of Sam clapping and insisting that Jesse twirl her too, but I was lost in the hazel eyes staring into mine. I wanted to be mad at myself that this was getting so complicated, but if I was being at all honest, it had always been complicated. And if today was any indication, I was in no state to be jumping into complicated when I, by myself, was a wreck. But I thought, just for this song, or just for this night, I could pretend I wasn't and that everything was fine. Tonight, I could believe this was easy, and the fluttering feelings in my chest could stay.

* * *

The last of the small group was trickling out to their cars, and I was floating in a cloud of exhaustion and pride. Sam's Aunt Zinnia came and wrapped me in a hug and smoothed my hair.

"You did a beautiful job."

She paused like Sam always did when she was waiting for information from some unknown source.

"And I'll say to you…it's okay to follow your gut. Tonight, and always. It feels like you're asking for permission, and I'm supposed to tell you that you have it."

I opened my mouth to ask how those things were connected, but she was already gliding away.

These psychics are sometimes more trouble than they're worth, I thought, even though I knew that was a lie. Sam and Zin were treasures.

I shook my head and started pulling tablecloths off tables and gathering up trash and dishes.

"Leave it," my mom said, looking almost as tired as I felt.

"Oh, it's okay. I'll be out of your hair in a minute, I—"

"All of it will be here in the morning. Go get some sleep. We can clean up tomorrow."

My shoulders relaxed at her words.

"Yeah. Sleep sounds fantastic."

"You worked hard, Laur. Get some rest."

Jer was packing up the very few leftover desserts, and the look on his face was adorable.

"Your table over here was pretty popular."

"Was it? I didn't notice."

He tossed me a smirk and snapped up the container.

"I heard your mom tell us to go home, and I'm not arguing. You ready to go?"

"Yeah. I forgot for a minute that I have no car. You don't mind taking me home? And mayyyyybe bringing me back in the morning?"

I flashed him my most winning smile.

"I'm sure you'll figure out how to repay me."

He got the eyeroll he deserved. He threw an arm around my shoulder and pulled me close while we walked down the driveway to his car, dropping a kiss on my head.

"We're not terrible together," he added.

I knew he meant working together and pulling off this party, but it sounded like it could mean more.

"Perhaps we're not."

Chapter 24- Jeremy

Her gaze may have been focused out the window of my car, but her fingers were actively tracing each of mine. I thought about driving for the next half hour and seeing if she noticed. However, I reluctantly steered us toward her townhouse. I was acutely aware of the parallels between this scene and the one that went terribly wrong after Sam and Jesse's engagement.

I now knew the outcome if I tried to be *good* and stay away from her, *and* I knew the outcome of giving in and being absolutely selfish. Being selfish felt a million times better, even if it made things a hell of a lot messier. It hadn't resulted in the silent treatment when we crossed the line on the Fourth of July. Which was why, no matter how bad of an idea, I was not going to try to walk away if she invited me in tonight. The best I could do was not invite *myself* in and accepting her good judgment if she didn't.

"Do you really think I might have ADHD or something?" she asked, still playing with my fingers.

"I don't know, Laur. I just… I don't think there's any reason for you to feel that awful. I think it's worth trying to figure it out because you deserve to enjoy your life. It sounded like maybe you haven't been lately. That's all."

"Maybe you're right. I'll try to make myself call for an appointment."

"Do you want me to set it up for you?"

"Oh. That's sweet. I can do it. I'm just the worst about making phone calls. It's why all my client appointments are done online."

"I make phone calls literally every day to our suppliers. So, if it's an issue, tell me, and it'll be done."

"Okay. Thanks, Jer. For everything," she said, yawning, as I pulled up to her complex and we got out.

"Do you think I can blame the hypothetical ADHD for why I suck at relationships? Or do I have to shoulder the responsibility for that one?"

I appreciated her attempt to bring things back to the light as we meandered up to her door.

"Have you considered the possibility that these previous men simply weren't very good in bed?"

She snorted.

"And you think you're any better?"

Her voice was teasing, but her eyes were saying something else. She was already backed up to her house, and it was too easy to step forward to cage her in.

"Baby, I *know* I'm better," I murmured in her ear.

"Prove it," she whispered back.

The earth stopped turning then. We hadn't discussed this like we had at the Fourth of July, and I didn't know what domino I was knocking over by doing what I wanted to do next, and I didn't care.

"Do you want to talk about anything first?" I asked, the words coming out slowly; I wanted her to hear them.

My hands were practically vibrating with how badly I wanted to put them on her body.

"Nope."

She threaded her fingers through my belt loops instead. Our eyes found each other as the word left her mouth. We both knew there were reasons we shouldn't do this again, but none of them seemed to exist while we stood right here. She opened the door from behind and crossed the threshold. I followed, and in a moment, I had one hand on the back of her neck and the other on her hip, pulling her into me and twisting us to press her back against the door.

Our mouths crashed together harshly, teeth grazing and our tongues frantically trying to get enough of each other. I dragged my thumb down the side of her throat and felt her heart racing at her pulse point. Her nails raked through the hair at the back of my neck as she arched against me. I traced my fingers from her throat up her jaw until my hand was gripping her hair and tilting her head back, allowing me to press my tongue to her neck and taste the salt on her skin.

The little breathy sound she gave away when I bit down lightly spurred me on, and I gripped her under her thighs and picked her up, her dress bunching up around her hips, and carried her to the kitchen. I placed her on the counter, stepping in between her legs and enjoying being able to look straight into her eyes before our mouths met again.

"Jer, please," she groaned, grasping my hand and placing it high on her inner thigh.

"You want me to touch you, Princess?"

"*Yes.*"

"Are you saying I *am* better in bed?"

"I need more evidence. And I swear to god, if you don't put your hands on me, I'm going to—" I captured the rest of her retort with my mouth and gave her what she wanted.

"You're so wet," I groaned, tugging her panties to the side and pressing a finger inside her.

"Fucking finally," she gritted out. "More."

I added a second finger, sweeping my thumb over her clit. I relished being this close to her and being able to go slower, less afraid of snapping one of us back to reality than I was last time. We were both choosing this now, regardless of the consequences. Maybe we were both stupid, but she felt so right.

"So tight, so perfect. You're so, so good, Laur."

Her hands traveled from being tangled in my hair to gripping my biceps to digging into my shoulders, and I had to stop myself from losing focus.

"I'm going to... Jer, *fuck,*" she moaned, tightening around me.

I kept steady pressure as she rode out her orgasm, only stopping when she put her hand on my wrist.

"Good girl," I said against her lips.

"Why do I like it when you talk to me like that?"

I huffed a laugh.

"Do you want me to stop?"

"Not even a little."

"Good. Bedroom?"

"Shower."

"Good call."

I picked her up and carried her up the stairs to her room, not hating her mouth on my neck while I climbed. I set her on her feet in her room, and she disappeared to start the water. She reappeared and turned her back to me, gesturing for me to get to work on her buttons.

"How pissed will you be if I rip this dress off of you?"

She gasped.

"Very. I went to four thrift stores looking for a dress to match your stupid vest."

My heart swelled at the fact that she took that much time making sure we matched.

"But I'll make it worth your while."

I could hear the smile in her voice as she reached behind her and undid my belt. The chore of undoing seven thousand loops on buttons was made infinitely better with her hand down my pants.

She was finally free, and I pushed her sleeves down her arm gently, letting the dress pool at her feet. She was left in only a green lace thong.

"Jesus, Laur."

She flipped around and returned the favor, unbuttoning my vest and dress shirt, and I helped make that journey more fun for her.

"Shower, now," she demanded.

I dutifully freed her from her underwear and followed her into the now steam-filled bathroom.

The reality of the shower was not living up to the fantasy.

"Was this shower made for hobbits?" I complained, trying to get a turn under the water and feeling like I was awkwardly smooshing her against the wall.

She laughed and kissed my chest, but the angle at which the water hit my head went almost directly into her eyes on its way down.

"This is wholly unsexy," I decided. I started laughing in earnest now.

She was shaking, trying to hold in her giggles. "Just get clean and get out. I have to wash my hair, and I can't even move my arms with you in here, you fucking giant."

I surrendered and hurried up, wanting her back in some sort of open space where I could have my way with her. I kissed her hard, my fingers digging into her ass before I got out, hoping it would encourage her to go quickly. Hair hastily dried and a towel around my waist, I laid myself out on her bed. Her sheets smelled so good—sweet and floral mixed with whatever fabric softener she used, and I wanted to stay there forever.

Fuck. Where did that thought come from? I wondered a little surprised at the strength of that want.

I felt my body relax as I pushed the surprise away and concentrated on staying awake—I wasn't going to miss this because I was dog-tired. I had at least two more orgasms in store for her. The water had been off for a few minutes, and it was taking Herculean restraint for me not to go in there and toss her over my shoulder. She finally emerged, wrapped in a matching fluffy white towel, her hair braided in pigtails down her back. Her eyes were wide, but a playful smile still played on her lips when she saw me taking up most of her bed.

"Come here, baby." I patted the bed next to me.

"Ah, your sex voice is back. Good, I like it."

That made me chuckle.

"I don't think I have a 'sex voice,' but if you like it, then we're good."

She crawled on the bed and ended up straddling me. I started at her knees and slid my hands up her thighs, sinking them in at the crease where they met the rest of her body. Her pupils took up most of her bright green eyes when I met them. She dropped her towel and let my gaze roam over her unhurriedly. Her skin was pale against the brightness of her hair, and the smattering of freckles down her chest and arms made me want to kiss all of them. Our eyes met again, and that was that. I grabbed the back of her neck as gently as I could and pulled her toward me, loving the feeling of her breasts pressed against my chest and her fingers now winding their way into my hair.

"Reach up and grab the headboard," I muttered.

She did as I asked, and I grabbed her ass firmly and nearly lifted her off me, making her squeak in surprise. I settled her exactly where I wanted her and dragged my tongue all the way up her slit to circle her clit. I repeated this over and over, stopping to suck harder every time she whimpered until her legs were shaking under my hands.

"Mmmmm, let go, baby," I murmured against her center.

I latched onto her clit and felt her come apart around me. I would do this all night long to feel her walls crumble like that again and again.

I put her back where she started in a similar fashion, but she was ready for me to move her that time. She collapsed on my chest, her breathing coming back to normal, and I made lines up and down her back, trying to see how many times I could watch goosebumps spread across her skin.

"You're not so chatty now," she said into my neck, changing the game and sending goosebumps down my arm.

I laughed.

"I can be if you want. Do you want me to tell you how good you taste? And how I was lying here thinking I would do that all night long to feel you come apart above me over and over."

"Do you plan these things out ahead of time, or do dirty things naturally roll off your tongue."

"All natural, of course."

"Hey, Jer?"

"Yeah? Everything okay?"

"Oh, everything is perfect. I was going to ask if you were planning on fucking me anytime soon or if I should go get ready for bed."

I felt the smile on my shoulder.

"So sorry for giving you a recovery period. Next time, I'll do with you want I want," I threatened playfully, digging my fingers into her sides and making her shriek.

"Don't tickle me!" she yelled.

I stopped, but I flipped her to her side and dropped my own towel, grabbing her hand and putting it where I wanted it. I rocked into her grip and bit down on her neck, letting her know I wasn't done with her.

"Then keep your attitude in check, Garrett."

"You like my sassiness."

I smacked her ass lightly.

"Maybe."

I leaned over to her nightstand and fumbled around for a condom.

"And don't think we're not going to get into your toys at some point," I promised while rolling it on.

"Oh my goddddddd, I expressly forbade you from looking at anything else. I moved everything after that night."

She reached up to cover her face, and I grasped her wrist firmly and pinned it above her head.

"Ah, ah. You're sexy as hell, and I love it."

She bit her lip in a way that made me insane. I reached down to line myself up with her entrance and tugged that lip between my teeth while I pushed into her. She whimpered, and I switched to her tongue, sucking it into my mouth.

"You know that, right? How fucking sexy you are?" I asked, pulling back and pushing in again, groaning at the feel of her.

"I like it when you say it," she admitted breathlessly.

"That's a good enough reason for me to tell you as many times, in as many ways as I can dream up, then."

   I put my focus into exploring her and finding out which angle and pace made her react most favorably. Getting her to make those sounds was a recipe I needed to get right.

Chapter 25- Lauren

I felt his large arm around me before I opened my eyes. I let all the images from last night filter in through my sleepy haze, and my heart rate sped up thinking about it.

Christ, he's good in bed, I thought.

I knew it was more than that, though. His attention and the way he handled me was far and above more of a turn on than anything he did physically, but *damn*. I was sore in all the best ways. My runaway thoughts were reined in slightly when I remembered *before* the wedding shower and the issue with my car. But that was far less fun to think about.

I tried to squirm out from under his arm to go brush my teeth and make us some coffee or something, but the moment I moved, his grip tightened around my middle.

"Nope."

His voice was thick with sleep, but it still sounded sexy.

"I was going to make coffee. And you know, brush my teeth."

I couldn't believe he was still here, in my bed the next morning. It wasn't a sight I thought I'd ever see.

"You stay here. I'll make coffee. And pancakes. I know where all your stuff is now, so this can be a bonus for you letting me use your kitchen."

"I mean, twist my arm. I guess I'll let you make me breakfast."

"Before that, though… *I* need to eat breakfast."

"Are you not going to also have pancakes?" I asked, confused, until a smirk appeared on his face, and he reached under my oversized T-shirt for my underwear.

"Oh my god. You are ridiculous. And insatiable. And…" I trailed off once his mouth was on me.

"Keep telling me what I am, Laur. I'm listening."

He laughed against me when I could no longer form sentences, but I couldn't have cared less. This was how waking up should be every day.

* * *

Pancakes devoured, I now had to deal with the fact that I had no car. I had Jer drop me at my parents' house to clean up. He tried to stay, too, but his time was better spent diagnosing what I'd done to my poor little Beetle. *So stupid.* I was busy collecting glasses and dishes and scraping bits of hardened petit fours off dessert trays.

"What can I do to help?"

I turned at the familiar voice because I was confused.

"You can't clean up your own wedding shower. You should be sleeping. Or happily doing things with your fiancé, whom for this moment I shall pretend is not my brother. What are you doing here?"

"First of all, I can do whatever I want. I'm the bride. Second, I hardly got to talk to you last night, and that's dumb. Third, I'm a nosy bitch. Something is going on with you and Jer because your energies were quite literally visible to me last night, but it's also seemed like you've been avoiding each other again for, like, two weeks. So, I need to know what is the what."

"So, what you're saying is that your cleaning help comes with demands."

"Obviously."

She picked up a napkin from the ground as if to say *See? Helpful!* I thought about holding back like I had been because I was trying to keep the focus on her and this wedding and not be a drama queen. But here she was, *asking*. So, it didn't count as being an attention whore.

"Well. If you want the story about last night, we'll have to back up to the Fourth of July..."

Sam arched an eyebrow at me but stayed silent, still pretending like she was helping me pick up. While I talked, I did put her to work helping me move the patio tables back to their original positions.

"You used fake astrology to get laid?" she asked.

"Well, kinda. I guess."

"I am going to turn you into a witch yet, I swear it. But let it be known that I am *furious* with you for not disclosing this earlier. So, okay, *that* happened, and then things got weird?"

"I guess? We just… were being too polite. None of the usual shit-talking, and it was weird. He was using my house to bake, but I told him I didn't want to talk about it if nothing had changed, and it hadn't. So, we ignored it. We're very mentally healthy."

"Clearly."

"Oh! Speaking of mental health, I think I have ADHD."

Sam looked thoughtful for a moment, her eyes focusing just past me, so I knew she was seeing or hearing or doing something psychic-y.

"Yes."

"Oh, you're a doctor now?"

"No, but I could tell you more about what the actual doctor will say if you let me read for you."

"Huh. Well, it would be nice to have some universal validation. I've been… struggling. And I think having a reason for it might help. I looked up, like, all these checklists this morning, and I swear to god, Sam, it's like seeing my life explained in bullet points."

"Oh, Laur. Can I ask why you haven't talked to me? I know I've been preoccupied. And I *know* you think I'm crazy for having this wedding so soon. But I'm not going anywhere. You can tell me things. I can still come over for movie nights—in fact, I insist upon it. But you're not, like, burdening me with your problems. If anything, I owe you a year's worth of listening to your issues without complaint."

I nodded, feeling a coil of stress in my gut loosen slightly. I had needed her. I still needed her. And I was only making things harder by trying to be *fine*.

"You're right. I'll be cashing in on those coupons soon. Like, in five minutes when I tell you what happened last night."

Sam's eyes lit up with the promise of good gossip.

Her eyes only got wider when I launched into the story about the heaters and the car and Jer coming to rescue me and then allllll the delightful things from after the wedding shower. I was worried they might detach from the sockets.

"*Lauren!*"

"Yeah?"

"Only you would tell that story casually. All of that happened in one afternoon?"

"Yeah, I guess it did."

She shook her head in disbelief. We'd finally completed thoroughly picking up the back deck and went inside to start washing dishes.

"And also, I thought my mystical car dragon was supposed to protect me from things like this?"

Sam had given me a little dragon statue to keep in my car. It was true that she'd explained the whole concept of a dragon from another realm protecting my vehicle probably six times, but I just thought the statue was cute.

"Your dragon cannot force you to make good choices about car maintenance, Laur. But the fact that you broke down in a safe place and were able to get help right away? I'm going to say it did its job exactly as expected."

I squinted at her, trying to think of a retort. But I couldn't. I'd have to thank my dragon.

"Fine."

"So… what does that mean? He dropped you off here this morning and what? Two or three more weeks of awkwardness until the couple-ette party? Or are you going to get over yourselves and be together?"

"Do not call it that. We need a better name. I've seen it called a Stag and Doe party, and I feel like that fits your nature vibe. Let's go with that."

"Hmmm. I do like that very much and I'm now planning invitations in my head. But do not try to get me off topic."

"Well, that's it, isn't it? I have no idea what to do, and I'm asking *you*. My psychic best friend. So, psychic already!"

A satisfied grin spread across Sam's face. She practically skipped to her purse, leaving me to finish the dishes, and pulled out her tarot deck. She sat at the counter and did her things, talking to herself or the universe, I wasn't sure, but cards started flying through her fingers.

"Right, right, right, obviously," she said.

I assumed she would address me if she needed some sort of response.

"Yeah, what does that *mean?*" she continued.

She huffed a breath and threw more cards down on the counter, and she ended with a smile.

"Well, they worked with me a little bit, but I still think your people are being stingy with their information. Bottom line: it is going to be so much easier to stop fighting this thing between the two of you. The image they showed me was like trying to build this wall, one of you on each side, putting up ridiculous things to strengthen it. Like feathers and tiny sticks and school glue. Because neither of you *wants* a wall there."

I bit my lip between my teeth. She was scarily good.

"Okay. We'll say that makes sense."

She rolled her eyes.

"I guess what I'm saying is that the wall is easy to take down. However…"

"I knew there would be a 'but.'"

"It's not. I mean, it kind of is, but not really. Just listen!"

I crossed my arms, dishes now forgotten.

"I'm going to stick with the wall metaphor if that works for you. If you take it down, great, but you're left with a mess of feathers and sticks and glue on the ground. Cleaning it up is tedious, and it's *work*. It doesn't mean anything bad is happening, it doesn't mean you shouldn't try to make it work. Just clean it up. Even if it feels… they keep telling me to say 'boring,' even though that's not the word I'd use. Cleaning it up will be boring, and you won't like it. Do it anyway."

No matter how many times she read for me, I always got a shiver down my spine when she said something so on the money that it was like the line between dimensions was thinning in front of me.

"Yeah. That makes too much sense."

And it was my biggest fear that I'd get bored or change my mind on a dime. But couldn't I push through that if I knew something better was on the other side?

Maybe. For Jer.

"Excellent. Now, let's get your car-less self home, shall we?"

Chapter 26 - Jeremy

Technically, I was off work. And yet my ass was in the garage looking at Lauren's car. I was going to fix it if it killed me because when she looked at me yesterday like she trusted that I could help her and take care of her, I swear to god, my brain chemistry changed. I was so focused on making sure I didn't fuck up and disappoint everyone in my life *again,* that I didn't think about anyone looking to me for help when shit went wrong. It felt *good.*

Unfortunately, I didn't have the fuel pump she needed in stock, but I found one that could be here relatively quickly, so I got that ordered and set up to change the oil.

Waking up with her back pressed to my chest and her bare legs against mine was scarily enticing. A list of reasons why I *needed* to go back to her townhouse tonight was forming in my head, and it hit me how absolutely fucked I was. A year. That's how long I spent hanging out with her, flirting with her, but constructing very firm boundaries in my mind around doing anything beyond flirting. It had been helpful when Jesse was a disgruntled-older-brother about the whole thing because it gave a whole other layer to that boundary. Obviously, it was a little hard for him to hang onto that once he was with Sam, and then the boundary started getting thin. And now I was standing here over her car, working for free, contemplating how to get myself an invite back to her bed tonight. Boundaries blown to hell.

"Shit."

"You good, bro?" one of the other mechanics asked.

"What? Yeah. No, it's not the car. I'm an asshole. I'll be right back."

I washed my hands and made my way into the main reception area, where Rachel sat.

"Hey. I need to know where to take someone on a date, like,

tonight. Something good."

"Oh? Are you ready to admit there are developments with you and Lauren?"

"Yes, developments, whatever, shut up. I haven't been on an actual date since I was in high school."

I'd slept with Lauren twice, and I hadn't taken her out at all. Because happy hour didn't count, even when I paid for her drinks behind her back. Rachel looked smug.

"What does she like to *do*?"

"Decorate. Thrift things. Go to estate sales. Watch bad movies."

"Oh! Take her to the drive-in. They play cheesy movies all summer. A little difficult to do any of the other things at night."

"Bless you, Rach."

"Wow, from 'shut up' to 'bless you' in under sixty seconds."

"Yes, gold star for you."

I returned to my closet office and looked up movie times. As a gift from the universe, they were showing *You've Got Mail* that night, and I knew that was one she liked. If I could do that and buy her gyros from her favorite food truck, I was pretty sure it would be a decent date. I started to text her, but I kind of wanted to hear her voice when I asked, so I pressed the call button instead. My nerves were bouncing around under my skin, worried that last night didn't push her into the same headspace I was in.

"Hey, is everything okay?" she asked.

"Yeah, everything's good. Can I take you out tonight?"

"Out... like, to soften the blow about how much it's going to cost to fix my car. Oh my god, am I going to have to get a new car?!"

"No, your car is going to be fine. On a date. Can I take you on a date tonight?"

God, I felt like I was in high school.

"Oh! Um, yes? Yeah, of course. What kind of date?"

I could hear her grinning as she spoke, and my nerves switched from anxious to something else entirely. I ran my plan by her.

"Greek food and a rom-com. Are you for real?"

"Is that not okay? I can come up with something else. I know you like—"

"You're completely ridiculous. Yes, it's okay. You do realize you'll have to drive. And let me eat a gyro pita in your car."

"I don't know why you think I'm this tyrant about my car. It's fine. And yes, I'm acutely aware of the fact that I'll be driving. I've had my head under the hood of your car all morning."

"My hero," she replied in a Disney princess voice.

"Trying to be, anyway. I'll see you at six."

"See you then."

* * *

After I finished what I could on her car without having the correct part yet, I swung by the florist and picked up a bouquet that was like an entire rainbow so it would match her house. I had way too much pent-up energy to sit around, so I thought about baking something non-wedding-related for fun. Except most of my shit was at Lauren's house. I searched my pantry to see what I could come up with and ended up with everything I needed for peanut butter rice crispy treats.

Not exactly five-star.

But it would work to kill some time and keep my brain busy.

While they cooled, I vacuumed my apartment and threw in a load of laundry. I'd been home so little lately that I didn't have much of a chance to get it messy, but I thought maybe I should invite Lauren over at some point instead of always being at her place. But her place was a thousand times cozier than mine. Just in case, though, I changed my sheets and cleaned the bathroom. A shower and a shave later, it was still too early to leave.

JEREMY: What does one wear on a date to the drive-in? Or a date, period?

LAUR: Your khaki joggers with the dark blue Henley and either the gray jacket or black hoodie if you wanna be comfy. Oh, and some jewelry. Because your rings are kind of hot.

JEREMY: Am I flattered or concerned that you have my wardrobe apparently memorized?

LAUR: I mean, you could be flattered, but I notice what everyone wears. I could tell you almost every item in Sam's closet right now.

JEREMY: Well, slightly less flattered when you put it that way. Any other requests, Princess?

LAUR: Be very careful calling me that. I don't know that you know what you're doing.

JEREMY: I think I know exactly what I'm doing.

LAUR: I'll see you soon.

She is so hot. I am so screwed.
As if to prove that point, I dressed in the exact clothes she told me to and put on no less than four rings and a leather bracelet. It might have been too much, but I was positive she would let me know and fix my appearance to her liking if needed.
Armed with flowers and dessert, I hopped in my car for my first date in a long time. All ideas of how I was going to screw this up were sealed in a jar somewhere in my brain, and I was full speed ahead into how I was going to be this person she saw when she looked at me.

Chapter 27 - Lauren

Had I expected Jer to ambush me and make me talk about what was going on between us after last night? Yes. I had gotten away with brushing him off before, but last night was…something else. Had I expected him to *call me* and ask me out on a date with zero discussion about the fact that we're apparently going on dates now? No.

I thought Sam was going to have a coronary while I was on the phone. As soon as I said the word *date*, she was practically on top of me so she could hear him talk. I made her keep her thoughts to herself and shooed her out the door to the appointment with her wedding caterer. Obviously, I commenced a pop-playlist-fueled-cleaning-frenzy rather than be left alone with my thoughts.

But then his text arrived, and damn it if all the thoughts didn't come rushing in. Heat spread through my entire body by the end of our back and forth, and I found myself sitting at my island, staring into space. My mind drifted to weeks ago when I asked him if anything had changed on his end, and the memory of his *no* sat on its haunches, ready to pounce.

You stay there, I demanded.

It was possible something had changed between then and now. His vibe today did not convey that he was taking me out to tell me he wasn't interested.

Quite the opposite.

I re-entered my body and glanced at the clock.

Shit.

I had a whole thirty minutes before he was picking me up. Happily, my hair looked fucking amazing when I took it out of last night's braids, so I only had to get dressed and do some sort of makeup.

I put on a white pleated skirt with embroidered daisies and a lime green tank top. A pair of knee-high socks, my white sneakers, and a denim jacket finished my outfit, and I put on the largest white plastic hoop earrings in existence. The whole ensemble felt happy and loud, and it matched my mood perfectly. I was finishing off my eyeshadow with glitter when he knocked, and my stomach flipped. I felt ridiculous like I didn't even know what a date was anymore.

I swung the door open to the most colorful bouquet I could have imagined. My eyes widened, and that feeling in my stomach turned from butterflies into squirrels at a rave.

"These are *beautiful.*"

"I thought they matched your house."

The earnest expression on his face as he stepped across the threshold made me want to melt.

"Let me put them in water and get my bag."

I motioned for him to follow me.

"Motivation still hasn't struck, huh?" he asked, nodding towards the half-finished wall.

"No. But rude to bring it up."

He chuckled and waited patiently. He had worn the exact outfit I suggested, and it inspired thoughts that were inappropriate for the drive-in.

"I have to get the twelve-foot ladder from my dad, and it's a whole thing, and now I don't have a car to go get more paint. So, it's your fault for taking so long to fix my fuel thingy."

"I am sorry that I do not have a 24-hour turnaround time for fixing your *fuel pump*, Princess. The part will be here Saturday. I put a rush on it."

He raised his brows at me in a challenge.

"Well. Now you make me feel bad. Thank you for fixing it. I mean it."

"And I mean it when I say it's not a big deal. Well, it is a big deal that you'd been ignoring your car's desperate cries for help, but, you know, everything else is fine." He shot me a grin.

I rolled my eyes, but I couldn't wipe the smile from my face if

I tried. I walked past him, flowers sorted and my purse on my shoulder, when he wrapped his fingers around my wrist and tugged me toward him. His cologne immediately enveloped me, and I was forced to look up into his melted-caramel eyes, my breath stuttering.

"Yeah?" I nearly whispered.

He leaned down so his lips brushed my ear, and goosebumps erupted down my arms.

"You look fucking gorgeous."

His hands grazed my lower back, making me shiver. He cradled the back of my head in his giant hand and tilted my face up even further. His mouth ghosted over my lips. I tried to stand on my toes to close the distance, and he pulled back slightly, clearly teasing me.

"Are you waiting for permission? Because you can have it."

My heart rate was now at a dangerous level, I was certain. He let out a laugh I felt in my chest before he finally gave me what I wanted. His lips were soft against mine, and I melted into him. He trailed open-mouthed kisses down my neck and let out something between a growl and a groan when he got to my shoulder.

"We should go if we want to get pitas and make the movie on time," he said, sighing.

"Right. Movie. Got it."

I ran my fingers through my hair, and we headed out of the house. My inner teenager was having a conniption that I was going out with Jeremy Ash. My brother had ensured I was off limits to any of his friends for most of high school, which was difficult because he was friends with *everyone* back then. But that had never stopped me from admiring Jer from afar. He was cute then. He was beautiful now. So, present-Lauren was getting the better end of the deal.

Chapter 28 - Jeremy

I did *not* want to be in the car going to get Greek food. I wanted to have her on her kitchen counter and be under that skirt. But that was *old-Jeremy* behavior. *This* Jeremy went on dates and spent the night and called the next day. It was a whole new world. I did take advantage of the skirt by resting my hand on her thigh while I drove, but I almost passed the food truck in my distracted state.

The sun was setting when we pulled up to the ticket stand at the drive-in, and I happily handed over the money to get to see Lauren's happy face from the passenger seat. I guided the car to a spot, backed in, and popped the hatch. Lauren had dutifully hidden the bag of food from the kid at the gate, but I was pretty sure he was high and didn't give a shit about much of anything.

I set up the pillows and blankets I'd brought along and helped her into the back of the car.

"Give me your drink and candy order, Princess."

She tried to glare at me, but the pink across her cheeks made it feel harmless.

"Dr. Pepper and all the sour candy. Do I have to wait for you to eat my pita since this is a date?"

"You can do whatever makes you happy."

She grinned and dug into the bag while I made my way to the concessions.

As the movie started, I returned with her requests and climbed in beside her to see if she left me any food.

"Try the falafel pita pocket. It'll change your life," she said seriously while wiggling closer to my side.

I had to agree that they were good. All the food was amazing, but my life had changed plenty in the last week, and I didn't know if I could handle any more.

The movie was all but background noise to me, but I tried to focus on it instead of her in case I needed to participate in some sort of post-date analysis of the film. When we were finished, I cleared the remnants of our dinner and laid down on the pile of pillows I'd stacked up.

"C'mere."

I held out my arm, and she slid in next to me, her head fitting perfectly on my shoulder.

"Your jacket is scratchy. There's no way you're comfy in that, is there?" I asked.

"Are you trying to get me to take off my clothes?" she replied without missing a beat.

"Well, technically speaking, yes. But I have more blankets to cover you back up."

She rolled her eyes and shimmied out of her jacket, leaving her arms bare. I pulled the blankets up over both of us and tucked one in underneath her.

"There, now you're a burrito."

"I wanna be a pita pocket."

"Fine. You're a pita pocket. Are you going to change my life?" The words were out before I realized how they might land. "Sorry, that was maybe—"

She laughed at my discomfort.

"Would you kiss me already? I had expectations about going to the drive-in with Jeremy Ash, and tucking me in like a food product was not on the agenda."

Oh, thank god.

"I live to exceed your expectations."

She had broken out of the blankets and had her hands in my hair, pulling me down to meet her mouth almost before I got the words out. I couldn't decide where my hands needed to be. I wanted them everywhere. I grazed my fingers up the back of her thigh and squeezed where it met her ass. Lightly, I traced paths up her stomach under her shirt to meet her bra line and back down again. All the while, she was kissing me like she had all the time in the world. Her mouth moved slowly; she bit my lip and then ran her tongue across it over and over.

It hit me that we *could* have all the time in the world. If we wanted it. We didn't have to rush anything here. I could lie here and kiss her and hold her hand and wrap her in my arms, and it was fine because the point was being together and not hooking up. That thought made my heart swell because it wasn't even something I'd known I wanted. But here it was in front of me, and I wanted it desperately.

"Okay, so now explain to me what's happening because you distracted me, and I'm lost."

"What? You've never *seen* it? I thought this was a repeat for both of us; I'm so sorry. I never would have tampered with your first experience with *You've Got Mail*."

She caught me up and snuggled back under my arm, and I relished that as much as the feeling of her nails across my stomach. The movie wasn't all bad, either.

* * *

"You did not disclose the fact that you had peanut butter rice crispy treats in the car. You let me think that Sour Patch Kids were my only *option*, Jer. That's where the betrayal lies."

"Betrayal might be a bit strong, no?"

"Well, it depends on how good they are, I guess. Let's try them out."

I placed the pan on her counter and cut two, handing her the large piece. She sank her teeth in and rolled her eyes.

"*Absolute* betrayal!" she got out with her mouth full.

"I'm so sorry, Laur. I'll never forget to present all your dessert options ever again."

"Thank you. I'm a reasonable sort of person, Jer. You have to do better, is all."

She grinned at me and took another giant bite of her treat. I wrapped my hands around her waist and hoisted her up onto the counter so I could stand between her legs.

"Tonight was fun."

"Tonight *was* fun," she agreed.

"I want to keep doing this, Laur."

"Eating delicious desserts?"

"No. Well, yes, I want to bake for a living. But no, not in the context of right now."

"Hmmm. I haven't the slightest idea what you mean, then." Her words held humor, but her tone was serious.

"I think this thing with us… it could work. I want to keep you."

"Oh?" She asked, her eyes now wide.

"Yeah. Can I?" I let the moment hang between us for a breath, hoping she answered the way I wanted her to. *Needed* her to.

"Yeah, Jer. I think you can." Her voice was soft now, and I searched her eyes for any hesitation, but she seemed calm. I kissed her lightly.

"It's late. Do you want me to pick you up before work tomorrow?" I asked.

"No."

"Oh. Okay. Is Sam—"

"I don't want you to leave. If that's all right."

I rested my forehead on hers, not knowing how badly I wanted to hear those words until they registered.

"Let's go to bed."

"Okay. But I get to take two more rice crispy treats with me," she whispered in my ear. I laughed but cut her two more and followed her upstairs.

Chapter 29 - Lauren

He walked me backwards until I sat on the edge of my bed before kneeling, making us about the same height. I pushed a piece of hair off his forehead and found myself cupping his jaw, running my thumb along his cheekbone. The skin around his eyes crinkled like he was amused.

"You're just very pretty," I explained.

"Oh yeah? So are you. I'd even go so far as to say that you would win should our beauty be judged."

"Well, of course," I agreed, making him smile.

I moved my hand to trace his bottom lip when he pulled my middle finger into his mouth and swirled his tongue around it before letting it go. Heat surged from behind my navel, and I sucked in a breath. I wasn't quite sure what we were doing in this little bubble, but I wasn't in a hurry to pop it.

"That felt...surprising."

"Surprising good or bad?"

"Good. Definitely good."

"Then maybe once more to make sure?"

He looked into my eyes as he did it again, and I was pretty sure I could hear colors at that point. I was not inexperienced by any stretch of the imagination, but the things this man did to my insides made me feel like I was in over my head in the best way possible.

"What are you thinking?" he asked while lightly pressing kissing along my neck. My whole body shivered.

"I...I don't want to tell you," I answered honestly.

He pulled back, and I felt the loss of his warmth immediately.

"Why?"

"I tend to... overshare. Or word vomit. Whatever you want to call it. And I don't want to do that, and then you leave."

"I, for one, like your overshares. I feel like I get a glimpse into your brain when you go on off on a tangent about breakfast pastries, you know?"

He leaned forward again and kissed his way down my sternum, and I arched into him and hummed my approval.

"So, tell me what you're thinking."

"Fine," I sighed. "But you have to get up off the floor. It's very hard to concentrate with you down there."

I leaned back and rolled to my side, and he joined me, his hand now on my hip, pulling me closer.

"I was thinking that I don't know what to do with you."

"How do you mean?" he asked, concern clouding his expression.

"No, no. Not a bad thing, I promise. You just… you make me feel like my mind isn't racing. Like I can be in my body and be with you and feel things. There are no outside thoughts trying to bust down the door. And that's new. For me."

He'd moved from my hip to holding my hand, putting pressure on different places of my palm.

"I very much want you to be in your body," he murmured.

"What are you thinking?"

"How there is literally nowhere else on the planet I would rather be right now."

My mouth quirked up at his quick answer.

"Do you think we could just do this tonight?" he asked.

His voice was low, and he pressed a soft kiss on my lips while the question registered.

"That…sounds really good. Let me get ready for bed, yeah?"

I kissed him and pushed myself up to go get my pjs and wash my face. He was still looking at me with a sweet smile, all stretched out on my bed when I came back.

"There are extra toothbrushes in the middle drawer in the bathroom," I said, grinning back.

It was such a small thing, but it felt like this choice—*not* sleeping together and doing something as normal as him having a toothbrush at my house—was a bigger one than any of the others we'd made so far.

* * *

I woke up with Jer's arms wrapped around my middle, holding me to his chest. After orienting myself, I relaxed into him and started playing with one of the rings on his fingers rather than trying to untangle my body from his.

"Morning," he rumbled in my ear.

"Sorry, you can go back to sleep; I wasn't sure how to extricate myself without waking you."

"Mmmmmm, no."

"No to what?"

"No to you extricating yourself. And no, I don't want to go back to sleep. I want to do other things."

He took the hand I was using to play with his rings, brought it behind my back, and settled it onto his cock.

"*Oh.*"

"Only if you want. Sorry, I should have led with that before I—"

He tried to pull my hand away, but I only laughed and squeezed through his boxers. He let out a hiss and lightly bit down on my shoulder.

"Can we stay like this?" he asked, grinding into my hand.

I only nodded and reached under the waistband of his boxers to take him out. He reached under the oversized t-shirt I'd slept in and dragged his fingers up my center. His hands tugged my underwear out of the way, and he put the lightest pressure on my clit.

"Do you need me to—"

"No, god, could you—"

He laughed, and I felt it vibrate in my chest.

"Do you want to grab a condom?"

I let out an exasperated sigh.

"I can. But I have an IUD because I couldn't be trusted to remember to take the pill, and I haven't slept with anyone other than you since my last annual visit, and if we're doing this for real, you and me…".

I was glad he was behind me, and I wasn't having to watch his facial expressions as I blurted this out.

"I haven't slept with anyone else either since my last physical and never once without a condom," he said, his hand rigid and splayed across my stomach.

"Okay, so then, we're agreed?"

"Jesus, Laur."

His laugh sounded against my ear, his hand returning to where I wanted it.

"I may not last thirty seconds. Fair warning."

He reached down and brought my leg over the back of his, opening me to him. In one slow motion, he was buried inside of me, and *god*, he felt so good. The heat from his skin was radiating around my body.

I groaned into his bicep, no longer resisting the temptation to sink my teeth into it.

"*Fuck*, Laur. You feel fucking amazing."

He held me tighter to keep me against him while he found his rhythm, hitting the spot that had stars forming behind my eyes over and over.

"That's…please don't stop. I need you *right there*."

"Laur…do you want me to pull out before I come?"

I shook my head, pretty sure I would murder him if pulled out right now. His hand drifted up from my ribs to my throat, and he held me against him with only the slightest pressure.

"Fuck. I'm going to need you to touch yourself, Princess. Because I'm barely hanging on here," he rasped.

I didn't even think I needed to; I was on the edge with him. Before my fingers reached their destination, he hit my G-spot one more time. I felt the thousand bands of tension that had been stretching tighter and tighter all snap together, and I didn't know what sounds fell from my lips. Jer's hand tightened by a fraction while I fell apart. His rhythm stuttered shortly after, and I felt him spill inside of me, nearly incoherent praise groaned against my neck.

His arms loosened their hold, but they stayed around me, not letting me drift away. We were both sufficiently out of breath and lay panting together. He slipped out of me a minute later and scooted over so I could turn and look at his face.

"Jer… I. Jesus." I still couldn't catch my breath.

I covered my face with my hands and willed myself to calm down. Laughter or tears threatened to force their way out, and neither felt like an appropriate reaction.

"Hey," he said softly, pulling my hands down. "Are you okay? Do you wish we hadn't decided not to use a condom? We can go back to—"

"What? No. That was the most…like so, *so* good. I'm just… I'm overwhelmed, and I don't know why. I feel completely ridiculous."

Even as the words came out, tears sprang to the corners of my eyes, and he wiped them away.

"I know we both have morning breath, but can I kiss you?"

"Yes," I answered, thinking that sounded like the remedy to this entire debacle.

He was gentle against my mouth, his tongue finding a leisurely rhythm against mine. It might have been a minute or twenty that he held me there, but I felt the wave of emotions peak and subside. I pulled back when my brain was securely connected to the rest of me.

"I'm sorry. I feel better now."

"Yeah? Good. And don't apologize."

He ran his hand over my hair and down my neck.

"That's normal, by the way," he said softly.

"I can assure you that is *not* normal for me. I've never cried after sex. Ugh."

He laughed at my scrunched-up nose.

"I'm not trying to mansplain your body to you. But with an intense orgasm, it can, well, from what I understand, it's like a big high and then kind of a crash. There's nothing wrong with you. That's what I'm trying to say."

"Pretty confident in your skills, then, huh?" I teased him.

"Less so, now," he said, huffing a laugh.

"I've never, well, *finished* without extra *help*…or whatever. So maybe it was a little out of the ordinary. You can enjoy your well-earned confidence; don't let it go to your head."

"Oh, it's already there. I doubt I'll even be able to fit my ego in my car."

"You're hilarious. But back to the point—I'm fine now. And that wasn't super mansplain-y. Well, maybe it was, but I think you're right, so I'll forgive it. I need to clean up, um, I'll be right back."

He laughed and started looking around for his clothes.

"I'm making you breakfast, so take your time."

I let out a giant breath once I was in the bathroom and heard him walk toward the stairs. I was hurtling toward something with Jer that I didn't expect, and the momentum was so strong that I didn't think I could stop it now, even if I wanted to.

An even scarier thought? I *didn't* want to.

Chapter 30 - Jeremy

Lauren's fridge left much to be desired, but there were eggs and everything I needed for pancakes. Only because all my stuff was still there; otherwise, we would be eating pickles with a side of ketchup. I made a mental note to grab her some staples the next time I went to the store.

I had prepped the pancake batter and was waiting for the pan to heat when she entered the kitchen and wrapped her arms around me from behind.

"You know, if you're not careful, I could get used to this treatment and actually start acting like a princess."

She let go and started making coffee.

"I will take my chances."

I flipped the first pancakes and started beating the eggs. I glanced again at the half-finished purple wall and thought about our conversation from the car-breakdown day.

"Did you get a chance to make an appointment for the ADHD eval or whatever?"

"Would you believe me if I said yes, I got right on that and have an appointment on Monday?"

"Not when you put it that way, no." I raised my brows at her.

"That's just as well. It shows you have good instincts." She plopped down at the island and scrolled through her phone. "I did look at like a hundred online checklists, and I've diagnosed myself with ADHD. Does that count?"

"Definitely progress."

I finished the pancakes, quickly scrambled some eggs, and put her plate in front of her.

"Do you want me to call and make the appointment?"

"No, it's fine. I'll get to it."

"Laur... I'm not asking because I think you *can't*. You seemed so overwhelmed that day, and I don't want you to keep feeling like that. So, if I can help, please let me help. But if you tell me to let it go, I'll do that, too."

She looked at me, her annoyed expression fading somewhat as she took a large bite of pancake.

"You don't have to call. Just stand there and look at me, and I'll do it."

"I guess I can bear that hardship."

She rolled her eyes but got on the phone with her doctor's office.

Approximately five minutes later, she was punching in her appointment to her phone calendar.

"Next Friday. Happy?"

"If you are."

She dropped her faux attitude at that, and we finished breakfast in a comfortable silence.

"I gotta be at work at eleven. Do you need a ride anywhere? I promise I'll try to have your car done tomorrow if the part gets here on time."

"Ah, no. Sam's picking me up soon. Today is bridesmaid dress day!"

"Oh, that's cool. I probably need to rent a tux soon, right?"

She almost snorted. It was cute. "As if this wedding would have you dressing in a regular tux. So silly. I'll be figuring out your suit situation. Speaking of, I need your measurements and sizes in case I see anything today while I'm out."

"I think you're familiar with my most impressive measurement."

Lauren *legitimately* snorted at that. "You didn't just say that. You're worse than a teenage boy."

"Sorry, I had to."

I could have given her my inseam and sizes, but it was much more fun to pretend like I wasn't sure and have her measure me. I stretched out on her couch when she was finished and laughed when she did, too, right on top of me.

"Hi there."

"Hi. Thank you for breakfast. And everything before breakfast. And last night. Five stars for all of it, really."

She laid her head on my shoulder, and I could feel her heartbeat against my chest.

"Definitely five stars. I…this is going to sound dumb, I think. But I'm going to say it anyway," I said, stroking her back.

"I hope so. I've said a crap ton of dumb stuff to you, even in the last twenty-four hours."

"Nothing you said was dumb, Laur. I guess I don't know if you need space or if it's like, a given that I'll come here after happy hour tonight or see you this weekend? I haven't done this in a very long time. You're also welcome at my apartment anytime. It's not as homey as your place, so—"

"Oh. Ummm, I don't know either. We're both working tomorrow, so it might make sense for you to stay here?"

"Okay. That seems… practical."

Her head lifted so she could look me in the eyes.

"Is that all right? You seem disappointed with that answer."

I cleared my throat. This was such an uncomfortable space. Being vulnerable with people was not something I did often.

"I guess I want to know how you feel rather than what you think."

Her face softened, and she laid back down, snuggling into me.

"Well, the less practical part of me wants you here all the time. Preferably cooking for me and being shirtless so I can admire your tattoos while you work."

"That can be arranged."

"How do you feel?"

"I am afraid I'll never leave if you don't kick me out. But I'm going to try to be more reasonable than that. I guess I'm saying, don't be afraid to tell me to go home, okay? I won't take it personally."

"Yes, you will."

"Yes, I will. But I'll understand it anyway."

I dropped a kiss on her head and resolved to get up and go to work in five more minutes.

* * *

All the oil changes in the world couldn't have brought me down. I was thoroughly disgusting when I got off shift, though, grease and sweat are a stellar combination. I discarded my coveralls and cleaned up what I could before heading home to shower. I had approximately eleven texts from Laur. Most of them were her looking sexy in what I assumed were bridesmaid dress options, but one photo in the middle stopped my scroll.

LAUR: We stopped at this bakery in Centerville and they're looking for a part-time person. Sam and I both chatted with the owner, and obviously, she loved us because we're sort of dynamic, but anyway, we told her all about you, and Sam showed her photos from the shower, and she said you should reach out. Her name is Delaney. Photo is of the job posting!

JEREMY: You look amazing in all of them. And I'll for sure send her my portfolio. Thanks, baby ♥

LAUR: It does things to me when you call me that. Even more so when you're in my bed. See you in a bit.

I groaned inwardly and adjusted myself, now forced to carry my jacket in front of me on the way out to my car. I was going to have to get my shit together. Tonight was the first time we were hanging out with Jesse since we stopped pretending we weren't into each other. He'd calmed down about me flirting with Lauren, thanks to Sam and whatever magic she did, but it was possible it might be a different story once it was a little more upfront.

Maybe not. Lauren never took issue with him and Sam.

But in my head, I knew it wasn't *exactly* the same because Laur was his younger sister. Maybe I should have thought about talking to him before right this minute, but it was a little late now.

I was late getting to The Bar because I knew I'd be distracted all night if I didn't send over at least an introductory email and my portfolio, which looked a hell of a lot better after I let Sam work on it. It was only part-time work to cover two weekday mornings, but it would be a great first step, and I'd still be able to work at the garage and keep my income stable. My chest felt light like I could breathe fully after being deprived of air. My brain, on the other hand, warned me to be on the lookout for potential toxins in that air, that things didn't all fall into place and stay that way. That there had to be a catch. All those thoughts could fuck right off, though.

I walked into The Bar and slid into the seat next to Laur while she was excitedly showing pictures on her phone of the dresses from earlier to Gen. I shrugged off my jacket and greeted the rest of the table. Gen and Danny, and occasionally Gen's husband or a date Danny brought, were our new additions to our weekly happy hour. I'd decided to forgive Danny for the shit he gave me when we hung out because he was kind of hilarious. And Gen was cool. Her husband was a dick, and I was glad to see he wasn't around.

Lauren finished her slideshow and angled toward me. I wasn't sure how she wanted to play the situation out in public.

We probably should have talked about that, too.

"Hi," she said, her green eyes meeting mine before she leaned over and pressed her lips to mine briefly.

"Hi."

"Oh, is this finally a thing we're acknowledging? That's exciting!" Gen said, a wide grin on her face.

Lauren rolled her eyes, but no one was exactly surprised. Because we were, apparently, completely obvious for quite a while.

"Yeah… I'm gonna go grab a drink. Vodka soda?" I asked her

more quietly.

"Thanks, Lover!" she said loudly, apparently leaning into us being open with our friends.

"Word choice, Laur. Honestly," Jesse grumbled, but he waved me off, so I knew he didn't have any real anger behind it.

Okay then. That was easier than ripping off a band-aid.

I grabbed drinks and put in an order for food before sitting back down. While waiting, I checked my phone to see a response from Delaney, the owner of the bakery. She wanted to meet with me and have me bring some samples of my recent recipes on Monday.

Holy shit. This might be happening.

I made my way back to the table, feeling almost unstoppable. Out of habit, I stopped myself from reaching for her until I realized I could, and I let my hand rest above her knee. I pulled up the email on my phone and set it in front of her while everyone at the table chatted. Her eyes widened, and she bit her lip as a smile took over her face. Her fingers were warm when she put her hand on top of mine and guided it up to her thigh instead. I let out something between a sigh and a laugh because she was going to be the death of me.

Chapter 31 - Lauren

True to his word, Jer got my car back to me by Saturday evening, and he stopped short of making me sign in blood that I'd never miss an oil change and always bring my car to him if something stopped working. I was very happy to have my little yellow bug home. He'd baked at my house on Sunday morning to have some new things to take to his interview, plus he still had a few other items in my freezer.

Now, it was Sunday night, and I was spread out in my bed like a starfish, wondering how it was even big enough to fit both of us when he was here. His absence was tangible. I knew I was being dramatic, and I didn't care. I slept better with him here; I hadn't begun a project in the middle of the night in over a week. I sighed and tried to get comfortable regardless.

LAUR: I want to text you that I miss you in my bed.

JEREMY: Oh yeah? You should do it. I think I'd love it.

LAUR: Nah, it's probably a little too intense. I better not.

JEREMY: Always the voice of reason.

LAUR: You're going to do great tomorrow, you know.

JEREMY: I hope so. If not, I'll rely on my exceptional good looks and wink at her or something.

LAUR: I'm pretty sure she's, like, late forties with a husband and kids.

JEREMY: You say this like cougars don't hit on me all.the.time.

LAUR: There are certain things I don't need to be made aware of, Jer.

JEREMY: Noted. Thanks for the vote of confidence. I'll see you tomorrow night? I can bring dinner over.

LAUR: Can't wait.

JEREMY: Night, baby

LAUR: Goodnight 💕

Sleep came easier after that.

* * *

Jer had texted the next morning that he thought things had gone well. She had him fill out some paperwork for references and a background check, which, to me, sounded like the job was as good as his. I didn't *love* that he'd have to go to work at some ungodly hour twice a week, but he was so excited it was hard to worry about it.

"You're less chaotic. What are you doing? Meditating? Yoga? Getting laid on the reg?" Christian asked in an accusatory tone while we were both between clients. I hadn't worked with him for any length of time since Jer and I were unofficially official. Or whatever we were. I shrugged.

"Getting laid, then. You finally did something about the lumberjack man."

I almost snorted then.

"That's a very personal and invasive question, Christian."

"Says the woman who explained to me *in detail* her night with the man with the fetish for—"

"Okay! Please don't make me revisit that! Yes, Jer and I are kind of together. Like he texts me and stays over and takes me out. It's *nice*."

"Oh, I'm sure it's *very* nice. That man is solid like an oak tree."

"You can't have him. No matter how pretty you are."

"Straight men that look like him are a tragedy."

"*Jealous*."

He hummed in resignation and went to set up for his next appointment.

I offered to pick up lunch for both of us later to make up for my sassiness. When I walked into the café, my eyes landed on a couple sitting at a table off to the side of the order counter. Something acidic rose in my throat when I realized that half of that couple was supposed to be *mine*.

Jer's back was to me, and he was sitting across from Rachel Turner, one of the prettiest girls to ever grace the halls of Emberwood High. She ran in the same circle as Jesse and Jer in school, but I didn't know her well otherwise. She was laughing and rolling her eyes at him, her hand swatting his shoulder until her gaze landed on mine. Her mouth opened, and she looked like she was going to call out to me, but I turned on my heel and got the hell out of there.

What the fuck? What the actual *fuck?!*

I stopped once I made it to the alcove of the pharmacy entrance next door and tried to dislodge the lump in my throat, swallowing hard.

"Laur…" I jumped at his closeness, not having heard him approach.

"Do *not* 'Laur' me. You fucking asshole," I hissed.

He stepped back like I'd physically hit him.

"Whoa, whoa. What is it that you think is happening?"

"You're out with Rachel fucking Turner after telling me you

wanted to 'do this' with me," I got out, adding air quotes to express my disdain for his vague explanation of what we were even *doing*.

Maybe this wasn't supposed to be exclusive to him. Tears suddenly overflowed from the corners of my eyes, and I frantically pushed them away with the heels of my hand.

"No no no no. No, I'm not. I am the third wheel on a lunch date between Rachel and her *boyfriend*, Mike Delgado. They both work at the shop, and we all decided to grab lunch together. He was in the bathroom when you came in, Laur. I will walk you back in there and introduce you to them both, I swear to god."

He'd stepped back toward me, his fingers tentatively reaching for my hip. I turned slightly, out of his reach.

"You're not there with her? Because that's not what that looked like." Embarrassment crept across my collarbone and up through my cheeks.

"Can you please come sit with me?" His voice was strained, and the look on his face only conveyed fear.

I nodded once and followed him to a bench in front of the pharmacy. I sat with at least a foot left between us.

"I... Lauren, look at me, please."

Reluctantly, I took a deep breath and affixed my gaze to his.

"I would not, ever, do that to you. Okay? I get that I do not have a great track record as a boyfriend, but I'm not... I'm not that guy."

The embarrassment had now fully settled in and made itself at home in the pit of my stomach. "

"I...You're saying you guys have never..."

He cleared his throat and sighed.

"Rachel and I have known each other a long time, and we hooked up a grand total of once. Years ago. It was a non-event, but I'm not going to lie about it."

The green flame of jealousy sparked but stayed under control.

"Oh. Well, I kind of hate that. But neither of us has exactly been saintly in our pasts, I guess."

"I'm sorry. I truly didn't think twice about hanging out with them because they're just my work friends. We occasionally go to lunch or grab a drink after work, but it's not often. I should have thought about it, but please—"

"Jer, just. Okay. It's okay. I'm not going to tell you that you can't hang out with your friends… I didn't know she was a friend. And I'm sorry for calling you an asshole." I swallowed hard. Those words didn't want to come out.

"Hey…it obviously makes you uncomfortable, and if I'd thought about it, I would have realized that I'd be losing my mind if you were at lunch with a guy who had ever touched you. So, I won't, going forward. Okay?"

"What? You can't not go out with your friends. That's…"

"Laur, it's not like we're talking about me never seeing my best friends again. If you want to get to know them, I can invite them to happy hour. You're not making me choose because there's not a choice to make. I told you I wanted to keep you, and I meant it."

"You're ridiculous."

The fight left my body as he spoke, though. I wouldn't have asked him to choose, but thinking about him *ever* being with Rachel Turner, with her perfect warm, bronzed skin and wild curly hair, conjured images in my brain that were unkind.

"Oh, absolutely. There's this girl who makes me completely insane. Now, will you please scoot over so I can touch you?"

I scooted down the bench a few inches, and he met me in the middle.

"I'm doing the thing, Jer. And I don't *want* to do the thing."

"What thing?"

"The thing we talked about. How we bring out the worst in ourselves in relationships."

"But look at us, communicating openly about it."

"Yeah. Maybe. I'm still sorry."

"Everything is fine. Let's get you the food you came in for, and I'll walk you to your car, yeah? How's it running, by the way?"

"Fine. *Show off.*"

He wove his fingers through mine and pulled me off the bench back toward the café. Thankfully, Rachel and Mike politely ignored our existence while I ordered food to go, and Jer kissed me at least twelve times before he let me leave.

"I'll get tacos for dinner tonight, okay?" he said after finally letting me sit down in my driver's seat.

"How about *I'll* get tacos. It's far past my turn, anyway. I'll see you later."

"I'll see you then."

I watched him walk back to the café, his hands in his pockets, and I cursed my temper for making me look like such a jealous monster.

Chapter 32 - Jeremy

I was grateful I was in the office that afternoon and not in the garage. My hands shook after I left Lauren at her car, all the adrenaline having left my body. When Rachel told me Lauren stormed out of the café after seeing us, my stomach lurched. I was an idiot not to think about how I would feel if Lauren was at lunch with some guy friend I didn't know.

Everything's fine. You explained. This isn't the same as before.

When I'd been with Kat, I'd flirted openly with other women when we were in a fight. I would pretend I had no idea what she was talking about when she called me on it, but I was well aware of my actions. She'd done the same to me—sitting on my friends' laps, dancing with other guys, whatever, but it didn't change the fact that I'd been a complete dick. Today *wasn't* that, but it scared the shit out of me anyway. Lauren held my heart in her hand and squeezed when she called me an asshole. The fear that coursed through my body thinking she might be done with me before I even got a chance to test the waters as her... something.

We should probably put a label on that.

Thankfully, Rachel didn't press me on what happened in front of Mike. She didn't even press me on it when we returned to the shop. She'd come from a toxic relationship similar to mine and Kat's, and now that she was dating someone decent, she understood that I'd do whatever I needed to make Lauren a priority. She *did* request that invite to happy hour, but I figured it was too soon to make that call.

By the time I got home to shower before heading to Lauren's, I was spent, but there was no way I *wasn't* going to her house, so it was an iced coffee on the way over to hopefully wake me up. To be safe, I got one for Lauren, too; although tacos and coffee did not sound like a great combination.

Even though we'd left things settled at the café, and she'd texted me twice saying she was sorry for overreacting, I still felt like there were weights tied to my ankles as I walked up to her door. I knocked and heard her yell to come in.

"Hey, I come bearing coffee, if you want it. I needed a jolt of something after work."

I held out her cup.

"Coffee always, yes. But maybe after tacos because yuck together. Anyways, eat! Try an empanada; it will change your life."

"You said that about the falafel before. How many times is take-out going to change my life?"

"Well, it depends on if you're getting take-out from the right places, Jer. Hopefully, a lot."

I shook my head and tried the food. It *was* good, but I couldn't say my life felt different after. I didn't want my life to feel different. It finally felt like I was on the upswing of all the shit I'd put myself through.

"So, tell me about the job. What's the what?"

"Ah, well? I think everything is good. I did have to tell her about my misdemeanor charges before she ran the background check, but she seemed like she was willing to look past that if everything came back as it should."

"I'm sorry, your what now?"

"Oh." I cleared my throat. "I got arrested after a fight with my ex-manager when I was twenty-one. Misdemeanor assault and disturbing the peace."

"Did you go to *jail?*"

"I mean, for a few hours, yeah. Until my grandma came and got me. My parents had already washed their hands of me by then. This was kind of the bottom of my spiral before I decided I had to get my shit together."

"I can't believe you're a *felon*. Do you have any prison tats?"

I laughed at her ridiculousness.

"I am not a felon because I was neither charged nor convicted of a felony. I got community service, and I picked up a lot of trash."

"That story doesn't make you sound hardcore at all."

"I'll try to come up with a better one, so I don't embarrass you in the future. I don't want anyone to think you're dating an upstanding citizen or something equally as awful."

"That's very considerate, thank you."

She grinned, and we cleaned up the remnants of dinner. She got happy all over again when she remembered her iced coffee was in the fridge, so that was a bonus.

I sank into her couch, which I had learned was velvet and not whatever other fabric I thought it might be, and willed myself to stay awake. We needed to have a conversation. Laur had other ideas. She immediately crawled into my lap, facing me—her body in this position was now familiar. Her legs were smooth under my thumbs until they broke out in goosebumps.

"Laur, can we talk about today?"

"I'm certain that we can. But do we have to?"

She wouldn't meet my eyes, and this was a difficult feat, being that her face was a total of three inches from mine.

"I promise it'll be painless."

She sighed, but at least she looked at me then.

"You realize you're very important to me, right?" I asked, my tone cautious.

"I… yeah, I think so."

"Okay. Well, then, know so. I'm extremely into you."

She squirmed in my lap, and I had to stop her before she distracted me.

"I just… I don't want you to assume the worst when something happens. And maybe I don't deserve the benefit of the doubt with my history, but I want you to know that I trust you, and I hope you can trust me. At least, eventually."

Her expression softened, and she melted into me a little more.

"Jer, I do trust you. Today was... well, it was embarrassing. But I kept thinking that there was *no way* this thing between us could be this easy, and when I saw you with Rachel, my mind was like, 'Aha! It isn't that easy!' And I let it dictate my actions. I'm so sorry."

She rested her forehead against mine and wrapped her arms around my neck. It was easy to pull her tighter and breathe her in.

"For the record, getting here would not be classified as easy. We were both idiots. But I agree with you that it feels like we've been together this way for a long time, and it's hard to remind myself that it's still new."

"Mhm," she murmured, her mouth dangerously close to mine.

"And one last thing?" I asked as she pulled back to look at me again. "Can we stop saying 'this thing' when talking about us? Like, can I call you my girlfriend and be done with it?"

Her face slowly lit up.

"Are you asking me to go *steady*? Are you going to let me wear your letterman jacket?"

"I think it's still in my closet. I'll bring it over next time."

She leaned in to kiss me, but I gripped her sides tightly.

"Is that a '*yes?*'" I asked, poised to tickle her.

"I'm going to need to think about it, Jer. This is all very sudden."

She couldn't even pretend to hide her smile at this point because she had no poker face whatsoever. She was very amused with herself, though.

"Such a brat," I said in her ear before I dug my fingers into the spot in her sides that I knew would make her lose her mind.

She squealed at a pitch previously unknown to the human ear before she gave in.

"Yes! Okay! You're my boyfriend! I'll order a shirt with your face on it tomorrow!" I stopped tickling and let her right herself in my lap and breathe. "Unfair. But I'll allow it because, yes, I was being a brat."

She stuck her tongue out at me and gasped when I closed the

distance between us and sucked it into my mouth. I kissed her in earnest then, glad we were done with that conversation. The fatigue that had been weighing on me was nearly forgotten when she tugged lightly at my hair and kissed me back with the same intensity.

Chapter 33- Lauren

Every morning, I was surprised to wake up and see what position I'd ended up sleeping in. I rarely had insomnia when Jer slept over, and I realized that I didn't have a 'normal' way that I slept. Today, I had my head on his stomach, and the rest of me star-fished out, my shins and feet hanging off the bed.

This cannot be normal.

I slid off him and righted myself to my pillow like a regular person, but he rolled toward me and tugged me against his chest.

"I kind of liked you there," he said, his voice thick with sleep.

"My feet were numb," I whispered. "Go back to sleep."

"You first." I rolled my eyes. I had no intention of going back to sleep because now my brain was awake, and I needed to do all the things. "You're thinking too loud."

"I have to call and confirm reservations and hunt down some RSVPs for the Stag and Doe party today. I feel motivated *now*, so I think I should do it now.

"Fine, fine. Go make coffee. I'll come down and help you make phone calls or whatever in a minute."

I gave him a long series of kisses down his neck, and he almost didn't let me out of bed.

This event had been ten times easier to plan than the shower since there were only about twelve of us going, and we'd only had to reserve a table at a cute bar over in Centerville that had a great cover band on the weekends. I'd ordered cute stag and doe pins and stickers for everybody, as well as some very witchy-looking crowns for Sam and Jesse. Jesse inevitably wouldn't wear his, but I figured he would for a few photos to make Sam happy. Otherwise, it was shaping up to be a low-key event, as requested.

Coffee was made, and I'd already called and left a message for the bar manager to confirm our table. I knew they wouldn't be open this early, but I felt like my voicemail allowed me to check the task off my list anyway.

"What do you need from me, baby?" Jer asked, coming up behind me and wrapping his arms around my stomach.

"Find out if Danny is bringing a date and if Hasan and Chase from the rec league are even coming."

"You got it."

He shot off a few texts and started making me eggs and toast. I texted Gen. It was weird that she hadn't gotten back to me about coming.

LAUR: Hey girl! I wanted to double-check that you were going to be able to make it to Sam and Jesse's party! Lemme know ☺.

I was almost done with breakfast before I heard back.

GEN: I'm so sorry, Laur, I meant to text you before. I don't think I'm going to make it.

LAUR: Boo! I hope everything is okay. I know Sam will miss you.

GEN: Yeah, I'm sad to miss it. We can chat soon.

I sent her six heart emojis for good measure. I *knew* this had something to do with Penn, but I didn't want to push her. We were friends, but we weren't the kind of friends where I could force her to tell me her business like I did with Sam. Yet, anyway.

"Danny is coming solo. Hasan can't make it, but Chase will be there and is bringing his girlfriend, Annie."

"You're amazing. That's all my tasks completed before nine. Well, as long as the manager calls me back. I could probably conquer the world today, if I wanted."

"No doubt."

"Can I tell you a secret?"

"Of course. I'm an excellent secret keeper," he whispered conspiratorially.

"I can't wait for this wedding to be over."

He barked out a laugh.

"You and me both, baby. And I know you're pulling way more weight than me right now, so if you need help, please tell me."

"Are you going to ask for my help with the cake?"

"Not a chance in hell, no."

"Thought so. We're good. Once this party is over, I become a helper rather than a planner. The wedding is all Sam and Zin. And Jesse, whatever. He'd show up in joggers and marry her on the baseball diamond if he could."

"You're not wrong. Hey, do you want to go to that bar this Friday night? Sam and Jesse already said they probably can't do happy hour because of engagement photos or something. We could scope it out, listen to the band, whatever."

"That's a fantastic idea. Then I'll know if there's anything else I need to think of before the party. You're so smart."

"I have my moments."

He kissed me in the way that made me forget about my to-do lists, and I was happy to let him.

* * *

My doctor's appointment was scheduled for mid-day on Friday, which meant absolutely nothing could get done beforehand. I sat and wandered my house, thinking about all the things I *should* be doing with my time and doing none of them. Impossibly, the clock did eventually progress forward, and I left. I'd been going to the same doctor for years, so at least I didn't have to figure out how to park somewhere new or where I was going. I did have to fill out a couple of forms, so I attempted to focus on that and not worry about what my doctor was going to say.

Jer sounded so reassuring when he told me I wasn't lazy or

losing my mind, but what if the *professional* disagreed and told me to, like, get my shit together.

Well, she can tell you how then, *because you've been trying forever.*

He'd helped me make a list of bullet points last night of the things I'd told him, plus some more I added that I thought might not be typical for everyone. Now that I was here, though, some of the things on the list felt silly.

Who forgets *to eat? That's dumb.*

But it was also true. I sighed and resigned myself to whatever this woman was going to say. I turned in the papers and waited.

When all was said and done, I wondered what, exactly, had just happened. I'd been doing a fair amount of reading about people's experiences getting diagnosed as adults with ADHD and how annoying the whole process could be. Honestly, a lot of those people's doctors sounded like gaslighting assholes, and I didn't think mine was, but I was still prepared for the worst. It wasn't the worst, though. I walked out of that office feeling like my entire life made fucking sense.

She had been so *nice* about everything. I showed her my list, and she read through it a few times before nodding at me and agreeing that we needed to go through the rating scales together and try to help me get some control back in my life. I could have cried.

You did cry. A little.

I left with a prescription to try and some articles and book recommendations to read before my follow-up appointment next month. She assured me I could listen to the audiobook when I admitted that sitting and reading an entire book was unlikely. She encouraged me to also find a therapist, and I wondered if it would be an issue for me to go to Jesse's. He seemed to like her so much, but I didn't know if that was against doctor's ethics to see siblings or something. I would ask.

I wondered if I could still do a cartwheel while I was on the way back to my car, because that's how relieved I was that maybe

I was on the verge of containing the chaos that was my life.

LAUR: I have the best news.

JEREMY: Oh yeah?

LAUR: I officially have the ADHD.

JEREMY: Oh! The appointment went well, then? I'm so happy you're happy, baby.

LAUR: I'll tell you more tonight. But yes. Thank you for making me go.

JEREMY: Anytime. See you in a bit.

I stopped short once I put my car in drive, realizing that my first instinct had been to text Jer, not Sam, not Jesse, not even my mom. He had so quickly become my first-to-call person when something happened, good or bad, and that was terrifying and exciting all wrapped into one tight little ball. So motivated was I by the outcome of that appointment that I drove straight to the pharmacy to drop off the script without waiting two weeks while it sat in my car.

* * *

The bar was super cute. Sam and I had been to scope it out, but that had been on a weeknight, and the crowd wasn't the same.
"We would be derelict in our duties if we did not try at *least* four appetizers, right? So, we know what to recommend for everyone?" I reasoned.
"Obviously. I assume anything that deals with bread and cheese?"

"You know me so well."

I flipped my hair, which I'd curled into loose waves. He disappeared to the bar, and I sipped at my vodka soda. All the worry I had about getting bored with Jer was fading into memory at this point. He was a magnet, tugging me into his force-field anytime he was close.

"Hey, guess what?" he asked upon his return.

"Tell me. I can't wait."

He chuckled.

"The bartender here, Caleb, is a guy I used to hang out with. Okay, we used to party together, but he's a good guy, honestly, and he's working during the party next weekend. So, I asked him if he could make some sort of signature shot called a Stag and fruity drink called a Doe for when we're here. He was totally down."

"Oh, that's a fantastic idea! You're brilliant."

I grabbed the font of his shirt and pulled him down to kiss me briefly.

"I've had my fair share of good ideas. Recently, anyway." He smirked down at me, and I melted a little.

After another couple drinks and testing every carb-plus-cheese offering, I was certain this was the happiest I'd ever been. Every time Jeremy's jeans brushed against my bare leg, or he rested his hand on the back of my neck or played with my fingers was enough to drive me insane. Happily, blissfully, insane. About this time, the best, and only, local cover band started to set up on the small, raised platform in the corner of the bar, and employees were moving tables to make room enough for people to dance once they were tipsy enough. I was already tipsy enough.

"Do you want to dance?" I asked after the band introduced themselves.

"With you? Always."

It was possible that literal hearts and stars were going to come out of my eyes at any moment. With that, I slid off my stool and steadied myself with the table when my balance checked in my heels.

I tugged Jeremy's hand toward the dance floor, my heart stuttering when he readjusted and threaded his long fingers through mine.

"You sure you're good to stay upright on those stilts?"

His words were teasing, but his voice was lower and a bit more gravelly than normal, letting me know he might be having the same internal battle as me when it came to keeping my thoughts appropriate. Instead of letting either of us get caught up in that conundrum, I grasped his other hand and pulled, forcing our bodies flush and looking up at his hazel eyes, watching them darken.

"Nope. So, make sure I don't fall."

I unhooked our fingers, but placed his hands exactly where I wanted them on my lower back, and I traced purposeful circles on the back of his neck, tangling my hands in his hair. The band switched to an acoustic song from one of my favorite 90s bands, and I took that as a sign from the universe that we were exactly where we were supposed to be. Sam and her *trust your intuition* sermons were rubbing off on me, and *Jimmy Eat World* had me in my feelings.

"You are going to get us in trouble," he murmured next to my ear while simultaneously sliding his hands down and pulling me impossibly closer, his fingers squeezing my ass through my dress.

"That's the general plan," I whispered back.

For whatever reason, even though we'd been *together* for a little while, this date, after officially declaring ourselves as something real, had the atmosphere feeling heavy over us. The barely contained groan he let out had electricity buzzing over my skin that had nothing to do with the vodka.

His lips traveled lightly against my jaw and brushed across my lips. I stopped breathing, trying not to launch myself at him. He pressed his mouth to mine, his lips soft and warm, before he pulled back only slightly, causing me to lean in to chase that feeling. He let out a low chuckle that I felt in my core, and then he was back, demanding entrance with his tongue, slanting his mouth over mine, and deepening the kiss. My brain was fuzzy already, but when he tugged my bottom lip between his teeth and bit playfully, I snapped back into the moment and tangled my hands in his hair with more intensity. I only vaguely registered the fact that we were still at least swaying, giving the impression that we were dancing and not making out in front of a bar full of people.

Jeremy's thumb ghosted over my cheekbone before he gripped my neck under my curls and pulled back, making sure I was looking him in the eye.

"Do you wanna get out of—"

"Hey Lauren," a less-than-friendly voice interrupted and cut through the haze that had gathered around us. I blinked several times and focused on the intruder to our moment.

Fuck.

Standing in front of us was a guy I'd gone on four or five dates with from a neighboring town not quite a year ago.

Shit. This *town.*

The bar we were at was in Centerville. I rarely ventured out of my bubble of Emberwood, and I forgot to be on the lookout for anyone I might know. He was a personal banker I'd met when I physically went into a bank branch to deal with a lost debit card.

"Charlie," I nearly whispered, still not recovered from that kiss. "Hi."

Please, please go away.

"How are you doing?" I continued.

He had light brown hair, brown eyes, and an easy smile, and I'd liked him. Until I didn't. He'd made a comment about how I'd have to tone down my very vibrant home décor if a man ever lived with me.

Immediate pass.

But no, I hadn't been a grown-up about it, and I'd stopped returning his messages.

"So, is this why you stopped answering texts?" gesturing to Jer, "or is he a one-time thing? I wasn't sure if you spread your legs for anyone or if I should count myself as special even though you couldn't be bothered to—"

"Charlie," I ground out.

He looked at me expectantly.

"Back the fuck off, guy."

Jer had dropped my hands and was now in front of me, blocking me from Charlie with his towering frame.

"Hey, man, I'm doing you a favor. She'll fuck you over, and I wouldn't want you to think she was more than a mediocre lay."

I choked on the breath I could barely take in, thankful I couldn't see Jer's face as I ran to our table, grabbed my bag, and got the hell out of that bar before my tears left the corners of my eyes.

Chapter 34- Jeremy

My hand was around the guy's throat before the last word was out. His eyes widened in fear, and I leaned in close.

"Do not ever find her name in your fucking mouth again, or they will have to wire your jaw shut when I'm done."

I shoved him hard, causing him to trip into one of the high tops around the dance floor, sputtering. I whirled around to find Lauren gone, and panic broke out across my skin.

"You good, J?" Caleb called above the din from the bar. I nodded and motioned that I'd leave, assuring him there wouldn't be more of an issue.

Lauren's bag wasn't at our table, and I swore. I jogged to the exit, pulling out my phone to call her, when I caught the eye of someone staring at me. My next breath caught in my throat when I realized it was the owner of the bakery. The one I'd assured days ago that my previous assault charge was due to a youthful indiscretion, and I was now a productive member of society. The one who now saw me manhandle a guy in a bar.

She raised her brows at me in disbelief, and I shook my head to try to convey that I was sorry, but she was turning away and back to the other woman at her table.

Fuck. FUCK.

I didn't have the brain space to think about how I'd ruined the only job opportunity I had because I still needed to find Laur.
I continued outside, now ready to call her, but I saw her tell-tale red hair on a bench down the sidewalk.

I approached slowly, hoping she hadn't walked out because of my reaction. I hadn't been in a fight in a long time, but I didn't see a way for that guy to walk away without putting my hands on him.

Maybe that's a you problem, I thought warily.

"Lauren," I said softly, kneeling in front of her. "I can take you home. I'm sorry if my reaction freaked you out…"

She met my eyes, and her tears made my gut twist. Gently, I placed my hands on top of her thighs and made small circles with my fingertips.

"I left as soon as you stepped in front of me. Why, did you kill him?" she sniffed, rubbing her arms.

I huffed out a laugh and reached up to wipe away the tear clinging to her jaw.

"He's alive, but I'll assume he left through the side exit. Kind of a pussy, Laur. Not sure what you saw in him." She let out a tight laugh. "Too soon?"

"Maybe only a little."

"Here." I slid my jacket off and put it around her shoulders. She looked like she might refuse it, but she was undeniably cold in that dress. "Can I drive you home?"

She shook her head, fresh tears welling up in her eyes as she looked away from my gaze.

"I can't talk to you right now. I texted Christian to come get me."

She tapped her phone screen on the bench next to her. I didn't know why she didn't want to talk to me, but I wasn't going to cross any boundaries after what that asshole had said to her. I couldn't imagine she was feeling great, and I wanted to fix it. Hell, I wasn't feeling great either, and I wished someone was there to fix that, too. But I pushed the job I just kissed goodbye to the back of my mind.

"I'm not going to make you get in the car, Laur. But I do hope you change your mind. You didn't do anything wrong. That was all on him. I'll go sit on the other side of the bench, and if you reconsider, or if you want to talk, you tell me."

I did exactly that and angled my body to make sure I'd know if she looked at me.

She only said she couldn't talk *to you.*

I pulled my phone back out to tap out a message to Sam and

then to Laur.

It took me a minute to think about how to approach our current situation. I didn't know exactly what was happening in her head, but I got the feeling she was embarrassed, and I had to figure out how to make her see the situation for what it was, which was a guy being a dick because he couldn't have her. It was very simple. For me, anyway.

JEREMY: For the record, I'm not worried that you're going to fuck me over.

JEREMY: Well, that's not entirely true.

She dragged her eyes from her phone over to meet mine. "Is this supposed to make me feel better?"
"I thought you weren't talking to me?"
"I'm not, I'm exclaiming *at* you. You're not allowed to talk back." I nodded and went back to my phone.

JEREMY: I think you can absolutely wreck me if you want to. I guess, when I say I'm not worried about it, I mean that I can't imagine a scenario where it isn't worth it.

She sucked in a breath, but she didn't look at me. This time, she texted back.

LAUR: How can you say that? Charlie was a dick, but was he wrong? I don't know. Which makes it worse. It sucks to have your insecurities validated. Worse with an audience.

JEREMY: I am well versed in believing the worst about yourself, but Lauren, you know that guy was pissed because he had you and lost you. And you do know that I'm not new here, right?

LAUR: What do you mean?

JEREMY: We might not have been close, but I've at least been around for the last few guys you dated, and I watched guys fall over themselves for you in high school. I know your M.O., Laur, and I'm telling you, you're worth the risk. I also think I've proven that I'm difficult to avoid indefinitely. You tried and failed. I'm far too charming. More than anything, my history is the one that's a concern, not yours. I shouldn't have put hands on him. I should have walked away.

The whole texting instead of talking thing was a benefit right then because my throat tightened when I thought about Delaney looking at me inside. Like I was kidding myself in thinking I'd grown up at all.

"I wish you weren't trying to make me feel better. I am trying to come back to reality after living in a delusional little fantasy all day that my life is finally getting on track. This conversation is making that difficult."

Air caught in my chest at her words. I hated that one asshole's comment brought her here from how happy she was earlier.

"Am I allowed to talk now?"

"Fine."

She'd angled her body towards me, and I felt like, in terms of body language, that was a good sign.

"You weren't being delusional or living in a fantasy. You're doing *well*, Laur. You kick ass at your job, your house is amazing, your boyfriend is kind of obsessed with you. His reputation leaves a little to be desired, but he's all in with you."

Her eyes fluttered closed. I couldn't tell where her head was or how to proceed.

"Your reputation is fine, Jer. It's mine that is apparently a problem. I just... I need some space to get my head straight."

"Understood."

I didn't like that answer, but at least it made sense. I could use some space, too, to figure out where to go after fumbling this chance that had been *right there*. I *got* feeling like it was a pipe dream to outrun your former self. But that needed to wait until she was taken care of.

"Now, can I take you home? I swear I'll be quiet if you want, but I'm freezing my balls off, and it doesn't appear that Christian has texted you back."

She sighed in resignation, stood, and walked past me toward the parking lot, leaving me to follow behind her.

Her phone buzzed as I unlocked the car, and she slid into the passenger seat. She relaxed noticeably in reading her text, and I was going to assume that my message to Sam had been received earlier.

"Sam's headed to my place."

"Good."

"Thanks, Jer," she added quietly, turning up the heat on her side.

"Anytime."

It was quiet for the remainder of the drive, and she shrugged out of my jacket when I pulled into her complex.

"Can I walk you—"

"No."

Hurt must have shown on my face because her expression softened.

"Not because of anything to do with you. If you walk me up, you will kiss me until I forget my own name, and I will have to start all over in dealing with this when my brain starts working again."

I sighed. "Okay. I'll watch from here like a stalker to make sure you get inside, and I'll count on Sam to make sure you're good. Can I call you tomorrow?"

"Yeah. I'll talk to you soon."

"Night, Laur."

Chapter 35- Lauren

"Honey, I'm home," I called, trying to not immediately infuse my house with negativity and embarrassment.

"Welcome, darling. I have all the combinations of bread and cheese I could think of. Pizza, pretzel bites with cheese dip, brie and crackers, and quesadillas from *Romero's*.

"How did you have time to go get all of this?"

"You realize it's almost ten? Jer texted me an hour ago."

"It simultaneously feels like I was dancing with Jer ten minutes ago and like it's two a.m."

Sam sighed and started loading a plate with food for me. "Tell me what happened."

"That doesn't sound like a good time for either of us."

I bit off a large chunk of pizza to emphasize my point.

Sam's blue eyes narrowed at me. "Remember all those times you talked me off a ledge in the last year? Was that a good time?"

"No," I got out begrudgingly.

"Right. I'm here because you're my best friend, and you needed me. Not because I expect entertainment. Eat. Hydrate. Tell me who I need to hex."

Tears sprang up again as I nodded. I knew things between Sam and me would change when she moved in with my brother and when they got married in a few weeks, but her showing up tonight helped me remember that it didn't mean I'd lose the person who knew me best.

I hydrated. I ate like I hadn't already overloaded on carbs and cheese three hours ago. And I spilled my guts about everything. Mine and Jer's official relationship status, my appointment and diagnosis, and how stupid I felt for thinking everything was looking up only to have the consequences of my past self's actions show up and punch me in the gut. I didn't even censor what

Charlie said, even though his words made me want to vomit.

"We're going to go back through that enormous life update point by point in a minute, but hold the phone. Charlie... like 5'9", lanky. Banker."

"Yeah."

"Went toe-to-toe with Jer. 6'3", looks like he belongs on a calendar." A laugh bubbled up from my chest as I nodded. "For the record, I'll be working a return-to-sender spell tomorrow for our friend, Charlie, but I can't imagine him coming within 100 yards of you after whatever Jer said to him."

I shrugged.

"Laur... you are the most confident person I've ever known. I one thousand percent understand people getting under your skin, but what is it about this guy that has your energy feeling like it's underwater. It's a weird sensation, and I haven't gotten that from you before ever."

"What if he's right?" I whispered.

"*Charlie?*"

"I mean I *know* some of the things he said were right. Except for the fact that I'm a mediocre lay because I'm *not*."

"Obviously not."

"But what if I'm putting all my eggs in this basket that what I have with Jer is special? What if it's not special, and I drop him because he says he likes chocolate sprinkles more than rainbow sprinkles? I've ghosted guys over such little things, Sam. With Charlie, I should have been able to say, 'Hey, it's not going to work out, all the best!' but I *didn't*. So, is he so off base that I'm fine for a hookup and otherwise kind of a bitch? Like, do I expect them to be perfect, or do I have terrible taste? I don't know."

"Charlie said you'd have to change your house, right? If you ever wanted to live with a man? That was him?"

"Yep."

"So, that tells us he's a misogynist who also has no taste in interior design. The taste thing is forgivable, but the misogyny thing, not so much. So, even if you think they might be 'little things,' your intuition is so much stronger than you give yourself credit for. Don't berate yourself for trusting the vibes—they don't lie."

I didn't know that I believed her. It felt like I had done this far too many times. Not all the guys I'd ghosted had been bad guys, no matter what Sam said. Even if she was a psychic.

"I kind of want to paint 'Trust the Vibes' on my living room wall now."

I could already picture it in my head in some great 60s-style lettering.

"Maybe tomorrow. Tonight, sleep."

"Always the voice of reason. Speaking of which, any sage wisdom on what I say to Jer?"

"Um, you could say 'hi, last night sucked.' Because that man is *gone* for you, my friend. But I also know that if you need some space, he'll give it to you. Your energies are so complementary when they're together, and he's not going anywhere."

"Maybe he should, though. I think so much about what's right for me that maybe I'm neglecting what's good for him."

"If you could see his face when he looks at you from across a room? I don't think you would be questioning that at all. So, to all of it, I still say sleep. Figure it out tomorrow."

Chapter 36 - Jeremy

That was not the ideal end to tonight, I thought as I watched Lauren disappear into her townhouse and headed for my apartment.

I was so *angry* at myself for not having a solution to this situation. The whole thing with that fucking asshole reeked of high school drama repackaged in adult wrapping paper, and my fists clenched around the steering wheel thinking about it.

Before the clusterfuck that was *Charlie*, I'd been thinking that was probably the best date I'd ever been on. She made me feel like life could be fun, and there didn't have to be a shoe waiting to drop.

She was in rare form tonight. My chest tightened at the memory of her putting my hands where she wanted them and pulling at the roots of my hair. I'd never had a truly healthy relationship before, and we'd jumped into this one like skydivers who didn't double check their parachutes and were hoping for the best. But the thing was, it was *working*.

And that one moment. That one fucking minute had thrown a wrench into everything. I ran my hand over my face, suddenly tired in a way that reached my bones. My phone buzzed as I pulled into my apartment complex.

JESSE: Hey, man. Thanks for tonight. I don't know what happened, but Sam texted and said you took care of whatever it was and made sure Laur got home.

JEREMY: Of course.

JESSE: Do I need to kill anyone?

JEREMY: I am pretty sure that guy would sooner piss his pants than go near Lauren again, so I think we're okay.

He responded with a thumbs-up, and I idled in my parking spot for a few minutes, trying to catalog the range of emotions I'd cycled through that night.

JEREMY: Do you have a minute if I stop by?

JESSE: Yeah, of course.

JEREMY: Be there in 10.

Their rental house was nice. I kind of wondered what sort of magic Sam had used to score it until I remembered that it was her aunt's doing.
That woman is terrifying.
I jogged up to the front door and knocked twice before opening it.
"Kitchen!" Jesse called.
I met him in there and sat my ass on a barstool. He slid a beer to me from across the counter without asking.
"I fucked up, man."
His eyebrows rose a fraction as he drank from his own bottle. "With?"
"Not with Laur. I...I know it's weird that I'm dating your sister. I probably should have had that conversation a while ago."
I glanced at him, hoping he knew I was being genuine because I didn't have it in me to do a deep dive into that on top of everything else tonight.
"Jer. You've been my best friend since Little League. In high school? I wouldn't have let you step foot near Lauren," he admitted, earning a laugh from me. "But now? You're good, man. I hope it all works out."

I sighed in relief to have that officially out of the way. "Me too."

"So, what did you fuck up, then?"

I let out the rest of the story from the bar about Delaney and how I'd completely screwed myself out of a job. If anyone *got* doing a job you were good at but didn't love? It was Jesse. He had been the one to push me to sign up for school instead of just talking about it when he'd moved back.

"I don't even think I'm looking for advice. Not really, anyway. I'm so *pissed off* at that guy. And at myself."

"If it makes you feel any better, I might have properly punched him. If anything, I think you showed restraint."

I huffed a laugh. "Thank you for recognizing that I could have done much worse."

"Anytime."

We finished our beers and moved on to less loaded conversation, but I did find I felt lighter after getting the situation off my chest. It didn't fix anything, but I wasn't carrying it alone. I made him swear he wouldn't say anything to Sam because I didn't want Lauren to know and get all in her head like it was her fault I didn't get the job.

"I'll do my best, man. You know she, like, *knows* things though, right?"

"Yeah. I don't know how you handle that. Your best will have to be good enough."

He shrugged in apology, and I made my way to the car to finally take myself home. My phone buzzed when I sat down.

SAM: You're a good apple.

JEREMY: Is this like an inside joke I don't get?

SAM: No. The opposite of a bad apple. She's upset but okay. Just wanted you to know. Night, Jer.

JEREMY: Thanks, Sam

The knot of worry sitting in my chest loosened slightly for the first time since I left Lauren at her house. Nothing was solved, but she was okay, and that was what mattered right now. I'd deal with the dissolution of my most promising job prospect tomorrow.

* * *

I'd arranged for Saturday off a while back because I needed to prep everything I could ahead of time for the rehearsal dinner desserts and the wedding cake. However, I had planned on doing that at Lauren's house. Where all my stuff was. So, instead, I sat and typed out texts and deleted them for a solid forty-five minutes. Finally, I had no choice. I at least had to go pick up my ingredients and pans and bring them back to my apartment to get started.

JEREMY: Hey. I swear I am trying to give you your space... I took today off to get the cake layers done and frozen for the wedding, and I need to at least come and get my stuff. Totally fine if you don't want me to use your kitchen. I didn't want to show up unannounced. You know that I miss you already, right?

LAUR: I'm sorry, I didn't mean to fuck up your plans. I'm headed to work in ten, so I won't even be home. Feel free to work here as long as you want, you know where the key is.

JEREMY: Thanks—I don't know that I can ever go back to my oven, honestly.

LAUR: I miss you too. I'm not upset with you for anything that happened last night. I'm upset with me, and I need to work it out. Okay?

JEREMY: Okay. But if you decide you want someone to explain to you all the reasons you're not at fault, please say the word.

LAUR: Noted. Happy baking.

That was one crisis dealt with. At least partially. The next one was going to hurt a lot more. I sat down at my computer and willed the words to come to me that would make this any easier.

Delaney,

Thank you so much for the opportunity to interview and go over my portfolio. I want to apologize for the incident you witnessed at Prime last night. While I do not believe that moment to be a representation of my character, I understand that my actions speak louder than my words.

Thank you again for your time. I wish you all the best in finding the right person for your shop.

Sincerely,

Jeremy Ash

That was that.

* * *

Getting into the rhythm of baking did help calm me down. I also took advantage of Lauren's stereo and played my music loud enough that I could feel the bass in my teeth. I worked for several hours, cleaned, got what I needed to into the freezer, and locked her house back up. I thought about staying until she got home, hoping we could talk, but she'd been clear about what she wanted.

So, I left.

In total, I'd had too many cups of coffee and a protein bar that day, and I felt that choice in my stomach. I stopped in town to get something quick from the café, scarfing down a sandwich without even tasting it. I glanced over at *Books and Broomsticks* on the way back to my car. I remembered how helpful Sam had been the last time I was feeling lost, and I found myself wandering over there before I even made the decision. The bell chimed, and the scent of lavender and rosemary washed over me.

"Mr. Ash, what a pleasant surprise."

I looked over to see Sam's Aunt Zinnia shelving books, her long silver hair tied back in a loose braid.

"Hey, Ms. Crawford. I was getting some food and thought I'd see if Sam was around."

"Ah, she is meeting with her photographer today, so she won't be in until late this afternoon. Anything I can help you with?"

Zinnia was one of those people who could see right through you. She didn't make me uncomfortable—she was very warm, and I'd never seen her be judgmental. She *knew* too much.

"Oh, no, I'm good. Was just saying hi. I was going to tell her I got the cakes done and frozen today, so I'm right on schedule."

"That's wonderful. I'll pass along the message. Are you sure you wouldn't like a reading? On the house, of course. You've done such a lovely job with everything for the wedding."

"Oh! No, that's okay, I'm—" I tried to finish the sentence, but the words wouldn't quite come out.

She smiled at me and went to sit at one of the small tables off to the side of the store's displays. I sat down across from her, feeling like I was awaiting my fate. A well-worn deck of tarot cards flew through her fingers.

"Do you have a question, or shall we see what comes up?"

"Um, no questions in particular," I lied.

She gave me a smile that said she knew very well that wasn't the truth.

Lying to a psychic is a bold move.

"Samantha told me about reading for you the other day, how strong your grandfather's spirit was."

"Did she? It was kind of a mind-blowing moment, to be honest. I... well, I miss him."

"He misses you. He's quieter today than she described. I think he got out a lot of what he wanted to say last time. But he still wants me to tell you he's here. And to tuck in your shirt."

I barked out a laugh at that. He complained about my clothes constantly when he was alive.

She started laying down cards on the table.

"Your work situation feels stuck right now, and I can see your frustration. Though, you're hiding it well from most everyone else. Is that your intention?"

"I... yeah, I guess it is. I don't mean to hide it like, deceptively. It's just my own issue."

"That much is clear, yes. Know that you don't need to. It's not benefiting you to keep it to yourself, and if anything, it's slowing down the process of you getting unstuck. Regardless, things will shift soon."

I blew out a breath. She was calling me out on a pretty serious scale. It was terrifying.

"That's good. That would be very helpful."

"I'm going to describe an image that your people are showing me, and you can take from it what you want or see if it makes sense."

I nodded.

"They're showing me you holding on to a rope and being led along a path, but you don't know where it's going. You're following it because you think you should or you feel like it's the only way.

"What you *can* do is plant your feet and yank that rope toward you and see exactly what it is that's been pulling you along for all this time. When the rope is gone, you'll see all the paths before you, and you can choose freely. They want me to be clear that this isn't only about work. This is about all the big, beautiful, scary things in your life." She looked at me pointedly and, therefore, didn't need to add the words *like Lauren* or *like your family* at the end of her explanation.

I swallowed hard. "That makes a lot of sense, yes. Um, do my *people* have any advice on how to do that? With the rope?"

"Certainly. Examine what you've lost. Often in life, we are driven far more by the fear of losing than the promise of gaining. And I say *examine* because it's not about wallowing in past hurts. It's about observing how they occurred, how you've changed, and overcome. You've already dealt with those. You don't need to let them keep calling the shots, so to speak."

"So, really fun things to think about. Lots of heartwarming memories."

She shot me an apologetic smile.

"Thank you, so much. This was… eye opening."

"Anytime. I mean that."

I stood and pushed in the chair, both reluctant to leave and poised to run out of the shop at the same time.

"Oh, and Mr. Ash?"

"Yes, ma'am?"

"Sometimes, what seems like an ending is only an intermission. Have a good rest of your day, dear."

"You too, Ms. Crawford."

I shuffled out of the shop and back to my car. I supposed it was too much to ask that she tell me everything was going to be fine and there was nothing I needed to do that was in any way difficult or sad.

Probably.

Chapter 37 - Lauren

Slowly, things seemed to settle back to normal between me and Jer. I was well and truly humiliated by what Charlie said at the bar, but there was also nothing I could do about mistakes I'd already made. Jeremy seemed more cautious around me, or maybe I was being more cautious around him, but I felt like we were *almost* back to a pre-Charlie dynamic.

I tried to convince Gen to come to the Stag and Doe night at least twice, even offering to style her hair for free on Friday, but she was firmly out. Sam and I were going to have to kidnap her soon to figure out what the deal was. Regardless, the week seemed to speed up the closer we got to the party. This was one of the last big events before the wedding, and I was so happy for Sam and my brother but also excited to have my brain space back when it was all over.

Speaking of brain space...the prescription for the ADHD medication had been sitting on my counter since last week, and I hadn't taken it yet. I didn't know why, exactly. Part of me was afraid it would change how I acted, which was the whole point, but on a deeper level, who I was. The other part was afraid it would change nothing, and I'd have to reckon with this being my life. Sam noticed me staring at it when she came over to get ready to go to her party.

"I thought you were excited about trying it out to see if it helped?"

"I was. I am. I'm just nervous."

"About?"

"I don't know for sure. Maybe that it will stifle my creativity or something? That might be dumb. I know I'm chaotic, but that's where a lot of my best ideas come from, too."

"That's not dumb at all, Laur. But I also think that trying and *then* making that determination is probably the only way you're going to find out. Your doctor said there are other medications if this one doesn't work, right? And you're going to start seeing Dr. Merrill?"

"Yeah. You're probably right. I'll start it tomorrow."

"And hey, I'll bring over a pretty tumbled carnelian crystal and stick it on top of your prescription bottle. Boom. Creativity-infused meds." Sam grinned at me; her blue eyes lit up.

"You're the best. Thank you."

"Now let's get ready because you promised me pretty hair."

* * *

The Stag and Doe party was near perfection. The signature drinks were delightful, the band played all our 90s requests, and everyone seemed to genuinely have a lot of fun. As the night wound down, I felt like I could see a light at the end of the tunnel. Even if the tunnel was full of love and friends and all the happiness in the world for my brother and my friend, I still looked forward to doing what I wanted with my free time—or having free time at all.

The next morning, I slipped out of bed and let Jer sleep. I started the coffee maker and stared down the prescription bottle on my counter. I was looking forward to putting the crystal on top. Then they would be *fancy* meds. I unscrewed the lid, took the pill, and proceeded to distract myself by scrolling through pictures from last night and editing them as I went.

You did kind of a kick ass job.

I patted myself on the back in my mind. When I was done, my gaze landed on that stupid purple wall, and I sighed. It was going to look *so* good when it was finished.

I pulled up my dad's text thread and sent him a message about the ladder.

DAD: Yeah, I'm heading to the store soon. You want me to drop it off?

LAUR: Ohhhh that would be excellent. Yes, please!

DAD: See you soon, kiddo.

I wondered if I should make Jer hide if he was out here when my dad showed up.
Yeah. That's probably an okay idea.
It didn't matter that it was my house, that I bought, and I was twenty-four. I didn't want my dad to see Jer's bedhead. I took a picture of the paint labels and sent them to Heather since I knew she opened this morning at *Garrett's Hardware*.

LAUR: Morning Heather! Any chance you could get someone to mix up a gallon of this paint for me and I'll be by to grab it in a bit?

HEATHER: You got it! You need me to pull rollers or anything else?

LAUR: Nope! I've got the rest.

She sent me a thumbs-up emoji, and I happily pulled out some bacon and eggs to make breakfast for Jer.
Look at you, being all domestic. And checking shit off your list before nine am.
It was silly that I hadn't finished that wall. It took a total of five minutes to get done what I needed.
"Holy *shit*," I said aloud to no one while holding a piece of uncooked bacon between my fingers.
I swallowed hard and put the bacon in the pan, the sizzles and pops filling the silence. I tried to mentally feel around inside my

brain, looking for the constant noise—the song lyrics, the random thoughts about creating a cat statue for my living room, the suppressed to-do list that was always on the verge of overwhelming me. But it was quiet. Like the aftermath of a wicked storm when the sun came out like none of it ever happened.

"What is this magic?" I asked, still talking to the empty room.

"Oh, are you doing magic now too?" Jer asked, sauntering into the room, shirtless, his sweats low on his waist.

"Not me personally, no. But, um, I took the ADHD meds a bit ago. And now…I don't know how to explain how I feel, exactly. Except different."

"In a good way or a bad way?" His brows furrowed slightly in concern.

"No, this is fucking amazing. I've already taken care of the whole purple wall shit, and I'm making breakfast. *I'm* making breakfast for *you*," I explained slowly, gesturing to the bacon and flipping it while I was at it.

"Well, sweet. That's what you hoped, right?"

"Yeah…I just didn't know that this was a thing I could hope for. Is this how everyone else's brain works? Like you have one thought at a time and then you can do the thing you were thinking about and then move on to the next thought? *That's* what is happening in your head?"

"Um, I mean, yeah, I guess? If I'm stressed or something, I do feel like my thoughts race or get jumbled together, but on a good day, yeah, that sounds normal."

"Jeremy Ash. Why has everyone been walking around operating like *this*, and no one fucking told me?!"

"To be fair, I *did* tell you. That's why you went to the doctor in the first place."

"Fine, fine. You're not on my shit list. But you're the only one. Everyone else has been gaslighting me my whole life! I want to send emails to all my high school teachers and tell them they were *wrong*, and I'm not 'flighty and only interested in boys.'"

"Your teachers said that about you? Like out loud?"

"Yes! To my mother. In front of me!"

"Jesus, that's kind of harsh."

"I mean, I *was* very interested in boys. But also, other things."

He laughed and wrapped his arms around me, adjusting the heat on the bacon.

"Want me to finish this for you?"

"Absolutely not. I'm doing things. Don't steal that from me."

He held up his hands in surrender and moved to get himself a mug.

"Oh, also, my dad will be here in a sec. Maybe be elsewhere." I shrugged, and he shook his head.

I took the bacon out of the pan and set it aside to get ready for the eggs. As if on cue, a knock sounded at my door, and I shot a warning look at Jer, making him disappear into the hallway toward the downstairs bathroom.

"Hey, Dad!"

"Hey, kid. Where do you want her?" he asked, holding the twelve-foot ladder at his side.

"In the entryway is fine."

He brought it in and set it down. He looked so much better than he had even six months ago, and it made my heart so happy. His rehab had done wonders, but being back at work and having a purpose at the store again had done more.

"There ya go. And, Laur? Do not, under any circumstance, use this ladder on your stairs while you're home alone. I don't need a call to take you to the ER later."

"Noted. Jer is coming over in a bit. I'll make sure he is on ladder watch."

"Right. Won't it be hard for him to get here since his car is outside?"

He delivered this blow without a hint of inflection in his voice, as though he was legitimately concerned for how Jeremy was going to make it here. Until he cracked a smile.

"Um, well."

"Right. Tell him I said thanks for fixing your car. It's runnin' good?"

"It is."

"Good. I'm late, but I'll get this back from you later this week. Have fun."

"Bye, Dad," I murmured, a blush still on my face from him calling me out for hiding my boyfriend in a closet like I was sixteen.

"Well, that was embarrassing for you," Jer said, laughter in his voice.

"Shut up and eat your bacon."

I finished the eggs, we ate, and I convinced Jer to go pick up my paint so I could get started with the edger. I pinky-promised not to get on the ladder until he got back.

In total, it took about two hours to finish the first coat of the top of the wall. And that was even factoring in Jer claiming he thought I was going to fall, and he *had* to put his hands on my ass. For safety.

"Please let me distract you while this coat dries. It's not fair to be above me in those shorts for *hours* and not let me touch you."

"You touched me plenty of times."

"You're killing me."

I laughed and relented, pulling him down to kiss me. His hands were so sure when he gripped my hips, my waist, and my thighs when he picked me up.

"Am I killing you less now?"

"Only slightly."

He continued his tour of my body when he set me on the counter and didn't seem to care that I had paint in my hair and splattered over my clothes. My phone buzzed and lit up in the center of my island, and I reached for it. He grabbed my hand and locked his fingers around my wrist.

"Ignore it."

I did for a minute, lost in him. Until it buzzed several more times. This time, I reached for it, and he didn't stop me.

"I need to make sure it's not an emergency!"

"An emergency would be a phone call," he grumbled, but he kissed the palm of my other hand and went to get water.

SAM: Why did you and Jer fail to mention that the fight with Charlie resulted in him not getting the job at the bakery?!

SAM: It seems like that was an important detail in the story.

SAM: And then I wouldn't have asked the owner how the interview had gone and if Jer would be starting soon. I'm in Centerville for my final dress fitting. Yes, bad choice because I'm hungover, but we live and we learn, Laur. Not the point.

SAM: She didn't tell me exactly what happened, but she alluded to him not being a great fit her for shop. I only put two and two together when I pressed her on it.

SAM: I am displeased at being left out of the loop.

A slimy sort of cold slid down my spine and made its home in my stomach. Because *what?*

Chapter 38- Jeremy

"Was it, in fact, an emergency? Or may I continue distracting you now?" I asked, letting the last of my water slide down my throat.

"I guess that depends on your definition."

"Oh." That sounded more serious. "What's going on?"

"Tell me, did you ever hear back from the bakery about the job?"

I felt the blood drain from my face as she leveled me with a stare.

"I take it you already know the answer to that question, or you wouldn't be asking it."

"I'd like to hear it from you, though. Instead of in a stream-of-consciousness text thread from Sam, who assumed I already knew."

Fuck. Fuck, fuck, fuck.

I briefly wondered if Jesse had been forced to give up my secret or if something else had happened.

Not the point.

I took a deep breath.

"It's not a complex story, Laur. Delaney, the owner, was at the bar the night Charlie happened. And I already told you I had to disclose my previous misdemeanor for fighting, and well, that made it look like I was the same guy now that I was then. So, she had every right not to hire me. I sent her an apology email and moved on."

"You...you understand why this is a problem, right? You not sharing *any* of that with me?"

My heart was racing now, all the lighthearted bantering from earlier forgotten.

"I didn't want you to worry about it. It's not like I lost my actual job. It was a hypothetical part-time gig, and it would have been awesome to get experience somewhere, but it didn't work out. Sometimes things don't."

I reached for her hand, but she yanked it away. I sucked in a breath. That might as well have been a punch to the stomach. She was shaking her head, and I could see the tears welling up in her eyes. I *needed* to fix it, but I had no idea what to say.

"But this thing *would have* if it wasn't for me, right? Like if my stupid choices hadn't led to *Charlie* in the bar, you'd have the job you wanted and be closer to leaving the garage."

"Laur, that's not even a thing that crossed my mind. *I* chose to put my hands on him. Anything resulting from that is on me. And he deserved it. I can't think that I would feel better if I'd let him walk away. I would feel like I'd failed you."

"*That!* That right there. You did it *for me*. To protect me or for my honor or something. And Jer, I appreciate you being there for me, but you can't do this! You can't keep things from me that are important and like, impacting your life. It...it feels like you don't trust me with *real* shit. Like I'm a fucking helpless damsel over here who constantly needs saving, which, fair point, I have needed saving recently. And you've been here, and it's made me fall—it's made me feel safe with you. But the whole time, it hasn't been real because it hasn't been a two-way street."

My entire body froze when she spoke. Because it sounded like she was about to say she *loved* me. And if I fucked that up with this stupid god damned omission, I would never forgive myself. Tears were on her cheeks and clinging to her jaw. I wanted to touch her, to pull her into me, but I didn't want her to turn away again, so I stayed put.

"Laur, please don't cry. I can't even tell you what it's been like for me...being someone worth trusting. Being someone you can call when things go wrong is everything to me. I have never been that. I'm so sorry I didn't tell you about the job. I don't want you to feel like I don't trust you with real things. I do trust you. With everything."

I reached for her involuntarily, and she stepped back reflexively. I withdrew and shoved my hands in my pockets.

"Me crying doesn't mean you have to save me, Jer. I'm crying because I'm so fucking angry! At myself mostly, but I'm also so pissed at you for not telling me. You've pulled the rug out from under me, and I don't know what we're doing here. I'm obviously not good for you, and you clearly have no sense of self-preservation."

"Whoa, whoa, baby, stop. This one thing is not some sort of sign that we're not good together. We are fucking *great* together. Don't do that. Don't start questioning our entire relationship because of one mistake. I'm so sorry I didn't tell you. I should have told you that night. Things were so tense already. But I had plenty of time to tell you after. And I didn't. I'm sorry. I will apologize however you want me to; just please don't tell me this isn't real because it's the realest thing I've ever had." I was choking on my words by the end. She owned my heart, and she was dangerously close to demolishing it.

She took a deep breath. Then another. And another. Her tears were drying, and her voice was steadier.

"I will wait until I'm calm before I say anything else. But I need you to leave. Take your kitchen stuff. I'll go to my room so you can pack it up."

The only thing I read in her face was resolve. I wasn't going to change her mind on this right now, but thinking about walking away and leaving things this way was enough to make me want to crawl out of my skin.

"Can I call you later?"

"Please don't. I'll call you when I'm ready to talk to you." Her words sounded watery at the end of her sentence, and it was enough to bring the tears I'd pushed down right back up again.

"Okay. Just know that I do *not* want to leave right now. I want to stay and talk to you and fix this."

"Noted."

With that, she went upstairs and closed her bedroom door softly. All of my muscles were coiled like springs, and I clenched my fists until they hurt. I tried to calm down in vain, but I managed to get grocery bags from her pantry and haphazardly pack up most of my stuff, though I left the cake in her freezer because moving all of it could be a disaster.

I threw everything in my trunk and sat in my car for longer than was probably appropriate. I was *willing* her to text me to come back or to see me sitting outside and come out. Eventually, I felt like I could drive without being a danger to anyone else on the road and headed toward my apartment.

How had I fucked this up so badly?

Chapter 39 - Lauren

How had the best day I could remember having in forever turned into *this*? I held it together until I heard him leave, but all the embarrassment and anger forced its way out in sobs as soon as I let the walls down.

He had shown up and helped patch up all the cracks in my life. I felt taken care of, and like I could be *myself* even when I knew I was being a little crazy. And things were so good.

Yeah, for you.

And I let him do it without even questioning if I was there for him in the same way.

I searched for the definition of a narcissist because I was pretty sure that's what I was. It was completely screwed up that I would let this happen and make everything about me. I didn't feel like that definition quite fit, but I *did* look up selfishness as an ADHD symptom, and that was an eye-opening experience. It was hard to decide if I felt better or worse that my brain made self-centered my default mode.

What the fuck are you going to do now?

I wanted to shout at the stupid voice in my head that I didn't *know*. Because thinking about giving Jeremy up had my stomach in my throat. I'd never, *never* felt like this about anyone. But for that exact reason, I felt like maybe I should distance myself so he could properly assess how my issues had screwed up his life. He was too wrapped up in me, the same way that I was with him, to see clearly. Because if he could think rationally about the situation, he would be mad at me.

The even more screwed up thing was that I *knew* he was sitting at home worried about me. Because that's who he was. He should be worried about himself.

Damn it!

I was not the person you trusted to make the difficult, grown-up decisions. I thought about texting Sam, or even Jesse, since he'd be able to give a better perspective on Jer. But I couldn't quite face them yet. If I thought being told off by Charlie was humiliating, this was a different level of hell, knowing that I cost my boyfriend his job.

You could go talk to the bakery owner and explain the supreme douchebaggery that was Charlie's behavior.

As much as that would make *me* feel better, I had the feeling it would not help the overall situation. Having a random job applicant's girlfriend come and confront you would probably be off-putting to some people.

I had to get out of this room.

As soon as I left, I was, of course, faced with the almost-finished purple wall that was quickly becoming the symbol of my failures. It was stupid and completely unsafe. But I was determined to fix one fucking thing in my life by myself. I said a quick prayer to whatever archangels gave protection that I would not fall off this ladder, and I put the second coat on that damn wall.

When I stepped off the ladder for the last time, the new color now fully covering the old, I thanked the universe and cleaned up all my painting supplies.

These meds really are as close to magic as anything I've ever encountered. Though, I'd never tell Sam or Zin that.

I sank into my couch, my muscles angry at the repetitive roller motion I'd been doing most of the day. I went searching for inspiration on what I could now do to the purple wall to add interest. Was I avoiding having any productive thoughts about me and Jer? Yes. Did I come up with some awesome ideas for a wall covered in mixed-metal spray-painted animal figurines? Also, yes.

I may have eaten four Pop-Tarts for dinner and gone to bed still with paint in my hair, but at that point, what did it matter?

* * *

It was an ungodly hour when I woke up to someone knocking incessantly on my front door. When my heart rate went sky high, I had to remind myself that murderers didn't usually knock. I grabbed my phone, saw eight missed calls from Sam, and expertly deduced that she was likely the person trying to wake up my entire complex. I texted first so she would be quiet, and I could put on actual clothing. At least that stopped the pounding. When I finally wrenched open the door, she was practically on top of me.

"You can't ignore my messages for like a year. I thought you had been kidnapped by someone in a van promising discounted vintage clothing or something."

"I'm sorry. I needed to reboot last night."

She stopped then, her shoulders relaxing as she took me in. Her long hair was in a haphazard bun on her head, and she looked like she might be wearing the clothes she slept in.

"I know. I talked to Jer."

"Oh, god. I don't even want to know how that conversation went."

"It didn't go anywhere. He told me you were safe and un-kidnapped, but the rest was yours to tell."

I nodded, willing yesterday's tears to stay in the past.

"And I will. Tell you. But not right now. I've gotta make it through a full day of clients, and *you* are getting married next weekend. You have many other things to think about."

I didn't even have to force the smile I gave her when her face brightened automatically.

"I am. But that doesn't mean you can't tell me what's going on."

"I know. Really, I do. And I will spill my guts to you, but if I start now, I won't stop. And I have to function."

"Okay. I guess I accept your reasoning. Oh, and speaking of functioning." She reached into the pocket of her sweats and pulled out a crystal. "Carnelian for creativity. For your prescription bottle."

I took it happily and hugged her.

"I will say that it didn't seem to dampen my creativity at all, just focused it. Check out my finished wall!" I gestured toward my masterpiece.

"Oh my god! I'd gotten so used to the in-progress look. This is great. Have you figured out what you're hanging there yet?"

"Of course. It'll be a project for *after* the wedding."

"Okay. Well, if you need to get out of your house at any point in the next week, Zin and I are working on centerpieces, favors, and, eventually, floral arrangements with every spare moment."

"Count me in."

She hugged me again and agreed to leave me to finish waking up in peace. Now I had to do the absolute last thing I wanted to do before getting ready for work.

Chapter 40 - Jeremy

I'd slept like shit. It probably wasn't the best idea for me to operate machinery today, but I was going to have to get it together. I got in the shower, hoping it might wash away everything that happened yesterday. When I got out, my heart leapt into my throat when I saw a notification from Laur.

LAUR: I'm still not ready to talk to you. I'm mad. But I don't want to do the thing I always do and try to disappear. So, this is me saying I'm still here. Just not ready to talk yet.

JEREMY: Okay, Laur. I'll be here when you are.

She didn't write back, but at least I felt like I could take a deep breath for the first time since last night. Everything was fucked, but maybe not irreparably. I had to show her that I was in this *with* her and not treating her like a damsel or whatever it was that she'd said. So, yeah, I had to work out how to do that along with create the first wedding cake I'd ever made for something that wasn't a class assignment. Not a stressful time at all. I sighed, shoved my feet into my shoes, and went to work.

The thought of going back to my apartment and either drinking until I fell asleep or staring at the ceiling wishing I had a time machine was unappealing, to say the least. Instead, I drove the forty minutes to the only house that still felt like the type of *home* people talked about with nostalgia in their voice.

I knocked twice on the screen door, knowing she was there because her car was in the open garage.

"Well, do my eyes deceive me?" she asked when opening the door.

"Hey, Grandma. Sorry for showing up without calling."

"What an odd thing to apologize for. Come in. I've got chicken and noodles on the stove."

She held her arms out once I crossed the threshold, and I bent down to let her hug me. Her house smelled like it always had—some mixture of melted butter and cinnamon, no matter what she'd been making. I followed her into her tiny 1960s kitchen and pulled out plates and glasses.

"Can I help with anything?"

"I've got half a loaf of homemade bread in the freezer. Take that out, and pop it in the oven for a few minutes."

I shuffled around her in the tight space and got the bread set to defrost.

"So, I'm always happy to see you, Grandson, but even in my old age, I can tell you're not here just to say 'hello.'"

"On the contrary, being here in your kitchen solves a lot of my problems."

I wasn't lying. As I stood, there was a sense of being a kid and knowing my grandma would take care of anything I needed. It was warm and safe, and that fact alone had some of the ever-present tension leaving my body.

"Hmmmm. I don't believe you, but okay. Do you want to eat on the TV trays and watch *Murder, She Wrote*?"

"That sounds excellent."

I took the bread out of the oven and marveled at the fact that hers was *always* better than mine, no matter what I did. If I were a conspiracy theorist, I'd insist that she left something out of her recipe when she gave it to me.

My grandmother's chicken and noodles had magical properties that I was pretty sure not even Zinnia Crawford could match. The warmth spread from my stomach to the rest of me, and, for the first time in a week, it felt like I could take a break from my brain and watch Angela Lansbury solve a murder.

"How is the wedding cake coming along?" she asked when the

episode was over.

"I think it's going to be good. I hope, anyway."

"Have you told your mama that you're using my cake recipe? You know she never could quite get that caramel cake down, don't ya?" She almost whispered that last part conspiratorially, and I laughed.

"I, ah, I haven't talked to her in a bit."

Every time I felt like I made strides with my mom, things seemed to stall on one of our parts, and then we had to start again.

"You know she's as lost as you when it comes to how to bridge the gap between y'all."

"It feels more like a canyon than a gap, Grandma. And I don't know if I know that or not. Having a *normal* relationship feels like an almost impossibility at this point." I hadn't come to talk about my mother. The tightness in my chest was returning with a vengeance.

"Hogwash, Jeremy Ryan Ash."

"Whoa, middle name."

"Well, you're being ornery as all hell, Grandson. Your mama misses you. The two of you need to have it out, that's what I say. Stop all this tiptoeing around for no reason. And I know your daddy's another story, but, well, he's a proud man, and maybe he'll get over it, and maybe he won't, but that's got nothin' to do with you and your mama. She won't be around forever, and take it from me; you'll wish you'da fixed things when you could've."

"Okay, Grandma," I said, giving in. "I know you're probably right. It's just…hard. I worry if I try to 'have it out' with her, she'll let me go for good."

My voice broke in earnest at admitting that fact. I hated not knowing if my mother would be willing to push through the discomfort of confrontation for me. I hoped she would. When I was young, there was never a question in my mind that she'd do anything for me. It hurt that I'd fucked that up, too.

"Ain't ever gonna happen, kid," she said, her voice slightly softened after my confession. I nodded at her and started to clean up our dishes. "And you need to come around more often. I won't be around forever either, y'know. I might write you outta the will."

"You wouldn't dare. I need that cast iron pan."

She shot me a glare and turned on *Jeopardy!* while I loaded the dishwasher and put away leftovers. I hadn't made a lot of *right* decisions lately, but this was one of them. It might not have made things better in the grand scheme, but it made getting through that night a bit easier.

* * *

By mid-week, I was ready to throw rocks at Lauren's window and play her love songs on a boom box if she would talk to me. She had texted me every morning with essentially the same thing. She wasn't ghosting me; we would talk soon. That was the only reason I wasn't already there, rocks in hand.

Within the next couple days, I had to pick up my suit from the tailor, finalize the cake decorations with Sam, and write a toast for the rehearsal dinner. To say that the lack of sleep was catching up with me was a dangerous understatement. My nerves were shot. I laid on top of my bed, fully clothed and desperately in need of a shower after being on the garage floor all day in what was apparently the last throes of summer heat.

Why did you volunteer to make this wedding cake? And cookies for the rehearsal?

Because I wanted to do something for my friends, sure. But really because I wanted to do something else with my *life*. The more distance that came between me and the end of my program, though, the more ridiculous I felt.

Who leaves a decent job to go bake muffins?

The answer was probably no one. I'd been toying with the idea of trying to finance a little trailer and maybe have a traveling bakery. But I was so fucking exhausted from working my full-time job that I couldn't wrap my head around the minutia of having my own business. Which was *why* working for someone else, like Delaney, would have been a great way to test the waters and get some insight into the licensing, budgeting, and overhead costs of running a place. It wasn't like there were an endless number of higher-end bakeries to apply to within driving distance of Emberwood, and while six months ago, moving was a viable option, *now* it was not. The thought of leaving and not seeing Lauren put a physical pressure on my chest.

Fuck.

I closed my eyes and tried to remove myself from the whirlpool of disappointment threatening to pull me under. Instead, my throat tightened uncomfortably, and that feeling on my chest got heavier. I sucked in a breath through my teeth, and it wasn't filling my lungs. Water collected in the corners of my eyes, and I heaved myself off the bed. This was clearly not working, and my body's reaction was starting to freak me out. I watched the water from the pitcher fill up the glass for too long until it was overflowing onto my counter.

Shit.

I grabbed a towel to wipe it up and tried to force my ribs to expand to let air in. I stretched my arms above my head and pressed my hands against the low ceiling in my kitchen.

You're fine. Get it together.

I gulped down the water and told myself it helped. I was probably dehydrated from sweating all day. A knock came from my apartment door, shaking me out of my daze.

Who is here at almost ten?

My phone confirmed that I had no notifications. I took the three steps from the kitchen to the door and wrenched it open, prepared to tell whoever it was to leave me to my nervous breakdown. But it was a head of red hair in a messy ponytail and a familiar face looking up at me with something like trepidation.

"Laur," I rasped, my throat still too tight.

I leaned my forearm on the doorframe and swept her into me with the other arm. I didn't care that I was sweaty, and I didn't even stop to think that I shouldn't. I needed to feel something real that was outside of my head. My body relaxed into hers when she fisted my shirt and hugged me back. Keeping her snug against my body, I walked us backward so I could shut the door. I pressed a kiss to the top of her head, praying to whatever deity would listen that she wasn't here to break things off officially.

"What's going on, Jer?" she asked, her voice soft as she pulled back only slightly and met my eyes.

I guessed basically enveloping her on my doorstep and not speaking was an indication that something was wrong.

"Nothing. I'm just so happy to see you."

Partial lie, but also a lot of truth.

"Jeremy." She shot me a warning look. "Do not make me regret coming here by doing *that*. What is going on?"

Fuck.

I was doing the whole thing she was mad at me about.

"I'm sorry. I…" I clung to her for a moment. "This is hard."

I still couldn't breathe, and my hands were shaking.

"Well, you look awful. Sit, and I'll find you something to eat. Have you had water?"

I nodded about the water and let myself fall into my couch. She rummaged around in my pantry before joining me, folding her legs under her to scoot close to me and handing me some crackers.

"I… everything is falling apart around me, and I am making every wrong decision. I feel like an absolute imposter about everything I'm trying to do. From being your boyfriend to thinking I can make this cake, let alone change careers and buy a trailer to figure out how to launch some sort of ice-cream truck for baked goods. It sounds ridiculous when I say it out loud, but I can't fucking *breathe*."

I couldn't meet her eyes as I let the dam break. The words kept coming, and she didn't interrupt me once. I wiped my eyes with the sleeve of my t-shirt and fisted my hands to keep the shaking from becoming noticeable. Except she opened them and held them tightly, which was decidedly better.

"I think you're having an anxiety attack," she said, still quiet, her fingers tracing circles into my palms.

That makes sense. I've never been more anxious in my life.

"I've read about some things to help if you want to try them? ADHD and anxiety disorders apparently overlap a lot." She gave me a small smile and shrugged.

"Sure. I don't think it could get worse."

She walked me through some questions about things I could see, hear, smell, feel, and taste, and breathed with me. I did feel the weight on my chest lessen somewhat, and getting air was less of a feat.

"Better?"

"Yeah, better. I'm sorry."

One *I'm sorry* wasn't going to cover everything I felt compelled to apologize for, but it's what I had at the moment.

"For what?"

"Ah, for ambushing you at the door with my meltdown and not even asking why you're here. Among other things, but that seems most pressing."

"Did you orchestrate an anxiety attack at the exact moment I got here to prove that you trust me?"

"Huh? No. Is that—"

"That was a joke, babe. Just… that would be the only reason you'd need to apologize for having an anxiety attack."

I relaxed back into the couch.

"And I'm here because I needed to see you."

"Yeah?"

"Yeah. I was congratulating myself on being such an adult and *not* disappearing. Except, I was still actively not dealing with anything, which is sort of the bigger issue buried beneath my tendency to go radio silent on people. So, I got in the car, and now

I'm here. But we don't have to deal with us tonight, Jer. I...it's horrible to say, but knowing you're a little bit of a wreck makes me feel not as bad about my own chaos."

I huffed out a laugh. "I'm glad I could be of service. But I am not above begging you to deal with us. Tonight. Now. I can't sleep, and I am so worried I'm going to pass out while I'm supposed to be giving a toast at the rehearsal."

"Suit yourself," she said, eyeing me warily. "I've been sitting at home, or really, keeping myself ridiculously busy to try to avoid sitting at home, but whatever. I've been feeling like I've taken so much more than I've given with you. And I hate it. I don't want you to lose things or give things up because of me. And I don't want you to *want* to do that. I don't know if I'm making sense."

"You are. For what it's worth, I've never felt like I've given anything up for you. I want to be here. With you." I kept my fingers running lightly over her palms while we talked.

"Let me be here, too. With you. I'm not only super-hot arm candy, Jer. I can help you with things. I just want you to *know* that."

"I do know that, baby. You're... you're everything. Please let me prove that I can do this."

"Only if you do the same. Let me in." She stopped my fingers from tracing lines on her hands and held onto me tightly.

"If only you knew how far in my head you already were. But yes, I will tell you things. I'm all in."

Chapter 41- Lauren

In one exceptionally smooth move, I was sitting in his lap. His hands gripped my thighs like I might float away if he didn't keep me there.

"I'm all in, too."

His lips met mine with urgency, his tongue exploring my mouth as if this was the first time. I wasn't sure how long we got lost in each other, but my lips were tingling when he finally pulled back.

"I want to take you to bed more than anything in the world right now. But if I don't get in the shower, I risk seriously offending you."

"Yeah, you're kind of dirty. I mean, still hot. But yes, shower." I slid off his lap and giggled at the mock hurt on his face.

"You could have softened it a little, Laur. Do you need anything while I'm doing that?"

"I think I'll grab water and get in bed. Your room isn't, like, scary with only a mattress on the floor like some 90s-movie-frat-boy, is it?"

Maybe it was telling that I'd only been in his apartment a couple of times and never even bothered to go to his room. I accused him of not letting me in, but there was evidence that I was happy to stay on the outside sometimes.

You're making progress now. It's fine.

"Well, you can go see for yourself. But I promise I have a whole bedframe, a headboard, and even a complete matching sheet set and comforter."

"Thank god. It was a bit of a gamble coming over here so late."

He shook his head and tugged at my hand to lead me to his room. He was right; it was perfectly adequate, even if horribly under-decorated.

"I'll be right back."

He dropped a kiss on my forehead and went to shower, leaving me in his room. I got under the covers and was immediately relaxed in a way I hadn't been in days having the scent of him surround me.

I didn't remember hearing him turn off the water, and there was only a vague recollection of the bed dipping down next to me and his warm body pressed against mine before the world melted away.

* * *

I elected to go with Jer to pick up his suit. Then, we stopped by Sam's house to finalize the cake stuff one more time because Jer was kind of a wreck about making sure it was perfect. But I wasn't going to complain about seeing Sam before I had to share her with everyone else at the rehearsal that night.

"Jeremy. This is unnecessary. The ideas you've pitched me are phenomenal, and the cake is going to be amazing. I have all the confidence in the world in you," Sam assured him after he asked her about the peonies for the third time.

"Okay, but if you *don't* love it, am I still allowed to come to happy hour?"

"Unfortunately, no. Your invite will be forever rescinded." She tilted her head in sympathy. "You're a dork. Get out of my house so I can relax."

"Aren't brides supposed to be, like, stressed days before their wedding?" he asked.

"Maybe those brides don't have an Aunt Zin and a Lauren and a Jeremy who've made sure this is going to be an amazing day. And I would be happy to marry Jesse even if there's a downpour and the cake tastes like cardboard. All is well."

Coming from anyone else, that might have sounded cliché. But from Sam, who was ever the realist-erring-on-the-side-ofpessimism, it was kind of heart-warming.

"Well, if you think of anything you need last minute, let me know," I assured her, hugging her tightly. "Enjoy relaxing."

"*You* can stay if you want. Your energy is lovely. His is all staticky." She wrinkled her nose at Jer.

"I'll come back by later and do your makeup if you want."

She readily agreed, and I pulled Jer out the door before he could ask more redundant questions. We went to my house so he could start to thaw the cake and dye the buttercream perfect shades of lavender and cornflower blue.

"I can help you with whatever, you know. I took the rest of the week off so I can be where I'm needed," I assured him.

"That would be great. Even if that's you sitting there looking hot while I assemble the cake. And you can make sure I don't go overboard with the edible glitter."

"Sam won't be happy unless you *do* go overboard with the edible glitter."

"Fair point," he conceded. "I will give you a spoon of icing to eat if you come here and tell me when you think this is the right shade of blue."

I immediately hopped down from the barstool and awaited my spoon. His buttercream was fucking amazing.

"Open."

I felt my stomach flutter when the word landed. My lips parted, and he lightly touched the spoon to my tongue and let me lick off the frosting.

"Good girl," he added when I groaned at how good it was.

"That was hotter than it had any right to be," he said, his voice strained. "But I *have* to do this before I can do the things I want to do to you."

A shiver worked its way up my spine, and I stood on my tip toes to plant a single kiss on his mouth.

"Let's get to it, then."

* * *

Walking through the ceremony in Zin's garden, when it was just us and our families, was kind of magical. It didn't have the weight of the actual wedding day, where everything had to be perfect. And when Sam almost tripped coming down the aisle, we could laugh about it and continue on. Zin was officiating their ceremony, which would contain the typical elements of a wedding and a hand-fasting, which seemed like a sweet, symbolic way to show that their lives were being woven together. I stood in my spot and diligently paid attention to when I was supposed to fluff Sam's dress, hold her flowers, and hand her the ring. The meds made this easier, I had to admit. My thoughts weren't jumbled up and wrapped in noisemakers and blinking lights.

But in the few moments I wasn't zeroed in on my brother and my best friend? My eyes were on Jer. And his were on me. And it felt like we were in our own little bubble in those moments. The sun went down, and twinkle lights came alive in the trees and along the garden path, and all of it was so beautiful. I also didn't hate that they'd gotten the dinner catered by the taco truck owners who were responsible for me eating most days. Jer had made some ridiculous cookies with chocolate chips and jalapeños to complement the Mexican food. They shouldn't have been good. But that little kick of spicy with the sweet had me sneaking back to the table for thirds.

I'd been so ready for this wedding to be over because of the chaos it had wrought in its wake, but now that it almost was, I realized I'd miss the excitement of it.

Maybe your next hyperfixation can be event planning.

I shook it off, though, because I already knew what my next project was going to be.

Chapter 42 - Jeremy

In the end, the cake looked even better than the inspiration photos we'd been over. And it wasn't particularly complex in terms of decorating because Sam wanted live florals on the cake and not fondant or buttercream embellishments. I'd built it up in my head to be something it was not, and it reminded me why I went to school for this in the first place. It was fun. And baking for people made me feel like I was taking care of them in some way, like any comfort food would, I guessed.

As promised, Lauren had sat at her counter looking pretty and painting her nails while I worked, but she disappeared into her room after she realized I was in my own world.

I was finishing up when she re-emerged, and she let out a genuine gasp.

"Are you for *real*? Jer, this could be on the cover of a magazine. Like, send it to *Better Homes & Gardens* or something. Please. Better yet, send a picture to your mom. I think she'll want to see it."

She was tentative when she mentioned my mom, but it was a good suggestion. I'd been working on keeping my promise to let Laur *in*, which meant sharing some difficult things about my relationship with my parents. She continued to circle the cake from a safe distance, like she was afraid to breathe on it.

"Yeah? I think you're right. It looks good."

"Good is putting it mildly, babe."

"I hope you understand that we have to clear out your fridge and take out at least one of the shelves so this can fit in there with its box.

"You know there's only takeout in there anyway. Throw it out. I will happily forego food in my fridge to look at this when I open it."

"You think they're ready to do this tomorrow?"

"I think it's been a long time coming, yeah. It's going to be perfect."

"I think *you're* going to be perfect," I murmured, wrapping my arms around her.

"Obviously."

* * *

If anyone had ever asked me if I thought I could rock a purple suit, the answer would have been a firm no. But I had to admit, the color did something for me. Jesse was in a dark blue suit and a purple tie, and we were posing for photos before the ceremony. At first, it felt stiff, like we were having senior photos done, but eventually, we leaned into it.

"I don't know that I've properly thanked you for everything the past couple of months, and really the past couple of years, if we're honest. I know you were still trying to get your life back on track when I crash-landed back in Emberwood and expected you to help carry me through it. But you did it anyway. And now I'm here."

We were in a spare room in Zinnia's house that was acting as a dressing room for the time being.

"I think you're giving me more credit than I deserve. I mostly just went drinking with you and kicked your ass at pool. But I'm happy you're here now, too."

"Well, I can't bake. But if you end up marrying my sister, I promise I'll be helpful in some form or fashion. I'll build you something. I've got a whole collection of power tools now."

"You're well on your way to being a suburban dad, then."

"That's not quite the insult it would have been in the past," he said, laughing.

A knock sounded at the door, and Jesse's mom let us know it was time to get going.

"Let's go get you married, then."

The look on his face was hard to describe, but mostly it read as love. I wondered if I had the same look on my face when I looked at Laur and she didn't know it.

When I met her at the edge of the garden path to walk down the aisle to our places, she took my breath away. I knew she wasn't the bride, but I couldn't imagine anyone looking more beautiful. She was in a long, deep purple gown that matched my tie, and her red hair was swept up into an artful twist on top of her head. I was pretty sure that when the wedding photos were developed of this moment, I'd be able to confirm the same look on my face that Jesse had on his.

* * *

"We did it, you know," she said, sitting down next to me at the head table after photos and talking to what seemed like every single guest.

"What, exactly, did we do?"

"All the things we were supposed to. Along with a bunch of things we *weren't* supposed to. Because us? Together? Was not a thing that was supposed to happen. If it wasn't her wedding day, I might accuse Sam of setting up the whole rushed-wedding-timeline based on our joint astrological birth charts."

"I wouldn't put it past her."

"Right?! She's sneaky."

"Astrologically orchestrated or not, I'm glad we're here, Laur."

She sighed heavily and leaned into me. "I'm happy, too. Now, can we get food?"

"Stay here. I will bring you sustenance."

I left her and went to fill up plates at the caterer's station. Even though most of the guests had already been through, it all looked phenomenal.

"Hey, you're the baker, right?"

"What's that?" I asked, not sure she was talking to me at first.

"You made the wedding cake?"

"Oh, yeah. It's the first one I've done professionally, but yes."

"You could have fooled me," she said, surprised. "Listen, I'm the owner of the catering company, and I normally wouldn't accost a guest and beg them to work for me, but are you looking for more work?"

"Oh! Yes, actually. I finished school back in June, and I've been trying to shift from my day job into doing, well, this."

"Well, I have more work than I know what to do with right now, and I don't currently offer clients a dessert package because I don't have a pastry chef on staff. But if you want to send me your portfolio and what you're hoping to do, we can chat next week."

She tried to hand me her card, but I was still awkwardly balancing two plates, so she stuck it into my suit jacket pocket instead.

"I'm Jeremy, by the way," I offered, unable to shake her hand.

"Elaine. Enjoy the rest of the party."

There's no way that just happened.

I made my way back to Lauren, happy I was going to be able to share good job-related news with her this time.

Don't threaten anyone tonight, and you should be good.

Chapter 43 - Lauren

When I promised Sam her wedding would be perfect, even if it killed me. And given the timeline of ten weeks, I didn't know, then, if I was lying or not. Thankfully, I wasn't. Because that ceremony was so beautiful, I didn't think there had been a dry eye in the garden. Zin was always a bit of a master with words, but having her officiate the ceremony felt like some priestess of an ancient deity was giving a blessing for their marriage.

I watched Jer make his way back to me after chatting with the caterer for a while. The grin on his face when he sat down and explained that there was a new, maybe even better, job offer on the horizon made me forgive him for taking so long.

"Dance with me," I demanded when we were finished eating.

"What is the magic word, Laur?"

"Now. Before I go ask Danny."

"That was below the belt, Garrett."

"I like what's below your belt, Ash."

"*Jesus.*" He laughed. "You are going to make it very difficult for me to walk around."

I bit my lip and pulled him to stand. We wove our way between tables and heaters to the patio they'd cleared to make a dance floor.

"Sorry," I offered half-heartedly when he pulled me against him.

"Liar."

I grinned into his chest and wrapped my arms around his neck.

"You look like a fairy princess in this dress, you know."

"Oh? I was kind of hoping for, like, a Queen of the Underworld vibe. But I'll take fairy princess."

He only responded with a kiss, just this side shy of being inappropriate.

"I want to have you *out* of this dress."

"Can be arranged. But we can't leave until they cut the cake. It's kind of your main event, you know?"

"Nah. This is my main event," he murmured, his lips brushing against the shell of my ear.

He twirled me around, my dress flaring in the most satisfying way, and pulled me back against his chest, maybe harder than before, his lips back at my ear.

"I am completely and ridiculously in love with you, Laur."

I almost choked on the air when the words registered.

"You are?" I whispered, happy tears springing to my eyes for maybe the fifth time today.

"I am. You don't have to—"

"I am *so* in love with you, you idiot."

"Yeah?" he asked, pulling back so he could look at me. "That's good. I think I might have had to sink through a hole in the ground if I'd read that one wrong," he admitted, kissing me again.

"As soon as I get to try the cake that has occupied far too many minutes of conversation this week, we are getting out of here."

He agreed readily and let me go when I insisted I needed to dance with Jesse before the end of the night. My brother won major points for turning my best friend into my sister, and I thought he should know.

* * *

The speed with which we left the wedding and got back to my house was almost cartoonish in nature.

"I want you to wear a suit every time we go out," I said breathlessly, pulling at the knot on his tie.

"I want you to not wear a bra every time we go out," he responded after working the straps of my dress over my arms and running his fingers over my nipples, tugging them lightly.

"I don't think that's an equal request."

"I don't care. I love your tits."

He pushed me onto the bed and climbed over me, taking the shirt situation into his own hands and shedding it along with his undershirt. God, the likeness of his upper body should be chiseled in marble and put on display for everyone to enjoy.

"I also love your neck," he added, nipping at me there. "Your shoulders." More licking. "Your thighs."

He used his giant hands to grip my thighs and push them apart so he could kiss his way up them, purposely skipping where I wanted his mouth to land.

"Your ass." He pushed my legs up until my knees were below my chin so he could playfully smack my butt. "And you," he said finally, coming back up to kiss my mouth, plunging his tongue inside.

His weight on me was so deliciously satisfying. I groaned at the loss of it when he rolled over, dragging me on top of him. His hands worked on his pants and boxers until he could push them off with his feet, and he pressed his now very hard length up against me. He grabbed some pillows for himself and put his hands behind his head like he was on the beach.

"What are you—"

"Take what you need, baby. Please. I want to see you."

My brows quirked at the request—he was usually happy calling the shots when we were together, and I was good with that, but the look of want on his face had me feeling very good about this, too. I ground against him, relishing how his arms twitched like he wanted to reach out and grab me, but he was apparently committed to me running this show. I sank down on him slowly, loving how his breaths shortened and his lips parted slightly. I braced myself on his chest and found my rhythm.

"God *damn it*, Laur, you are so perfect. I love watching you. I love you."

"Oh my *god*," I groaned, still so affected when he talked to me in that stupidly low sex-voice.

I found my release quickly and gasped when he flipped us again and made up for not having not used his hands before as he lost himself in me. He collapsed into me, and we both worked to catch our breath.

"I love you, too," I said, realizing I hadn't said it back just now. To be fair, my brain was otherwise occupied.

"So, so, perfect, baby," he got out on an exhale.

He slipped out of me and rolled to the side, tugging me firmly against him and stroking paths down my back. It struck me, in that moment, how quickly life could change, and I started to understand why Sam and Jesse had said to hell with the traditional timeline and got married when they wanted. I hadn't felt like that about anybody before, but now, I got it. How you could simply not wait another minute to be with someone. Even though he'd only said he loved me earlier tonight, nothing about it felt new or unfamiliar. It was like he put words to what he'd been showing me for a long time, and it felt like home.

Epilogue - Lauren

Three months later: Christmas

"You already surprised me with the cabinet thing for all my baking stuff. What other thing are you giving me?" he asked as I practically vibrated in front of him; I was so excited.

"The 'cabinet thing,' as you so eloquently put it, was honestly more for me than you. Your stuff had taken over my pantry, and it needed a home. And it's a pie safe originally crafted in 1908 and beautifully refinished. I probably would have bought it even if you and your stuff didn't exist. *This* is just for you, though."

I tried to cover his eyes from behind, but I couldn't reach, so I settled for making him cover them himself and leading him to my garage.

Our garage.

I'd been making both of us park in the lot instead of the garage for days so that I could inspect my purchase and make a mood board of different theme options for him to choose from. He had been banned from peeking.

"I'm going, I'm going."

"Okay, open them!"

He did, and he took a minute to walk towards it, his brows furrowed together in confusion.

"What is... you bought me a trailer?"

"Not only a trailer. *This* trailer was used as, like, a mobile bar by the owner when he used to bartend at weddings and events and stuff. So, look, look, there's a generator and a small fridge in here," I said, stepping inside the little space. "So, you could keep your, like, macarons and cheesecake in there and then use these shelves for everything else that doesn't need to be refrigerated. And I have so many ideas for how to give it a glow-up. I mean, it's in good shape, but you could paint it, and we need to add the logo Sam made. It was just—"

He joined me in the trailer, his head almost touching the roof, and his mouth crashed into mine. He gripped the back of my head and held me against him, nipping and sucking at my bottom lip as he seemed to forget about the trailer for a moment.

"Lauren."

"Jeremy."

"You know this is too much, right? Like you have to let me pay you for this because… well, I mean, look at it."

"One, it's a Christmas present. And two, like you let me pay you for all the work you did on my car?"

"It's not the same th—"

"And how you let me pay when you retiled the bathroom after that pipe leaked last month?"

"Laur—"

"Let me do this, please. You cover half the mortgage now, so let me do what I want with my money. There's even more of it with the cosplay crowd. They've been kind to me with all their requests for insane hairstyles lately with that con in Toledo. Plus, the guy was moving out of the country and needed it sold. I got an absolute steal on this."

"Of course you did, baby."

We ducked out of the small space back into the garage.

"Do you think if we got it up and running, it could make up the difference, and you could leave the garage altogether?"

"Maybe, after a bit. I've got spreadsheets, you know, with all the costs and whatever for something like this. I didn't think someone would *present* me with a damn near perfect trailer."

"Hey. You should. Expect me to do things that help you. Like you want me to expect you to do things that help me. Now can we be excited about this and go look at my inspo boards for what to do with it?"

"If I can thank you properly after, then yes. Show me *all* the inspo boards."

"Hmmmmm," I let out, reconsidering. "Maybe you thank me *first*, then the boards."

I shrieked as he picked me up and threw me over his shoulder, hauling me back into the house and tossing me down on the couch. He kissed me more slowly than I expected after that ride, but I went with it and twirled my fingers in his hair.

"Thank you for getting me, Laur. I love it, and I love you."

"I love you, too, Jer."

"Okay, good."

With that, he resumed with a sense of urgency and gave me a *proper* thank you for the next hour.

This life we were making? Was unbelievably sweet.

Preview of *Rebuilding Romance from Ruins*, Emberwood Book III
Coming Dec 10, 2024

Prologue- Gen

Fall

I wished the tears I couldn't keep at bay were from how happy I was for my friends. Sam and Jesse's wedding was the most beautiful thing I'd ever seen. In reality, though, I was replaying my own wedding and how stupid I'd been to believe any of it. It was probably the wrong decision to come at all, but I hated the idea that I couldn't support my friends because my own husband was a colossal asshole. Soon-to-be-ex-husband.

At least there's an open bar.

The lavender gin fizz was purple and bubbly and made a lovely popping sensation over my tongue. The fact that this was my fourth one didn't diminish its delightfulness.

"Is that actually good? It looks like Kool-Aid and Sprite."

Danny had sauntered up next to me while I was leaning on a high-top table, watching other people dance. I side-eyed him, but all that accomplished was me noticing how well he cleaned up. He was in a light gray suit with his tattoos creeping up over his collar and across his neck, his jet-black hair pulled back.

"A little more of a kick than Purplesaurus Rex."

"You sure? That shit got me wound up as a kid."

"Everything gets you wound up, Vega."

"It's official. You're far too comfortable around me now. I liked you better when you were timid and overly polite." He lightly bumped me with his shoulder.

I almost snorted. He wasn't wrong. I tended to err on the side of wallflower when I first met people. Which was why they were usually shocked when they found out that, in addition to teaching pre-school, I wrote romance novels. But then they were less shocked again to find out they were sweet and clean romance novels.

As long as no one ever downloads your e-reader history, you have safely cemented yourself as the girl-next-door.

I sighed, not quite knowing that I liked that distinction. Sometimes it felt like *nice* was my only personality trait, and lately, that wasn't doing me any favors.

Maybe this is why Penn claims to have no idea who you are.

Because maybe *I* had no idea who I was.

"Sorry. You've opened the box. There's no going back now."

"I guess I'll adjust. You wanna dance? This dress should see the dance floor, no?"

"You dance?" I asked, a little surprised. I swished my long dress without thinking, feeling it flutter against my legs. The night air was cool, but the warmth from the heaters all over the garden kept the chill at bay.

"I'm Latin, Gen. El ritmo está en mi sangre."

"Okay. Let me think about that one a sec."

I paused and replayed his words.

"The rhythm is in your…something."

I'd made a New Years' resolution last year to learn Spanish. It had been coming along slowly, at least until Penn blew up my life, but I was trying, anyway.

"That sounds vaguely suggestive, Gen. Is your husband okay

with you harassing *very* attractive men in his absence?"

I winced physically at his words. I closed my eyes and took a breath, downing what was left of my drink.

"I don't think he has an opinion one way or another." I plastered what I was sure was an unconvincing smile on my face.

"I'm sorry… I didn't mean to step in something—"

"You're fine. We can dance."

I left my glass on the table and walked toward the speakers, willing the tears that had shown themselves to go back into hiding. The music switched from a fast-paced bop to a slow song the moment my foot hit the makeshift dance floor, and this was less than ideal. I supposed I didn't *need* to feel weird about it. I was free to dance with whomever I wanted. But it *did* feel weird to dance with anyone but Penn.

Not that he has danced with you in years.

"We don't have to dance, Gen," Danny said, reading what was clearly written all over my face.

I rolled my eyes and grabbed his hands, placing them on my waist. I wrapped my arms around his neck and let him steady me, the fourth drink hitting me in a wave. He wasn't wrong, anyway. This dress had cost me half a paycheck, and it deserved to be seen at least once. It was a lovely periwinkle organza that floated just right around my hips to the ground.

Happily, I could also breathe, since for the first time in a long time, I'd left my tummy-flattening shapeware at home. Pretending I didn't have a belly wasn't worth the lack of oxygen.

"It was blood, by the way. The rhythm is in my blood. You almost had it."

"Ah. That makes sense," I murmured, relaxing into his shoulder. He smelled good, like something woodsy, and I breathed him in.

"In some cultures, it's impolite to sniff someone while dancing."

"Oh my god, I'm sorry. I… I've probably had one too many

gin thingies," I mumbled, mortified. The world was slightly out of focus, and I was regretting my choices. I could feel my filter dissolving in my brain.

"Don't worry. It's not *my* culture. Just making conversation," he added, tugging me slightly closer.

"You're funny. I think I used to be funny." We swayed in silence for a beat or five.

"Are you okay, Gen?" Danny asked, his voice thick with what felt like concern.

I swallowed hard because the truth was dangerously close to spilling out of my mouth.

"Oh, yeah. Fantastic." I tried to hold it back. I really did. I blamed the pretty purple drinks.

"Penn is leaving me. *He's* leaving *me*. Just to be clear about that. Because...well, that's a story that would take longer than this song. But yeah, he filed for divorce last month. He hasn't finished moving out yet, but he'll be gone by the end of this weekend."

To his credit, he kept us swaying to the music while he took in that trauma dump of a outburst.

"*Fuck*," Danny murmured, his forehead now close to resting on mine. "I'm sorry. And I said...just shit. I'm sorry."

"Not your fault. All my fault, apparently."

"Yeah..." he started, clearly hesitating over what he was going to say next. "Uh, I've met the guy. I can guarantee you none of whatever is going on is your fault."

He said it with such finality, his dark eyes stealing my breath, like there was no room for argument. I hiccupped something that felt like a sob trying to force its way out of my throat.

"I'm sorry, I shouldn't have laid this on you. I shouldn't even be here. I'm going to get a ride home. Enjoy the wedding, Danny."

I pushed back from him, wobbling only a little, wondering who the hell I was going to get to take me home, but there had to be an option. All at once, I couldn't breathe, and I just needed to get out of this dress and take my hair down. My whole head was throbbing.

"I got you. Let's go."

He linked his arm through mine and held it tightly, steadying me. My brain told me to argue, that it was rude to make him leave the party; that it was rude for *me* to be leaving the party. But I felt myself coming apart at the seams, and I desperately wanted to make it home before that happened. It felt like a sucker punch to realize that Penn would be at the house when I got there, and there would still be no reprieve from the tornado of anger and grief and fear, and did I mention *anger,* swirling around me.

Get it together.

I didn't have the money to get a hotel room, or I would have done it in a heartbeat. My sister had offered me her guest room, and I'd taken it the past three weekends, but her house was too far for me to commute to work every day, so I was stuck in my house with *him* during the week, where everything I did was met with a snide remark or an eye roll, meaning I just hid in our…*my*… room anytime I had to be there.

I sighed heavily, almost letting it dissolve into something else, but I willed my emotions to get it together until I could lock myself in a closet and cry myself to sleep.

Danny's car was only a short walk, and I sank into the passenger seat, wondering if I'd eventually wake up from my life and things would be normal again.

Prologue—Danny

I was not equipped to handle this situation. What possessed me to insist on driving her home was beyond me. Maybe it was the nauseous feeling after the joke I made about her husband being mad about her flirting with me. That had taken a whole three seconds to not age well.

Cabrón. I was an asshole.

My abuelita told me my whole life that my mouth was going to get me into trouble that I couldn't charm my way out of, and I hadn't really believed her until tonight.

Gen gave me directions to her house as I drove, and I wished I had something to say to lighten the tension, but I didn't know that an amusing story was appropriate when your spouse was leaving you.

And the worst thing was, I would have bet money that her dick of a husband had been cheating on her. The few times we all went out together, he had no qualms about flirting with other women. Maybe not in Gen's direct vicinity, but that man didn't give a shit about her. I gripped my steering wheel like it was personally at fault for me being in this situation.

"Can I walk you up?" I asked when I pulled up to her house.

"Hmmm? Oh, no. I'm fine. Thanks for driving me...I'm sorry you had to leave the party."

Her eyes were struggling to stay open, and the blond waves that were pulled up into something intricate on her head had started to unravel and fall around her face.

"Yeah...I think I'll just feel better if I do, though. So, for *me*, let me walk you up, yeah?"

She just nodded sleepily. I hopped out and opened her door and let her lean on me as we made it down the drive. The front door swung open before we made it up the porch steps. Penn stood there, leaning against the door frame, beer bottle in hand.

"Hey, man," I offered in terms of a greeting.

"Danny," he replied, taking a long drink.

Well, this is fucking awkward.

"Thanks for the ride," Gen said, her voice much smaller than it had been earlier.

"Are you so hard up without me that you're fucking *him?*" Penn asked, his tone taunting, his words slurred.

"Jesus, Penn. He gave me a ride home because I drank too much."

She turned to me, unshed tears filling her eyes.

"I'm so sorry, you can go."

Like hell I can.

He grabbed Gen by her arm and pulled her closer to him.

"Don't apologize to him like *I'm* the problem. He should be thankful we even let him in this country."

Oh, for fuck's sake.

A smile played across my face because there was almost nothing I enjoyed more than fucking with racists.

"You know, man, my cousins… the ones who ran with the cartel back in Mexico, have a saying for men who put hands on their women."

I succeeded in getting his gaze to land on me. He loosened his grip on Gen, so she was able to wrench her arm away and step back.

"Muerto," I finished, dragging my thumb across my throat.

"Are you fucking threatening me, you illegal piece of shit?"

"I wouldn't dream of it."

"Get in the fucking house, Gen."

Penn lunged for her, and she let out a squeak, but I'd been ready for that move and caught him by the arm. I shoved him back against the house, my forearm now digging into his throat. I hadn't spent four days a week in the boxing gym for years to let this asshole manhandle a fucking woman in front of me.

"Go back to the car, Gen," I said as calmly as I could under the circumstances. She hesitated a moment before whatever sense of self-preservation she had kicked in and she took off down the driveway. I knew he was going to hit me as soon as I touched him, but I was good with it. If he had the bright idea to call the police after I left, I'd at least have evidence that he was the aggressor.

Penn shoved me and swung, his fist connecting with my cheekbone in what I could tell was a valiant attempt on his part. At least there would be a bruise. That only made me grin wider.

"Get the fuck off my property." He ended with a stream of racial slurs that weren't the most creative I'd ever heard, but I wasn't going to hit a white guy on his own porch and have to explain that to the cops.

"Don't touch her again, or I will become exactly who you think I am. *Pinche pendejo.*"

I turned and sauntered back to the car, only hoping a little that he'd come after me. I hadn't been in a decent fight in a long time outside of the gym. But, that would be counterproductive to getting Gen out of there. He didn't. He slammed the door instead.

Super tough guy.

I yanked open the driver's side door to find her bent over, her hands covering her face and her body wracked with sobs.

"Hey hey hey. You're good. Everything's fine."

I reached for her wrist and tugged gently to coax her to uncover her face. She used the other to wipe away the tears from her cheeks and the mascara from under her eyes.

"I'm so sorry, Danny. He… he wasn't always. I don't know."

She finally looked at me and reached out to touch my face. "Oh my god, he *hit* you? I'm so sorry. I'm *so* sorry. I should—"

"Stop apologizing. I *let* him hit me. He's kind of a pussy, honestly. You need to work on your taste in men."

She let out a choked laugh at that and then a heavy sigh, her blond hair now fully falling around her face, previous hairstyle forgotten. I started the car and headed for my apartment; glad I'd just cleaned, though I didn't imagine she'd be awake for long.

"I can, um, call my mom or my sister to come get me, but it will take them a bit. Or, maybe Lauren, she's closer."

"You can stay at my place, and I'll crash on the couch. It's not a big deal. But if, ah, you're not comfortable with that, I get it. I can take you wherever."

"Oh, you've already done more than enough, I couldn't ask you—"

"You're not asking, Gen. It's late, and if *that's* what you've been dealing with, I can't imagine how tired you are. Again, if you're not comfortable, I'm not gonna press the issue. But my sheets are clean, and I have an extra toothbrush, even."

Her lip trembled again, but she kept it together.

"Okay," she got out in almost a whisper.

"Okay."

I held her hand and rubbed circles into her palm as I drove, and she didn't seem to mind, so I figured she just needed someone to shut up and be there. I could do that.

Once we got to my place, I showed her to my room and shut down her thousand apologies and thank-yous as many times as I could.

Before she went to brush her teeth, she turned to me and asked, "Didn't, like, your entire family grow up here in Ohio?"

"Mostly, yeah. Why?"

"Just... your cousins didn't actually work for the cartel, right?"

I burst out laughing, and a small grin appeared on her lips. "No. But I've learned that sometimes it's best to play into the fears that people have when they're being racist pieces of shit."

She tilted her head and let out a sigh.

"He really is a piece of shit, isn't he?"

I shrugged, trying to convey an *obviously* as gently as I could, and she made a sound that could have been a laugh. While she was in the bathroom, I laid out a t-shirt and a pair of sweats on the bed and set a glass of water with some pain killers on the side table before making myself scarce. Really, I should have been tired too, but the adrenaline hadn't fully left my body yet, and I needed to wind down. After taking an ice pack out of my freezer, I peeled off my suit and tie and pulled on the sweats I'd grabbed from my room before sinking into the couch.

That was *not* how I envisioned tonight going.

Other Books by This Author:

Finding Magic in Misfortune (Emberwood Book I)
Rebuilding Romance from Ruins (Emberwood Book III)

The Tower

The Gem City Series

About the Author

Nicole resides in the PNW after thirty years in the desert and spends most of her free time with her laptop and an iced tea, enjoying the weather. A former English teacher, Nicole now stays at home with her awesome kids, home schooling and trying to visit every park in her city.

For infrequent and non-spammy updates, including ARC opportunities and the occasional free steamy novella, visit NicoleCampbellBooks.com and join Nicole's newsletter.

Acknowledgements

A huge thank you to everyone who worked on this book:

My beta readers are incredible and made this book what it is.

There would be no book if not for the wonderful women who work the childcare at my gym. You are all-stars for giving me time to write.

My editor, K.F. Starfell, for jumping in and giving such amazing feedback, in addition to being a great supporter.

My cover designer, @caravelle_creates for bringing these characters to life and creating something I fell in love with.

My readers, new and old, for embracing Emberwood and my new genre. So much love to all of you!

Last but never least: my friends, my husband, my kids, for being my biggest supporters even when I'm clearly being insane.

Milton Keynes UK
Ingram Content Group UK Ltd.
UKHW031947281024
450365UK00008B/484